"My paella is to die for. We can make a feast out of it."

"Thank you," Santiago said quietly. Indya found herself facing down his penetrating gaze head-on. She was far more aware of Santiago than she had been on their journey into the bay. He was so close, she could sense the rise and fall of his chest.

Santiago's proximity to her was dizzying. Intoxicating. She wanted to run her hands up his chest, feel the warmth of skin and bone beneath the palms of her hands. Taste the salt and sea on his skin. "It's what friends do." She paused, the heat that simmered through her making her reckless. "Are we friends, Santiago?"

How had she let that question fall out of her mouth? Her throat had gone dry and her skin was pulled so taut that she was sure she could peel it off and crawl out of it. Her heart was tight, her breath short, and everything...everything strained to reach out to him and pull him down for a kiss.

He surprised her when his hand came up to her cheek, cupping it gently. "Indya, I'm anything you want me to be."

Dear Reader,

Teenage motherhood and an early divorce have taught Indya Linares to be self-reliant. From her college degree to her fashion choices, Indya strives for excellence and has never learned how to lean on anyone.

Indya returns to Soledad Bay after a decade away from her hometown to help her aging parents run the Alba Beachside Resort after a hurricane nearly devastates the Gulf Coast town. Complications ensue when her facilities manager quits without notice, leaving her with a resort in need of repair and the biggest event of the year looming around the corner. When Santiago Pereira interviews for the position, she takes on the handsome, brooding man despite the way he makes her feel.

After his family immigrated from Venezuela, Santiago Pereira risked it all to stay with his daughter and launch a business. However, when his partner bankrupts them, he follows his family in the hopes of building a new life.

He never expected to meet a woman like Indya, competent, strong-willed and so beautiful. It makes him want more than he dreamed of when he set out for this seaside town, more than his father believes he deserves. A new country, a home and a love to make all his struggles worthwhile. If only Indya would let him in.

A Summer to Start Over is the first book in the Soledad Bay series, a cozy beach romance about a woman who seems to be able to do anything but who keeps her heart in check against a world that is quick to hurt her. Until she finds a cinnamon roll strong enough to love her.

Best,

Sera

A SUMMER
TO START OVER

SERA TAÍNO

SPECIAL EDITION

Harlequin®
SPECIAL
EDITION™

Recycling programs for this product may not exist in your area.

ISBN-13: 978-1-335-40231-8

A Summer to Start Over

Copyright © 2025 by Sera Taíno

For questions and comments about the quality of this book, please contact us at CustomerService@Harlequin.com.

Harlequin Enterprises ULC
22 Adelaide St. West, 41st Floor
Toronto, Ontario M5H 4E3, Canada
www.Harlequin.com

Printed in Lithuania

MIX
Paper | Supporting
responsible forestry
FSC® C021394

Sera Taíno writes Latinx romances exploring love in the context of family and community. She is the 2019–2020 recipient of the Harlequin Romance Includes You Mentorship, resulting in the publication of her debut contemporary romance, *A Delicious Dilemma*. When she's not writing, she can be found teaching her high school literature class, crafting, and wrangling her husband and two children.

Books by Sera Taíno

Harlequin Special Edition

The Navarros

A Delicious Dilemma
The Best Man's Problem

Soledad Bay

A Summer to Start Over

Visit the Author Profile page
at Harlequin.com for more titles.

To everyone who's ever tried to carve out a space that was not meant for them while still managing to preserve the spark of joy in their hearts.

Chapter One

Indya

The sun was edging closer to the horizon on the Gulf of Mexico when the engines on Indya Linares's Cobia 320 CC sputtered and died.

Indya turned the double outboard engines of the thirty-five-foot fishing boat over again, trying to get them to come to life, but they only choked several times before dying again. She'd cleaned the spark plugs and checked the fuel pumps before heading out to sea for a bit of alone time, hoping to prevent this very problem, but the engines still shut down. She wouldn't be surprised if the new fuel she put in was responsible for both engines failing. She guessed she had about forty-five minutes of sunlight left to sort things out, a glance at the app on her cell phone confirming her estimate.

It was Tuesday evening, an odd day of the week to claim a break for anyone who didn't work in hospitality. But Indya had been desperate to get out on the water. It had been a long weekend of check-ins and snafus at the Alba Beachside Resort in Soledad Bay, Florida, the hotel that had been in her family since her grandmother had bought it for a song more than a half-century earlier. Indya and her teenage daughter, Gia, had moved back to Soledad Bay from Sarasota at the start of the school year to help her elderly parents restore the hotel after a hurricane hit their hometown, very nearly destroying it.

But even after six months, Indya still felt like a rookie, trying to figure out what the hell she was doing.

But the coup de grâce in all of this upheaval was the abrupt resignation of the long-time facilities manager, Carlos, after he met his "soulmate" during a vacation to see his favorite band in California. He'd called to announce that he was following the newfound love of his life to the man's hometown of Seattle because, as Indya's teenage daughter, Gia, would say, "YOLO or whatever."

But "YOLO or whatever" wasn't going to change the pool filter or fix the damaged deck leading from the pool area to the beach. YOLO wasn't going to make FEMA move faster to fix the pool house roof. YOLO certainly wasn't going to get her hotel, or the town, back on its feet.

And "YOLO or whatever" wasn't going to get her boat back to the marina before the sun set, plunging her into the endless, relentless darkness of the open sea.

At least she wasn't adrift in a shipping lane. It could be worse, all things considered.

She hated having to send out the pan-pan emergency message and bother any nearby seacraft. Asking for help wasn't exactly in her vocabulary, but the prospect of floating out here on the Gulf in the middle of the night with her boat dead in the water was doubly unappealing. She'd been overconfident in letting her TowBoatUS membership expire and now she was facing the consequences for that failure.

After tightening the straps of her life vest, she dropped anchor and headed down into the small cabin to send the call.

"Pan-pan, pan-pan, pan-pan. All stations, this is the Gia Marie, *call sign Bravo Alpha Charlie. I am five miles south of Soledad Bay experiencing double-engine failure and in need of a tow. One person on board. Over."*

She repeated the call three more times, each one pushing her hope of rescue further and further away. She'd have to call Wilfredo, or Wil, the owner of Sunset Marina, where she kept a boat slip, and ask them to give her a tow. But that might not be until the morning, which put her in a vulnerable position and Indya didn't like vulnerability. Not one bit.

The response, when it came through, forced her heart into her throat while simultaneously flooding her panicked mind with relief. A man's voice, deep and accented, came across the radio.

"Pan-pan, pan-pan, pan-pan. Gia Marie, *this is the* Aragona. *Received pan-pan. Transmit GPS coordinates. Over."*

Indya scrambled to get her location across to him.

"Gia Marie, this is the Aragona. *ETA eight minutes. Do you copy? Over."*

"Copy Aragona. Gia Marie, *over."*

"Sit tight, Gia Marie. *On my way. Over and out."*

Indya let out a long, cleansing breath. If all went according to plan, she'd be back at the marina in about an hour. She radioed Wil on their frequency, letting them know of her situation now that she'd resolved it.

"You should've called me sooner!" they practically shouted. "It would have taken me no time at all to get to you."

"Come on, Wil," Indya said. "The marina needs you. You don't need my irresponsible behind inconveniencing you and taking you away just when business is starting to pick up again."

Wil, like Indya and every other business owner in Soledad Bay, was still recovering after Hurricane Adalis. It had forced everyone to make adjustments, and it would be years before they fully recovered completely.

Even across the FM static, Wil's voice climbed to higher and higher decibels with each word they uttered. "You're stuck in the middle of the ocean! That's not an inconvenience. That's a life-or-death situation."

"I'm just a few miles from the shore, I have a functional radio and there are boaters still out," Indya said, touched by her friend's worry, even if they needn't have been. "Why should I drag you out here, too?"

"*Dios mío*, Indya!" Wil exclaimed. "You know, it's okay to ask for help sometimes, *amiga*. You don't have to be a superwoman all the time."

"I just sent the pan-pan signal," she retorted, though she was fully aware that they were talking about more than just this instance. She'd always had to be the strong one, as the only daughter of parents who had been forced to work long hours all their lives to build up and maintain the business that took care of them. She was later thrust into the role of single parent to her daughter, Gia, after Indya's divorce from her father, Trent. And now, she had returned to Soledad Bay to help her parents get the hotel back on its feet. Being a superwoman wasn't a choice, it was a requirement to get through her life.

The sound of an approaching engine unraveled a winch of anxiety Indya hadn't realized she'd been carrying, a winch that slowly gave way to relief at the possibility that she would soon be back on shore.

"My ride's here. I'm going to share my coordinates with you, just in case."

"It's the least you can do to keep me from d-wording from worrying," Wil complained.

Indya smiled at this. Wil spent too much time on social media. "Come on, Big Bear. I always make sure you or someone else knows where I am. You taught me that much."

"I did teach you that, didn't I?" Now Wil was practically preening over the radio.

"You can be so extra sometimes, you know that?" Indya laughed before transmitting the information.

"Be careful. Oh, and tell whoever comes to get you that if anything happens to you, I will chase them down and give them a *paliza* that their ancestors from the beginning of time will feel."

"Dios mío," Indya chuckled. "I'll be okay."

"You better be."

Indya signed off in time to hear a man's accented voice come in from outside the cabin.

"Anyone here?"

Indya clambered up the stairs. The sound was caramel smooth without the crackle of a radio transmission dampening its effect, and it wafted over her like the aroma of a homemade dessert. Oddly comforting, but for no good reason.

"Thank you for answering my call. My engines choked and now I'm stuck." She stepped up to the stern of her ship, trying to get a better look at her would-be savior. He stood at his fly bridge, wearing a baseball cap emblazoned with a yellow lion on its hind legs, over a large soccer ball, against the backdrop of a red shield. She didn't worry as much as Wil did about shenanigans out in the water. She knew Krav Maga and carried a taser at all times. With her family and employees depending on her, Indya couldn't afford to have something happen and took more than the necessary precautions to make sure she came back to the people who were waiting for her to come home.

"Do I have permission to board, Captain?" the man asked as he stepped down into the main steerage of his vessel. Painted a fresh baby blue, it was an older but well-cared-for cabin cruiser, trimmed in wood that had been recently weather-treated, judging from the fresh, even gleam of its coating. The cruiser was longer in length than the *Gia Marie*, with inboard motors that she assumed were at least as powerful. If her assessment was correct, he could easily tug the Cobia back to shore.

"Okay, yes," Indya answered.

Tapping the brim of his cap, he returned to the navigation deck. He slowly maneuvered his boat alongside hers, water frothing between the two vessels.

A gust of wind blew the cap off his head. Indya watched it tumble down and across the deck like a leaf whipped in the wind. Across the mere few feet of water that separated their boats, she came face-to-face with the owner of the voice and was nearly as blown away as the flying baseball cap. There stood a tall, powerful man with wavy brown hair, its ends burnished bronze in the sunset. His legs were long and muscular beneath cutoff jeans. He wore a stark white T-shirt, under which a sleeve tattoo wove up his arm. The color made his dusky skin glow in the gold of the low sun. Worn-leather dock shoes completed his sailing attire. Indya dragged her eyes up his rock-hard chest, as if they were scaling a jagged sea cliff to his face. Strikingly drawn eyebrows and enormous dark eyes perched on a strong nose and the kind of full lips that begged to be kissed.

Indya didn't know where her eyes should settle. She consciously drew herself up to her full height and rested her hands on her hips, hoping it would make her look bigger and more confident than she felt. It had been far too long, in her divorcée life, since she'd stumbled on anyone this good-looking and it was making her palms sweat.

He waved at her, forcing her out of her stupor, and moved around his deck with the easy confidence that came from experience. Scooping up his cap and setting it on his head again, he held the thick braid of line in his large hand and lifted it up. "I'll toss this to you."

Indya stepped out of the way of the line, catching the standing end just as it landed at her feet. The natural hemp fibers scraped against her palms, which were thankfully used to the rough handling even with her expensive gel manicure, and tied it to the cleats, making sure to loop and secure the knot carefully.

The man stepped onto her boat, sure-footed despite the swaying currents and gusty wind that was forecast to pick up as the night progressed.

"Santiago," he said by way of greeting, tipping his base-ball cap again.

"Indya," she said in response, offering him her hand, which he accepted. Strong and rough, his hands were also a bit dry, probably from handling his ship. He had a few inches on her—and she was already tall to begin with. His eyes, upon closer inspection, were a hazel pierced through with vibrant greens and dark browns, a perfect complement to the coloring of his hair.

"A pleasure," he said, his accent wrapped around each word like silk. Many of Mami and Papi's friends had similar Spanish accents, especially among the older generation of transplants from the island. But Santiago's accent possessed a different melody and Indya's ear could not stop straining to capture every note. "May I take a look at the engine?"

"Como no," she ventured, pointing with her chin at the double motors, as if he didn't already know his way around a boat. She couldn't help but lapse into the language of her home when she met other Latinos, like a universal welcome to everyone who, like her, lived in the interstices between two languages and two cultures.

"¿Hablas Español?" he asked, his smile bright with surprise.

"Sí," she answered, unable to hold his gaze. He had a smile that made her think of sunshine and glittering things. He was really a stunner. *"Aunque nací aquí, soy bilingüe."*

"Born here?" He tapped his chin. "Your accent is distinct. Is your family from Puerto Rico?"

She nodded with a touch of pride that, despite having been born in this country, her Spanish bore the traces of her parents' cadence. *"¿Y tu?"*

He chuckled, his pride also evident. *"Venezolano.* Born and raised."

A pause hung between them, not altogether unpleasant, in which they took each other in. It wasn't invasive, but there was clear admiration in his eyes. A strong wave forcing their boats to thump together served as a reminder that they were here for other, more pressing reasons.

Indya cleared her throat. "So," she said, taking up his earlier question, her nerves driving her to sound repetitive at this point. "I already checked the engines. But you are welcome to take a look at them again."

Dipping his head in acknowledgment, he made his way to the outboard motors. She watched him go through the basic steps she'd completed earlier. She studied him carefully, her eyes falling on his sleeve tattoo, names in script etched in intervals on shoots between the vines. It undulated under sinews of muscles that flexed as he worked, and the movement mesmerized her. A shift of posture caused his arm to disappear from view, interrupting her line of sight and reminding her that she had, in fact, been staring.

She glanced at the sky growing pink in the distance. If this man hadn't come out to help her, she would have run the real chance of being caught out here at night, and no matter what Wil said, retrieving her would have been an unnecessary annoyance for everyone involved. Plus, being stranded at night was the very definition of not having a good time.

Indya stood next to him, forcing her eyes away from his forearms. "What do you think?"

He shrugged. "You said they gave out at the same time?"

"They did."

He rubbed his chin, nodding softly, as if to himself. "It might be the fuel. Sometimes bad fuel can—"

"Leave debris in the tank, clogging the fuel lines and forcing the engine to shut down. I kind of arrived at that conclusion myself, but it helps to have confirmation." She smiled to take the smugness out of her words. She was used to being right and she was even more used to people not taking kindly to that fact. "Think your boat could pull mine?"

A bemused smile crossed his features before he examined her engines again, then surveyed the boat, no doubt calculating the power that would be required and variables such as time, fuel and wind—things she had already taken into account while he'd been working, but kept to herself.

He nodded as if coming to a conclusion. "Yes, no problem. Want to stay on board?"

"It's probably best if I do," Indya answered.

"I'll catch your lead." He turned to step across the space left by the lashed boats and hopped down onto his deck.

Indya moved toward the bow of the vessel and unwound the thick rope she used to dock the boats. Securing the end to the fairlead, she tied a clean hitch, wrapping it around the gleaming metal before tossing it over to Santiago.

He tied the end around his own fairlead, knotting it so hard, Indya thought he would probably need a knife to cut the rope free again. He was strong, but despite his bulk, he was also precise and careful. His size should have intimidated her, but all she felt was curiosity and a lull of comfort provoked by the velvety silk of his voice. She thought she knew almost everyone who called Soledad Bay their home, but she'd never met this stranger before. She needed to know him. It was her duty as the owner of one of the most iconic hotels in Soledad Bay to be acquainted with any potential clients or business partners living in town. There was no other reason for her intense desire to know this Santiago.

As the sun sank lower into the sky, she went about the slow and methodical work of getting both boats back to the marina, awareness of the man in the cruiser chasing her at every turn.

Chapter Two

Santiago

Santiago carefully maneuvered his boat into Sunset Marina, the *Gia Marie* bobbing gently behind. Wil, the tall, lanky marina owner, was already on hand with three other boaters to take control of the *Gia Marie* and pull her in. Part of the marina was still closed after the storm, so they angled her toward a guest slip, where they tied her down for the night.

Santiago made sure his boat was safely parked in a nearby empty slip and secured before hopping onto the dock of Indya's boat and helping to tie the lines of the *Gia Marie* to the pylons. Santiago tried not to stare at the beautiful captain of the stranded vessel, who currently held one of the rough, thick lines in her pretty hands. She heaved right along with Wil and the others, her dark, wavy ponytail bouncing from the effort of pulling on the line until the boat slid into place. Santiago was no stranger to a woman doing a man's work but had not expected someone who seemed so well manicured and polished as her to be one of them. Everything about her screamed femininity, but it was not the fragile kind.

Santiago was a sucker for contrasts, and his need to understand this woman was growing into an irresistible impulse.

He reined himself in. His impulsivity had already gotten him in trouble in life. Now was the time for him to take things slow and be measured about his reactions.

"Indya!" Her name pulled him out of his reverie. He watched Wil drag Indya into a massive hug. A giant, single gold hoop earring that hung from one of several ear piercings knocked her on the nose, and Santiago had to bite back a smile. "You had me out of my mind with worry. Glad you found someone to help you out."

"Yeah, Santiago's been great." She released Wil and turned toward Santiago, inviting him into their conversation. "If he hadn't answered my call, I might have been stuck out there until the morning."

"Someone would have helped you, for sure," Santiago responded, though he was pleased, not only with the praise, but with the simple sound of his name on her lips.

"Maybe." Indya watched him unflinchingly, triggering a quiver of excitement low in his belly.

Slow down, he scolded himself.

Wil looked from one to the other. "I'll get Josh to take a look at the engines tomorrow morning. Just leave the key with me."

"Pretty sure it's just the fuel," Indya said, pulling a set of keys from a key holder in her pocket and handing it to them. Santiago secretly agreed and was confident in Indya's assessment that the marina's on-site mechanic would not find anything more.

Wil shrugged. "Maybe. But I'll get him to look at it anyway." They turned to Santiago. "Hey, thanks for helping out. Indy and I go back a long way. She's like a sister to me." Wil's hands flew as they spoke, running a mile a minute, which Santiago found charming and familiar. His younger sister, Miriam, had that same animated way of expressing herself, in total contrast to him.

Wil rubbed their tummy, distorting the sketch of a sailboat on the worn, light blue tee they wore. "I remember you. A couple of weeks ago, I drew up your short-term rental contract for a slip on the south side of the marina."

"How could I forget?" Santiago recalled Wil telling him that their pronouns were they/them, which Santiago had made sure to fix in his mind. "Your cat jumped on my lap and fell asleep."

"Misha?" Indya's eyes grew wide with surprise. "She's a hellion."

"No, she is my glorious feline queen and I will hear no slander about her," Wil retorted. They'd told Santiago that they had found her as a kitten hiding in one of the stored boats and had instantly claimed her. "If she sat on his lap, it means she likes him."

"That *demonia* doesn't like anyone," Indya snapped back.

"She seemed to like me well enough," Santiago interjected, suspecting that Indya would not appreciate him agreeing with Wil, an impression that was confirmed by the way she narrowed her eyes at him. It wasn't an exaggeration. The tabby had barely hesitated before landing in Santiago's lap, her purr like a jet engine. She had proceeded to knead his jean-clad thighs before settling in and promptly falling asleep.

Misha reminded him of Tigre, a neighborhood cat he had known back home in Caracas. He'd grown fond of her, though she was cared for by everyone on the block and considered property of the neighborhood. She had been similarly patterned as Misha—a light-brown-and-gold tabby with bands of black along her tail like a raccoon's. He thought of her often and hoped she was well cared for and doing okay. By the time he left Caracas, people could barely attend to themselves, much less the animals that called the city their home. Tigre had been taken in by an elderly gentleman who'd sworn he would leave his city in a coffin, not before. Tigre had been a sweet but sturdy beauty, one of the many beloved things he'd had to abandon when he left his country.

Sometimes home was a scrappy animal who came to your business for a meal each day and used the doorjamb of your building as a scratch post.

Santiago shook himself out of his memories. There was no use dwelling on them. It only served to augment the constant melancholy that had become a part of his psyche ever since he had been forced to leave Venezuela two years earlier. He'd spent too many months drowning in misery and anger, and it had been an utter waste. He was in Soledad Bay now, with a new approach to life and a different set of objectives.

"A fluke." Indya's voice cut across his thoughts. Her face was adorably petulant and Santiago was captivated by the contrast with the toughness she'd shown until now. "I get goose bumps just thinking of how that *malvada* stares at me every time I walk into the marina shop." She shivered in reaction to whatever image her imagination presented to her. "She's nothing but a wicked little beast."

"You just say that because she's mean to you," Wil answered, sounding wounded. "She's a sweetheart to everyone else."

"The fact that she lets Santiago get within hissing distance of her says a lot more about him than it does about her." She turned her nose up at Wil. "That doesn't make her a good cat."

"No, but it does make her a discerning one," they huffed, crossing their arms for emphasis.

Santiago chuckled at the banter. Indya's answering smile felt like the flash of a camera bulb, blinding him. It was perfect and made her face look fresh and much more vulnerable than it had when she'd been fretting over her boat. He looked away before he was caught staring. The sun had completely set and it was time for him to get going.

"Cat defamation aside, you can leave your boat in the guest slip until the morning if you don't want to bother with moving it," Wil said.

Santiago shook his head. "I'd prefer to just dock her for the night." He turned to Indya, now more able to take in her lovely face and lively expression without being blinded into silence. "You will get home safely, *sí*?"

"Yes, but—" Indya frowned, twisting her fingers together "—can I buy you a drink as a thank-you for your help, before you run off?"

Santiago's smile escaped despite himself. He had an early day tomorrow, and a to-do list as long as his arm. But she was absolutely captivating, and if he was honest with himself, he was loath to let her get away so soon. His grandmother had always said that the sea gave an endless bounty, and at this moment, he was inclined to agree with her. "You don't have to buy me a drink."

"I really do," Indya insisted. "But if you have somewhere to be…or someone to be *with*…"

"No," he quickly answered. He took a deep breath, then spoke again. "No, I don't have anyone waiting for me."

A glint of humor sparkled in her eyes and bled into the curl of her smile. He'd exposed himself, but God, she really was a finely made woman, from the top of her wavy, brown hair to the bottom of her boat shoes. She had the kind of gaze that could capture him like a crab pot and not let go. It was no wonder that every word out of his mouth laid his interest out for her to see.

"Hey, I'll get one of the boys to dock your vessel." Wil's voice broke the spell Indya had woven around him. They waved over one of the young men who'd helped pull Indya's boat into the slip. "That way you can throw back a few without worrying about getting behind the wheel."

Santiago hesitated before relenting, handing over his key to Wil. He was no different from most seamen who were possessive of their vessels and didn't easily tolerate anyone else handling them. But he was even more possessive of the *Aragona*. Ever since he'd relocated to Soledad Bay from Miami, the cruiser served as his temporary home until he sorted out permanent living arrangements, ones that preferably did not involve his father, with whom sharing a living space had the same effect as mixing bleach and ammonia.

"Don't worry," Wil assured. "They'll take good care of her."

"I have no doubt," Santiago answered. The marina owner had proven their reliability and Santiago trusted them. He swept his hand in Indya's direction, waiting for her to lead the way. Indya thanked Wil before moving inside to the marina's bar-restaurant. Patrons sat at small wooden tables illuminated by electric lantern centerpieces. Indya and Santiago wove their way past couples or groups of people having drinks at the bar after a day on the water. Wil had a couple of helpers Santiago already recognized as regulars at the marina, young men who worked just enough to fund their fishing habits.

"Are you hungry?" Indya asked as they settled into a pair of stools at the helm-shaped bar, complete with brass trim and wood spokes. "The marina has a small restaurant that serves sandwiches and simple hot foods."

Santiago glanced around him. He hadn't had many opportunities to explore the marina restaurant. Mamá kept him well stocked with food from the meals she prepared at Taste of Caracas, the supermarket she and his father owned together. Santiago didn't have to trouble himself with food very often, which was convenient, because the boat's kitchen, while functional, was also the size of a dollhouse and not particularly comfortable. "I ate earlier, thank you," Santiago answered. "I'll have to try it someday."

"They just reopened it. It was closed for repairs after Hurricane Adalis came through, as most of the town was." Indya rested her head on her hand, growing pensive. "Soledad Bay took a hit, but they were still very lucky."

"They? Don't you live in Soledad Bay, too?"

Indya huffed silently. "Yes, I do now. I was even born and raised here. But I moved away for over a decade to live in Sarasota and have only been back for a few months."

Santiago remembered the hurricane that arrived the summer before, sending fierce winds and dumping rain along the west coast of the peninsula before slamming into Apalachicola Bay. It ran up the coast and inland across north Florida and south Georgia before hitting the Atlantic again and sweeping out to open sea. But not before it left its mark on several coastal towns. Soledad Bay was one of the survivors, but only barely.

"I was in Miami at the time, but I remember it well."

Indya tapped her manicured nails on the counter. "Soledad Bay took heavy damage, but it's still standing. Not every town around us can say the same."

A Tom Petty earworm from the old-fashioned jukebox played as she spoke. Beyond her, wall-length windows looked out on the boats docked at the marina. Indya had a lovely, straight nose, full lips and a strong chin that made her profile look like it should have been imprinted on a coin.

Wil appeared, setting down a set of keys in front of Santiago. "Your boat's all set."

"Thank you." Relief flooded through him.

"I'll be right back to take your order," Wil said, hustling off again.

"You were really worried about your boat, huh?" Indya observed.

Santiago smiled at her directness. He appreciated the unadorned way she communicated. "I can't help it. I live on it."

Her surprised laugh washed over him and he decided he truly enjoyed listening to it. "You live on your boat? I thought that wasn't legal on a motorized vessel."

Santiago nodded. "This is true for long-term liveaboards, but the state of Florida allows it for short periods as long as you don't claim it as your residence."

"Oh, good to know." Indya grew wistful. "I've always wanted to do that. Sleep with the sound of the water surrounding me. Go out and fish whenever I want."

"Why don't you?" Santiago asked, genuinely curious. He knew very little about her, but she didn't seem like the kind of person who was meek about going after what she wanted.

"Truthfully, I'm spoiled and I hate being uncomfortable."

Santiago barked out a laugh that pulled an answering laugh from her. "You have a good point. It's nice, but I get tired of the tight space. I'm hoping to move into an apartment in a month or so."

Before Indya could ask more questions, Wil returned, beaming at them. "What will you two wild kids have?"

Indya pointed at the cold case. "The usual."

"One Corona Light with lime, coming right up. And you?"

Santiago lifted himself up and over the wooden counter, assessing the available beers on tap. "I'll take the local brew, please." He settled down, feeling Indya's eyes on him.

"You have good taste," Wil said. "No wonder Misha likes you."

"Maybe she just likes the smell of fish on me," Santiago replied.

"Misha is too wicked to be persuaded by something as common as the smell of fish. It's definitely you." Indya laughed. "Wil, put our drinks on my tab, please."

Santiago began to protest, but Indya put up a hand. "You rescued me. It's the least I can do."

"Neither of you are paying," Wil interjected. "This round's on me."

"Wil!" Indya scolded.

Santiago dipped his head in acknowledgment. "Thank you."

"Wow, *que machismo*," Indya said when Wil walked away, flip-flops clopping in their retreat. "You'll take a free drink from Wil, who you assume is male because of the way they present, even though they identify as non-binary, but not from me, who you actually helped, because I present as a woman?"

"Oh." Santiago's mental machinery began to scream and smoke. He hadn't thought of that at all, and was horrified to realize she was not entirely wrong. He knew better than to do that. "I didn't... Okay, maybe that was *un poquito machista*."

"¡Un poquito machista!" Indya exclaimed. "How about a lot!"

"Okay, okay. I just..." He rubbed his face, trying to find some way to recover his footing, and chose the truth. *"Mira*, I'm not used to women offering to buy me drinks.

If you'd like to, then you should be able to and the person you're with should be gracious enough to accept it. But you shouldn't feel obligated to buy me a drink. Meeting you is enough payment for me."

"Oh." She dropped her eyes, the vulnerable gesture sending a pulse of warmth through him. His instincts told him that she did not often reveal her soft underbelly, that beneath the direct language and can-do attitude, there might be a gentle and tender side of her that she didn't often show to the world.

As he surmised, the gesture evaporated under a wicked grin when she looked up again. "Nice save," she retorted.

"And, if I am honest," he added, unable to help himself, "I really wanted to impress you a little by offering to buy you a drink instead."

The humor sharpened her expression. "You wanted to impress me by paying for my overpriced beer?"

"Hey, I heard that," came Wil's voice from the other end of the counter.

"Just kidding. I love you and your prices!" she shouted in response. When she turned back to Santiago, he was laughing at her. "You already impressed me by fishing me out of the water. But you can impress me with some small talk. Where exactly in Venezuela are you from?"

Santiago set the beer down on the coaster with precision. He hated wet spots on wooden furniture, even the ones that didn't belong to him. Wood should be respected. "The capital city, Caracas. But I've lived in Miami for the last couple of years. Your people are from Puerto Rico, you said?"

She lifted her wrist to show him the red, white and blue bracelet with the tiny Puerto Rican flag painted onto one of the beads. "My grandparents were from Puerto Rico."

"Americana," he teased, eyes shining with mirth.

Indya's expression grew mordant. "I'll have you know that even the ones born on the island are *Americanos. Muchas gracias.*"

"They might have something to say about that statement," he said around a laugh. At her glare, he added quickly. "Your Spanish is very good, though."

She beamed at this. "Growing up, my mother only spoke to me in Spanish because she wanted me to be bilingual. Later, I studied the language throughout school as part of my degree." She spun her coaster, watching it whirl until it flattened and went still. "Do you prefer that I speak in Spanish?"

"I prefer English, if you don't mind," he answered. "It's a good way to get practice. Otherwise, I sound like I learned the language from a grammar book, which, truthfully, I did." Santiago's parents had worked hard to send him to good schools in Venezuela, and followed Miriam's studies closely here in the US. They'd wanted their children to become educated adults who would not have to struggle as much in their lives as they had.

"That's why you speak it so grammatically well," Indya observed. "Until I took it in high school, my Spanish was functional, but my grammar was all over the place, a point my native-speaking cousins never failed to point out." She chuckled to herself. "Teachers thought it would be easy for me to perfect the language. But learning Spanish grammar is work. I can relate to you wanting to speak English as much as possible, because I was exactly the same when I wanted to improve my Spanish."

He raised a finger, and very seriously said, *"La practica hace el maestro."*

"Practice really does make the expert," she repeated. *"Bueno*, English it is." She gave him a thumbs-up, which pulled another smile from him. Her voice was husky and warm, inviting him to listen and laugh along with her.

His eyes dropped to the cupid's bow of her lips, perfectly arched, full and thick, the blush color of a strawberry daiquiri. His eyes kept returning to the elegant shape, and he tried very hard not to stare. He pulled away on the pretext of taking a long swallow of beer.

"That's why I make sure that my daughter speaks Spanish every chance she gets. I don't want her to be monolingual," Indya said at length.

Santiago's interest sharpened. "You have a daughter? How old is she?" His enthusiasm seemed to catch Indya off guard and he hurried to clarify. "I ask because I have a daughter as well. Her name is Lisbet. She's ten and her mother tells me she is a terror."

India's shifted her entire focus to him, and it was intense, like having the light of a bright lamp shine down on him "She doesn't live here with you?"

He shook his head. "She lives in Venezuela with her mother. We separated a few years ago. When I came to the US, I had to leave her behind."

"I bet you miss her," she said quietly, studying his reaction carefully. It made him self-conscious, as if he was undergoing a test and was at risk of failing.

"Como el oxígeno." He pulled up his T-shirt sleeve, uncovering the top of his tattoo. He tapped at a spot just below his shoulder. "I added her name when she was born."

Indya leaned forward to study the lines of his daughter's name, the looping sweep of the *L* that led to the remaining letters, which sprang from the tip of the vine. Several names bloomed from other branches, but she seemed most riveted by his daughter's.

"Lisbet," she read. "It's a beautiful name. I had this one

done for my daughter when she was born." Indya lifted the T-shirt sleeve of her right arm up to her shoulder. On the firm, smooth skin was an arrow dragging a date across her shoulder. It was simple, the work of an hour, tops, but it was elegant. It suited what he knew of this lovely woman so far.

"It's very elegant." He dropped his finger to stare into dark eyes that threatened to pull him into their depths. "Like you."

She bit her lip, as if holding back a smile. He liked being able to shake her composure, because he suspected it was not an easy thing to do.

"Is there any chance of seeing her soon?" Indya asked after a few moments passed.

Santiago's sigh came from deep in his bones. "I'm trying to get her here, but I need to be more settled and government agencies move very slowly over there. If all goes well, we will celebrate her birthday in July." She would have arrived sooner if he hadn't financially imploded, forcing him to put off filing the paperwork to bring her to the US. But he was in a better place now, and working hard to make up for lost time.

Indya raised her glass to him. "Here's hoping you'll be with her soon."

Santiago raised a glass in response. "Amen." They both took a long draught of their beers before setting them down.

"So," he said, changing the subject. "Tell me about your daughter."

"Gia?" She chuckled. "She's fourteen going on forty and knows more than everyone around her, including her mother. Especially her mother." Her words carried a tender exasperation toward her daughter. "I named a whole boat after her."

"The *Gia Marie*." He nodded, the name taking on greater importance. "And her father?"

Indya stiffened, tapping on the counter again. "Her father lives here, in Soledad Bay. Just not with us."

"Ah. Sorry about that."

She shrugged. "It happens. It's been a long time." A phone vibrated and they both went for their pockets at the same time.

"Speak of the devil. I have to get going." She stood, flagging Wil down; they were swaying to the jukebox beat of Tina Turner's "The Best" while they sorted receipts. "Can you close out my tab? Gia needs me to come to her dad's house."

They twirled to a stop in front of them. "No problem, *chica*. Is my baby girl okay?"

"Gia is everybody's baby girl, I swear." She dug her car key out of her pocket and Santiago felt instantly bereft. He could have spent hours talking to her. "She left her schoolbag in my car and only just noticed. I'm going to run it over to her dad's on the way home. It'll save me a trip in the morning." She turned to Santiago. "Thank you so much for your help. Soledad Bay is not a big place, so I hope to see you around." Indya put out her hand for him to shake. "It was nice meeting you."

"Thank you for the drink." He wanted to tell her more, that stumbling on her boat had been the best thing that had happened to him in weeks, wanted to ask where she spent her time when she wasn't stalling her engine on the Gulf, but Indya was in a hurry. Instead, Santiago took her hand, holding its delicate warmth in his larger, more calloused one. The contact sizzled, warming his skin and making his heart shift in his chest. Her expression was that of someone who had also been caught off guard and hadn't quite recovered yet. He gently withdrew his hand from hers and moved to take out his phone to hopefully exchange phone numbers, but she had already turned away and, without looking back, bounded out the door and into the night.

Chapter Three

Indya

The town was quiet as Indya's Audi glided through the sleeping streets of Soledad Bay. Every now and again, a scaffold was visible on the sides of buildings still under reconstruction, and more than a few residential roofs were still covered in the blue tarp that FEMA provided to keep houses with roof damage from being further compromised by rain or bad weather. Businesses had been prioritized to keep people employed and services flowing. They'd applied for, and most had been awarded, emergency small-business loans, but even with the accelerated timelines, things moved slowly. When repair times dragged on too long, it had catastrophic consequences for a business's ability to recover.

Alba Beachside Resort had been lucky in that respect. Indya had been able to get the major structural damages under control. But Carlos up and leaving when there was so much left to fix had really set the resort back, all while she was still trying to provide the kind of service the resort was known for. Despite how hard she worked to project cool confidence, sometimes her to-do list overwhelmed her with anxiety, and she had no one to share it with. She couldn't trouble her parents with that—Mami had her hands full, shuttling Papi to his appointments. It was all on Indya, and she didn't have the luxury of breaking down.

She approached the road where her ex-husband lived. Trent's house belonged to his family. It was situated right on the canal, just a few blocks away from the sea. Indya remembered it well—they'd lived in that same house when they'd first gotten married, just two teenagers, recently graduated from high school, when Indya ended up pregnant with Gia. They'd gotten married, carrying the weight of a family when they were barely adults themselves.

Things quickly fell apart, as soon as it became apparent what kind of marriage Trent wanted—a perfectly traditional stay-at-home mother and housekeeper in a house with a white picket fence, a football team's worth of kids and two dogs in the yard. The whole suburban dream. He would work for his father's construction company, and be sole breadwinner and head of the family.

That was never going to make Indya happy.

Trent had resisted her going to college on the pretense that Gia was too young, even though it hadn't cost him a thing and Indya's mother had provided the lion's share of the childcare. Though it was to the economic advantage of the family for Indya to earn a degree and work at least part-time, Trent had been against it. When it was clear she would not relent on this, his resistance became passive-aggressive. He refused to split the housekeeping or child-rearing, not interfering but not supporting Indya, either. When she graduated and was offered a lucrative, entry-level position with an accounting firm in Sarasota, she packed her possessions and her daughter into the SUV she'd owned at the time and moved there.

If anyone asked Trent, he said it was Indya's fault that

the relationship had come to an end, because she'd wanted too much. If she had just done her womanly duty and taken care of her family, and at least waited until Gia was in high school before trying to do things like going to school or making a career for herself, they might still be together.

It never occurred to him that there were women the world over who managed to do just that, and their husbands not only did not force them to choose between their aspirations and their families but actually supported them because what was good for the wife was usually good for the family.

Imagine how that worked.

Indya gripped the steering wheel. There was no sense in rehashing this argument with herself. She'd had it with Trent, with his family, sometimes even with strangers who had too much to say over bodies and lives that weren't their own. Indya was not going to waste any more real estate in her brain on this. She'd come to terms with the end of her marriage and what she needed to do to successfully live her life. It did not include conforming to some outdated idea of womanhood.

She had a hotel to manage, two elderly parents to take care of, and a wonderful, if somewhat forgetful, teenager to raise. She had to lock in on those priorities and leave that painful past behind her.

Except that, every now and again, when she was at her loneliest, she couldn't help but wonder if maybe he had been right.

Indya pulled up to her ex-husband's house, the single-story Florida home illuminated by a street lamp, while inside, a golden light glowed in the space she knew to be the living room. Flickering flashes filtered through the curtains, which meant that the television was probably on. Indya maneuvered the car into the driveway before shutting off the motor. She braced herself—even after all these years, she and Trent would sometimes go at it, though they did their best to be civil for Gia's sake.

Stepping out of the car, Indya swung Gia's oversize backpack onto her shoulder. It weighed as much as a person, and Indya couldn't imagine how Gia biked around with the thing on her back.

Indya observed the landscaping and what looked like a cobblestone walk that hadn't been there before. Trent had always been good with his hands and had a DIY project ongoing at any given time. Even in the dark, Indya saw how much the house he'd inherited had changed in his care. Once little more than a middling Florida canal home, it was now a stylish bungalow that could hold its own among the toniest houses in Soledad Bay.

Indya thought fleetingly how useful someone with those skills would be to her now that her hotel was without a facilities manager, but she pushed the thought out of her mind. She'd never be able to work with Trent. He simply wouldn't accept a woman directing him, especially if that woman was his ex-wife.

She rang the doorbell, then fired off a text to Gia to let her know she was outside. She'd just pressed Send when the door opened and Trent appeared. His green eyes raked quickly over her, his dark blond hair glistening gold under the light of the moon. She still found him attractive after all these years. Too bad his ideas belonged firmly in the Paleolithic Age.

"Hey, Indya, didn't expect to see you out this late." He stepped aside to let her in.

Indya walked through the small, dimly lit foyer to the family room before her. It was a large room with a wall of windows facing the canal. To the right was a rich, oak-wood panclcd island which divided the open space between the living area and kitchen. A dining nook was wedged into the corner, and beyond the patio doors, a screened-in deck sat at the end of the gently illuminated pier.

The windows were part of the original design, but the beautiful, oak-wood flooring, stainless steel appliances and overall woodsy interior were all things Trent had added through the years. Even with the sunlight, the vibe of the house was that of a man cave.

"I'm guessing Gia forgot something." He adjusted the tie of his sweatpants, his white tee snug around his shoulders and loose around his waist. "Want to have a seat?"

"No, I'm good." Indya indicated the backpack with a quick tilt of her head. "Gia forgot her school bag in my car and she only just realized it now. Figure I'd drop it off on the way home."

His eyes flicked over her outfit. "Been out on the boat?"

Indya shifted on her feet. "Yeah. Haven't had too many chances to take the *Gia Marie* out since I brought her up from Sarasota." She clamped her mouth shut, suppressing the instinctive need, even after all these years, to justify her passions to Trent, even the ones she shared with him, like fishing and boating. He had always teased her about the hobbies that didn't revolve around maintaining the comfort of their family, but the edge to that teasing had told her he merely tolerated her interests and did not actively encourage them.

"So, uh, did you catch anything?"

No way was she sharing her boat troubles with him. "Not much. I wasn't out too long."

An awkward silence descended. Indya didn't want to linger and Trent probably had a game or sports program he was missing, given the way he kept fidgeting and looking back at the television. That hadn't changed much, either—his absolute obsession with sports. Didn't matter what they were, even sports he didn't understand well. He had always preferred to wind down with a game than do something as banal as spend time with his wife, who should be working anyway.

To Indya's immense relief, Gia burst out of one of the back bedrooms. Trent always kept a room for her, which he decorated any way she liked. She was a tall fourteen-year-old—no surprise, given her and Trent's height. But she looked even younger with her hair swept up in a messy bun and her face freshly washed. She wore her favorite short pink-and-blue-cotton pajama set. She'd gotten her olive coloring from her mother, but the dark blond waves and hazel eyes were all from her father's side.

"Mom!" she said, flinging her arms around Indya, nearly knocking the giant bag onto the floor.

"Hello, Little Miss Forgetful." Indya squeezed her little girl close to her. Her daughter was her partner in crime, spending every spare minute with her. Gia hadn't even had a proper sleep over, spending the nights she wasn't with Indya with either of her two sets of grandparents or her father. Even on those few nights with the people Indya knew would take care of her, she missed her little girl desperately.

"You're amazing, Mom! I have my notes for my science project, and if I don't bring them for tomorrow's work session, I'm going to lose points for participation."

"Science project?" Trent asked.

"Uh, yeah, Dad," Gia said, the hesitation clear in her voice, which Indya didn't like one bit. "We're building a hydroponic garden and each group is responsible for their own plot of land."

"That sounds like messy work," Trent said, smiling down

at Gia. "Be careful. You don't want to ruin those pretty little hands."

"Her pretty hands will be just fine," Indya snapped.

Trent cast a sharp glance at Indya. Gia, who was unflappable even on a bad day, simply shrugged away the sudden chill between her parents. "Most of the work is design stuff anyway. The digging and planting doesn't take much time at all." She hugged the bag to her chest. "We're going to have an Instagram page, too. That way, parents can follow our progress."

"Sounds amazing," Indya said, beaming at her. Gia was a STEM girl through and through, and it thrilled Indya to think of all the doors that would open for her. "I hope you don't have any homework to do. It's late and you should be headed to bed."

Gia shook her head. "I got everything done during study hall." She gave her mother and her father a kiss on the cheek each. "I'm going to bed. Swim practice was brutal today."

"Get upstairs then, *mija*," Indya said, catching Gia in her momma-bear hug. "You need your sleep to keep growing."

"I'm tall enough!" Gia protested.

"Doesn't matter," Trent added. "A growing young lady needs her beauty sleep."

"Okaaaaaay." Gia giggled before scurrying off with her insanely heavy bag to her room.

Indya waited for her daughter to be well out of sight before turning her attention to Trent. "The hydroponic garden is a semester-long project that she's very excited about. If it works, we're going to add one to the hotel and she will be responsible for taking care of it. Our chef can use the fresh vegetables in his dishes."

"Your chef's going to have to prepare it, because I noticed that Gia can't cook to save her own life."

Indya bristled. "She can. She just chooses not to, like her mom."

"She's not going to keep a partner if she doesn't even know how to boil an egg or do the bare minimum around the house."

Now, that got Indya going. "Or, maybe she'll find a partner who will do it for her. Has that ever occurred to you?"

"That's not realistic," Trent scoffed. "No man is going to marry a woman who can't even make scrambled eggs."

"You did."

"And we got divorced."

"How dare you?"

This was an old argument between them, a wound they couldn't help but press whenever their tempers flared. It always came back to how Indya was somehow the one responsible for their failed marriage.

Trent ran a hand through his hair, the tension so thick that the air between them crackled with it. He visibly backed down. "Look, I just want her to be happy."

"As if getting married at all costs is the only way for her to achieve that."

Trent threw his hands out in frustration. "Come on, Indya, I'm just saying that she should know how to at least take care of herself."

"Now, that's something I can agree with, but that's not at all what you said, is it?"

Trent glanced at the television, his limited attention span slipping away. "You don't have to get so defensive."

"I'm not—" Indya was beyond frustrated. There was no reasoning with him. "Listen, it's late and I have to get going. But please, check your chauvinism when it comes to Gia."

"It's not chauvinism. It's realism. If you want her to find

happiness in a relationship, she really needs to learn to do more than just build little hydroponic gardens at school."

"So, is it her not being able to take care of herself that worries you, or is it your fear that she won't find a relationship?"

Trent pursed his lips, shaking his head. "It's one and the same."

"Goodbye, Trent," Indya said, exasperated. "I don't care what you think. Don't spew that nonsense at Gia or I'll make sure she never comes to see you again."

"Court's gonna have something different to say about that," Trent retorted.

Unfortunately, being a card-carrying member of the Gold Star Sexist Club was not enough to get the courts to modify their custody agreement. And frankly, outside of those ideas, Trent was a good, even indulgent, father. He just really needed to get with the modern program, because of all the girls he thought he could persuade with the benefits of a traditional marriage, Gia was not one of them.

"Just talk less and listen more, okay?" Indya said finally. "Good night."

"Hey," Trent called out when she was nearly through the door. "Text when you get in. It's dark out there."

His words took the edge off her anger. He was so freaking annoying, but he also had that overprotective streak that some people would find endearing. She just didn't happen to be one of those people. "I'll be sure to do that."

She shut the door behind her and made her way quickly to her car. It really was late, and the next day promised to be a long one. She leaned back into the leather seat, thinking of Trent's words, which nagged at a tender place inside of her. She was a tough lady and she didn't apologize for her strength. On the contrary, it was one of her most im-

portant, necessary qualities. She'd needed that strength,
first to survive her divorce in her early twenties, then when
she'd had to learn to be a good single parent to her daughter while earning her degree and making inroads in the
good ole boy's club of the finance firm she'd worked for
in Sarasota. Now she was back in Soledad Bay to help her
elderly parents get the family hotel back on its feet. Tough
wasn't a quirk of her personality—it was her only mode.

But sometimes, she wondered if being so strong hadn't
exacted too high of a price. Powering up the engine and
pulling out onto the street, she reminded herself that, in-
tellectually, it took two people to wreck a relationship. But
she couldn't help that kernel of self-doubt that told her if
she had only been a little bit softer, she might be living
a different life now. Not that she missed her ex-husband.
She really didn't. But she did miss being a part of a family unit, having someone besides herself to depend on. She
never introduced the men she was dating to Gia, reserving
that step for the person she thought would occupy a permanent place in her life. That person, so far, had failed to
materialize, and she didn't expect the position to be filled
anytime soon.

She gave a passing thought to the man who had towed
her stranded boat back to the marina. Santiago had been
quiet, mild-mannered and handsome. He was new to this
area, too, though she hadn't had the time to find out his
whole back story. And he had a daughter who wasn't with
him, a torture she could not even conceive of. She'd thought
of asking for his phone number. But when Gia's message
came through, every other thought in her head had disappeared. Too bad because he would have been a nice person to have around.

Indya sighed as she pulled her car into her covered driveway on the side of her beachfront home and quickly got out, taking a survey of her surroundings. She had a human resources crisis to address now that Carlos was gone and there was so much work to be done on the property. He'd been with them for so long, he knew that hotel better than even Indya did. It was going to be a headache to replace him and get someone new onboarded quickly enough to address all the repairs. She tapped in her alarm code and stepped inside, wondering if it might not have been better if she'd just stayed out on her stranded boat until morning after all.

Chapter Four

Santiago

Santiago returned to his boat and went through his usual preparations. Despite his physical exhaustion from the events of the evening, he had a hard time falling asleep. He couldn't stop thinking about the woman he'd met. The memory of her pressed down on him, like an invisible weight, making its presence known no matter how he tossed and turned. When he did drift off, it was to the sight of her, laughing at some comment at the bar, or grasping the rough rope to help Wil and their workers pull the *Gia Marie* into the slip.

At dawn, his eyes were wide open again. He scrubbed the sleep from his face before sliding out of bed, tossing on a pair of sweats he'd fished out from his drawer and making his way across his tiny space and up the stairs to the deck of his boat. Only the dim night-lights of the marina illuminated the deck. In each slip, a boat bobbed gently with the swaying currents. Every movement slowly replenished his thoughts and his energies. Santiago's family were originally from a seaside town, and even though they had relo-

cated to the city when he was very young, he was drawn
to the water like a turtle returning to its depths after nesting in the sand. That energy flooded him now, despite the
lateness of the hour.

The sea sloshed against the sides of the boat, a half-
sleepy undulation that filled the air with its sibilant, swishing sound. He had always found peace in the salt and sand
of the ocean. Its power didn't intimidate him. He welcomed
its invitation to get lost in it. As he planned for the rest of
the day, he would need that strength and healing energy
more than ever. He had several interviews over the next
few days, with the hopes that one would come through.
He needed a job to settle and grow roots here, not only for
himself, but for his daughter as well, whose absence ached
like a constant, gaping wound.

He hadn't seen Lisbet since he visited Caracas the summer before last. Those two weeks hadn't been long enough,
and every day that passed since his return was one more
twist of the knife to his gut. Back home, he'd been well
on his way to achieving what few people dreamed of—
making enough money to support himself and his family
while doing something he loved. After years of property
and facilities management in some of the largest hotels in
Caracas, he had left to begin his own business as a crafts-
man specializing in woodwork, and he was brilliant at his
job. That was, until the national economy started to col-
lapse and Jose, his long-time friend and business partner,
had decided that their friendship was not strong enough to
resist the temptation to steal what he had not earned. He'd
liquidated the company and escaped to neighboring Co-
lombia without Santiago being the wiser. The only thing
that remained of all he'd built was an outstanding lease on
a building for a business that no longer existed.

What made it an even more bitter pill to swallow was that his father had warned him against leaving his management position to open the business to begin with. He'd wanted Santiago to use his degree to find a steady job in the government or the petroleum industry—the two most viable institutions in his country. He'd gotten the degree to make his father happy, but owning his own business doing a craft his grandfather had taught him had always been his dream, and he had been so close to making it sustainable. His father had called his business a risk he could not afford to take. Little could he have anticipated that his father would be right because he'd chosen the wrong person to trust, and it had altered his life forever.

He also couldn't have anticipated how his move to the US would complicate things for Lisbet, or how hard it would be for Santiago to bring his ex-girlfriend and his daughter over when they were ready. He and Natasha had never married, and as things had begun to deteriorate in their country, everything had become more expensive, including going through the legal channels to emigrate. The US made immigration as difficult as possible, but he was determined to do it properly and give his daughter the best opportunity of a secure life. So he did what he was told to do: Completed their paperwork. Attended the interviews. Paid the exorbitant fees. And he waited. *Dios mío*, how he waited.

After a rough start in Miami, he had finally found a stable situation. He'd been sure he could bring Lisbet and Natasha to the US. But then he'd been laid off from work and flung back to square one. Mamá had persuaded him to try Soledad Bay. A new start, close to his parents and little sister, in a town he could settle down in. It was everything he needed to build a life for himself and his daughter, if he could just nail down the employment part.

As the sun rose over the eastern horizon, past the endless deciduous forests that surrounded Soledad Bay, Santiago retired to the inside of his cruiser and its diminutive dimensions to get dressed and prepare for the day. The restricted space was the price he paid for peace. Mamá had offered him the guest room for his indefinite use until he could get on his feet again. She was so happy to have her family, including the possibility of her granddaughter, all together that she was prepared to do anything to help him.

But he couldn't imagine occupying the same living space as Papá. Not in a million years.

Santiago stepped onto the dock, taking a moment to find his land legs before striding in the direction of the parking lot. The marina's rental office, a large blue, two-story building, was on the way. Next to the building stood the dry-stack storage, three boats currently occupying the available spots, one on top of the other. Santiago's experience of the sea didn't involve modern-marina life, so every aspect caught his attention.

A cursory glance through the propped-open side door indicated that someone was already inside. Santiago moved in that direction—it would only take a few minutes to ask about Indya's boat and confirm that she'd gotten home okay. Wil seemed like the type who would expect her to check in with them. He didn't interrogate this impulse too deeply—in his opinion, it was the neighborly thing to do. It had nothing to do with wanting to know how she was.

Upon Santiago's approach to the lot, Wil stepped out, carrying a can of paint and a brush. They wore what Santiago suspected was their daily uniform—a pale yellow T-shirt emblazoned with a sunset in the center. The words "Sunset Marina" were superimposed in gold over the image. They paired it with a well-used pair of cargo shorts, if the frayed edges of the pockets were any indication. Santiago couldn't help but smile at their pink Crocs decorated with cat charms. Misha slinked ahead of them, her tail swishing lazily in the air.

"Are those in honor of Misha?" Santiago said, pointing at the charms.

"What? Oh." Wil smiled at Santiago's approach. They lifted one foot, admiring the decorations. "She's more than a pet. She's my aesthetic. Isn't that right, Mish-Mish?"

The well-fed tabby threw herself down on the ground, rolled over and offered them her belly. Wil set the can down and scratched at the soft fluff of her fur. They glanced up, a wide smile brightening their features. Santiago had been so captivated by Indya the night before that he hadn't appreciated the elegant symmetry of Wil's angular face, etched into the smooth, golden skin, or the sensuality of their full, if somewhat crooked lips.

"Go ahead. Give her a scratch." Wil's fingers were deep under the thick fur of the cat's chin.

Santiago hunched down as well, scratching the top of her head. Her purring grew as loud as a jet engine.

"She really does like you," Wil said between saying sweet nothings to Misha.

"Does she prefer Mish-Mish or Misha?" Santiago slipped down to scratch just behind her ear.

"Oh, Misha is her Christian name, but I just like Mish-Mish. She answers to both."

Santiago couldn't help but chuckle at the idea of a cat having a Christian name. "I thought I'd check in on Indya's boat. How's it going?"

A bright smile crinkled the edges of their eyes. "Josh came by this morning. He said everything looked good."

From the lot, a shuffle of shoes on gravel drew their attention. Santiago looked up, the sun temporarily blinding him. When his vision cleared, it resolved into the image of Indya. From his vantage point, hunched down near a Misha who was now on her feet, she loomed, long-legged and beautiful, over them. She wore a pair of loose, soft, mint green trousers and a white, mint green and beige polka dot blouse. Her brown heeled sandals allowed her pretty manicured toes to be fully on display, her skin a dark tan that glowed with good maintenance.

Misha's growl interrupted the tableau.

She frowned at the cat. "What did I tell you? That *demonia* hates me."

Misha gave her one last glare before darting into the bushes surrounding the marina office.

"Hola, Santiago." Indya waved.

He slowly got to his feet, trying to shake the stupor her appearance had plunged him into. *"Hola, Indya, que bueno verte otra vez."*

"It's nice to see you, too." Her nostrils flared as if she were dragging air into her lungs, but otherwise, she was as cool and composed as ever. Wil was already flinging their arms around her.

"Hola, chula," Wil sang into their embrace. "Are you checking on your baby?"

Indya blinked rapidly before turning her full attention on Wil. "Yeah. I tried to call, but obviously, you were out here, spoiling that evil cat even more than she deserves."

"I will not have you smack-talking my queen, okay?" Wil huffed in Santiago's direction as if to say, *Can you believe her?* "Josh came through not even half an hour ago and gave it a look. He said to stay away from that brand of fuel. It's too heavy for these types of motors."

"Bingo," Indya said, glancing at Santiago, who had also drawn the same conclusion.

"Don't worry. He drained it out, cleaned the tank and gave it a quick tune-up. Motors are as good as new."

"That's a relief. Think your guys can get her into my slip?"

Wil waved her question away. "Already done. I have the keys in my office. Let me go get them."

"And the invoice," she called out to Wil's retreating back.

They threw a thumbs-up over their shoulder.

Indya turned to Santiago. "Fancy seeing you here."

Santiago shrugged. He had come specifically to check on her boat and had no backup excuse to explain why he was here with Wil, other than an attachment to a cat he barely knew. He chose an approximation of the truth. "I was walking by and stopped to say hello to Misha."

Indya rolled her eyes. "She won't even let me touch her."

"Are you uneasy around animals?"

Shrugging, Indya looked to where Misha was creeping in the tall grass. "I'm not much of an animal person. Gia sometimes nags me to get a kitten or a puppy, but I always say no."

"Are you allergic to them?"

Indya shook her head. "No, it's more of a lifestyle issue. I don't think it's fair to have an animal cooped up all day in our house while we are out at work or school. We are barely ever home."

"You don't want them because you don't want them to suffer. It sounds to me like you are an animal person. You care enough about them to not own one if you can't give them a good life."

Indya pinched her lips together. "That's a generous take on the whole situation."

"No," Santiago said, observing her now-moist bottom lip, trying not to stare. "I just think you are coming from a more generous place than you give yourself credit for."

Indya's mouth fell open, as if she were going to respond, but Wil had returned with the invoice. "Here. I charged it to your card on file. I know you're probably playing hooky from work and have to get back."

"Love how you have my schedule memorized," Indya laughed, folding the paper and sliding it into her pants pocket.

"I just know you. You probably have this stop timed, down to the minute." Wil turned to Santiago. "Indya is a well-oiled scheduling machine."

"I live and die by my calendar," she said, smirking at Wil.

Santiago spread his hands. "My mother tells me I'm more punctual than the sun. She teases me about it, but I get it from her." His phone buzzed in his back pocket. "That's probably her now."

Indya pointed at the sound. "Well, you better get that. I know from experience that mothers don't like to be kept waiting."

"Especially yours, chica." Wil shook their hand in imitation of someone getting burned. "Oriana is not one to trifle with."

Santiago glanced at his phone, and it was, in fact, his mother.

Indya smiled brightly at both of them. "That's my signal to get going. Thank you, Wil. You are a lifesaver."

"No problem. I was going to touch up the paint on my boat before it gets too hot. Can't show up to the Salty Fish with the *Mittens* in the state she's in. She's not fit for the public."

"That's right. You have to represent," Indya teased.

Santiago knew he had just missed the context for something important, but his phone buzzed again and he had to tend to it. "She's being insistent. It was good seeing you again, Indya."

"*Igualmente.* We'll definitely see each other around town." She gave a small wave to them both before turning and heading to the gate. He watched her as she moved toward her car, a convertible, from what he could see. She must look striking with the top down, tearing through town with the sun on her face and the wind in her hair.

"She's beautiful, isn't she?" Wil said, interrupting his reverie. Santiago tore his eyes away with great effort, embarrassed that he had been so blatantly caught.

"She is, I mean, there's no question—"

"Yeah, it's hard to believe the price they were selling her for. Not many people are able to afford her at market price, but she was just sitting there at auction, waiting for someone to snatch her up."

Santiago whipped his head in Wil's direction. "What?"

"I know, right?" Wil exclaimed, clapping Santiago on the shoulder. Hard. "Luckily, Indya was in the right place at the right time."

"Her car," Santiago breathed, all the shock draining out of him. "Of course."

"Yeah. Indya has the Midas touch, you know? She's never put her hands on anything and not turned it into something special."

Santiago inhaled deeply. Obviously he needed more practice with the English language, because this conversation had given him whiplash. His phone buzzed one more time. "I really need to message my mother back. Other wise, she won't stop."

"Oh, no problem, dude. Have a good day!"

Santiago exchanged a quick goodbye with Wil, who walked around the back of the building.

Santiago scanned the parking lot, but as he anticipated, Indya was long gone. He leaned against his truck, catching his breath. He had the best and worst luck. Best because he'd seen her unexpectedly this morning after meeting her last night, and his mother always said good things happen in threes. But he also had the worst luck because, yet again, she had escaped without him being able to get her information. He wasn't going to ask for Wil's help. It didn't feel right to get her phone number from anyone but her.

He silently scolded himself. He had massive things to worry about with his job search, his parents' supermarket needing work and getting Lisbet to the US. He was attracted to Indya. He imagined anyone would be. She was an absolutely exquisite woman. But maybe fate was being kind to him by not making it easy to get to her. He had so many other things to think about, he didn't have time to romance anyone. It was logical when he thought it through like that.

But that impeccable logic didn't make him want to know her any less.

Santiago forced himself to reread the series of texts from his mother. They were lists of errands to run between his appointments and supplies to pick up. His parents were still rebuilding parts of the property that housed the supermarket, which had been damaged by rain and wind, and they needed supplies to continue the work. His father was doing what he could himself, but Santiago made sure to stop by each day to help him out. His father was difficult, but he was his father, and Santiago could never deny him his help.

Driving through Soledad Bay's downtown was like stepping into a postcard that had frayed at the edges. Brightly painted storefronts intermingled with buildings that were covered in scaffolds, or outright boarded up. His hands itched to grab a set of tools and get to work on them. He couldn't stand to see buildings looking so decimated and unloved.

On the ocean side, private beaches flowed in wind-carved waves directly into the sea. The placid blue of the Gulf Coast shared more in common with the Caribbean sands of his home country than it did with Miami Beach, with its unpredictable Atlantic waters bubbling and boiling whenever the wind kicked up. The gentle nature of the Gulf never ceased to soothe him. There was peace to be had here, the kind of peace he was desperate to share with his daughter.

After he'd found all the items on the list and filled out several applications for employment, he set out to deliver the things his mother had requested. He parked his truck and walked across the asphalt to the sliding glass doors of Taste of Caracas, the tiny supermarket his parents had opened when they moved to Soledad Bay all those years ago. At first, they had leased the building, starting small, but after Adalis, they took advantage of plummeting real estate prices—and the original owner's unwillingness to fix the damages incurred by the hurricane—to buy out the entire building. They had seen the potential of owning property and were now ready to expand the supermarket, even while it was still under reconstruction. The downtown of Soledad Bay was quaint and largely untouched by giant developers. Its fishing waters drew anglers from all over the world, as well as tourists who loved the largely underdeveloped beachfront that was as close to its natural state as any beach in the Panhandle.

Taste of Caracas was a treasure trove of predominantly South American products that re-created the atmosphere of the neighborhood bodegas of the city. On its shelves, customers could find a full array of offerings, as if they were shopping in a Venezuelan supermarket. In addition, a daily selection of warm lunch and snack options were available each day in the hot case for the midday crowd, both tourists and locals. By this time in the afternoon, his mother would have already restocked the *tequeños* and *buñuelos* so popular with the high school students who stopped in after the schools up the road released for the day.

Santiago rounded the supermarket storefront, wedged between a Cuban café and a Puerto Rican restaurant, and parked in the back. The workroom was simply a section of the storage room that was missing drywall and flooring. Papá was nowhere to be found, so Santiago left everything on the worktable before stepping into the store proper to greet his mother.

"Mijo," Mamá said as she handed change to a young man of about sixteen or seventeen. Her nails were always manicured and her makeup perfect, even on delivery days when she accepted the pallets of merchandise she and his father unpacked and moved onto shelves. Even in her typical cardigans, in deference to the air-conditioning, and sturdy black slacks with an apron on top, Mamá wasn't afraid of physical work. When he was young, before Miriam was born, she'd been a busy office manager in a corporate environment of suits and dresses before the family moved to the US. She still maneuvered as if she were making her way around a cubicle and not the back of a shop counter.

"Thank you for stopping by on short notice. What are your plans for tomorrow?"

He accepted the kiss she left on his cheek. "Nothing fixed. I have a list of places with job openings to visit and one interview in the afternoon." Santiago had focused on potential employers that needed his skill set—construction, facilities management, handiwork or even carpentry. No job was too insignificant for him to do.

Mamá's eyes lit up with excitement. "Cancel your appointments tomorrow morning. I spoke to my friend, Oriana Linares. She owns the Alba Beachside Resort here in Soledad Bay. Their facilities manager quit without notice and they need someone immediately to take over the position. She said none of the current staff has enough experience to do project management and they need that because of all the repairs the buildings require. I told her about you and she said she wants to interview you."

The name sounded vaguely familiar. It was one of the local properties along the waterfront with direct access to the beach. No doubt a brightly colored property, probably with its own pool and amenities. Large enough to be interesting, but not so large that he would be overwhelmed. Excitement pulsed through him. *"¿De verdad?"*

"Sí." She nearly clapped with excitement, her perfectly twisted bun on the top of her head bobbing with her movements. "You have an appointment early tomorrow morning."

He couldn't turn away from the opportunity. "I can't believe you did that for me. Thank you." Maintenance management was a respectable position and, in a local hotel, would be much more secure than his previous employment. It would put his skill set to good use and help him get one step closer to providing a home for Lisbet.

"Of course! You are my son and I want to see you set tled and happy right here next to me," she answered, wagging her finger at him. "But you have to be good, okay? Be responsible."

The hairs at the nape of his neck stood on end. He had heard that so many times in his life. *Be good, Santiago, Don't give any trouble.*

"Mamá, that time is behind me," he said, though even he knew that he was being facile. He hadn't committed just one mistake to make his family mistrust his judgment. He made several that began with his decision to stay behind in his country after his family left, even though all the signs had pointed to catastrophe. Every choice he made afterward was tainted by that one misstep.

He hoped this time, things would work out in his favor. But he needed his family to have a little faith in him.

"Where's Papá?"

An expression moved across Mamá's features, easy to miss if a person didn't know her well enough. She loved her husband dearly, but it pained her to see strife in her family, and she radiated with that pain. "He had an appointment with the insurance adjuster. He hates talking to them."

"He could have called me to go with him."

Mamá shook her head. "You know how he is."

"I know. He is still angry with me and won't let me help with those kinds of things."

Mamá's shoulders drooped, as if the weight of her optimism was too heavy for her. "He's not angry. He is only—"

"Disappointed?" Santiago tried to tamp down on the fury that threatened to overflow the barriers of his ingrained manners toward Mamá. As the only son, his father had always been hard on him. "But he's okay with me putting up drywall and flooring. He makes no sense." It wasn't right to continue to hold the past against him. Not when he was trying to get his life together again.

"I know you are making an effort, and in his way, he is also trying," Mamá said, as if reading his thoughts. "Just give him some time. He seems rigid but he loves his family. He only wants the best for all of us."

Santiago patted his mother's hand, grateful for her comfort and knowing there wasn't much she could do to make things easier between him and his father at the moment. "Do you know anything else about the job?"

His mother smiled, her pretty face wrinkling at the edges of her eyes where the joys and struggles of her life had left their mark. "I barely understand my job. How can I understand yours?"

Santiago laughed. His mother should have been on conference calls, speaking to clients about their finances and getting paper cuts, not burns from the hot case behind a shop counter. But it was work, and his experience in life had taught him that all work was dignified, as long as you did it to the best of your ability. He was proud of what his parents were able to build in a few short years and he just hoped he could live up to that expectation and provide his daughter with a life as stable as his family had tried to give to him.

Chapter Five

Indya

"**M**om, the air-conditioning!"

Indya broke off yet another mile-long stare across the dashboard of her Audi A5 to settle her attention on Gia, finding it difficult to focus on her daughter. Her thoughts had wandered randomly again to Santiago, to the night he rescued her boat, and how she'd stumbled on him the very next day at the marina's office.

"Mom!"

Indya blinked, clearing her vision. "What?"

"Ay, por el amor de Dios," Gia muttered as she opened the window to let the oven-temperature air seep out of the metal can that was Indya's car. "It's hotter than Satan's as—"

"Hit the pause button on that thought, young lady," Indya snapped in warning as she turned on the car and put the air conditioner on full blast, which was another mistake because now all they got was a faceful of stale, hot-car air. Sweat beaded on Indya's skin, and breathing was difficult when the air was so heavy. She knew better than to do that, and really would have preferred dropping the top, but Gia wouldn't tolerate her hair getting windswept before she had to be at school. She spent more time on those dark blond waves than was normal, even for someone as high-maintenance as Indya.

"Just go, Mom," Gia huffed, crossing her arms while tossing her hair over her shoulder as she fixed her gaze out the window. "My skin's going to be all greasy now."

"How tragic," Indya muttered, pulling out of their driveway, then heading in the direction of Gia's school, trying very hard to keep her mind from returning to the subject of Santiago and how his forearms looked when he had prepared and tied the rope to the—

"You haven't heard one thing I said just now, have you?" Gia complained, her pout even more pronounced with the clear gloss she'd over applied to her lips.

Guilt flooded Indya. One thing she'd always promised herself when it came to Gia was that when they were together, her attention would always be 100 percent on her, offering her the quality of her time even if the quantity could sometimes be lacking. But she was doing a terrible job of it now, and it was all because of a man she barely knew.

That was unacceptable.

At the red light, Indya rifled through her purse to find the packet of tissues she always kept there. "Here." She handed the packet to Gia. "Blot your lips."

Gia huffed but did as Indya told her, wadding the paper up when she was done before disposing it in a mini trash receptacle Indya had set up in her car. One of their bonding rituals was to go makeup shopping together and experiment with its application. Even before Gia started having crushes on the boys and girls at her high school, she had loved fashion and cosmetics of every kind. She wasn't allowed to wear a full face of makeup, but she was allowed to do up her eyes and lips. They got mani-pedis together, watched YouTube video tutorials on how to create the perfect eyebrow shape, and had some of their most meaningful conversations when they gave each other facials and skin treatments.

Gia was used to her mother's undivided attention, and did not respond well when she didn't have it.

"I said, is it okay if I go downtown with some of my friends after school?"

Indya's firm rule was that school nights should only be spent studying and participating in sports or clubs, while social activities should be reserved for the weekend. "Depends on how much homework you get. I don't want you up half the night, getting assignments done, because you spent the afternoon on the strip."

"I won't know how much homework I'll have until school's over." Gia sucked her teeth. "Come on, Mom, it'll just be for a little while. I can't just go from sitting at a desk for eight hours to going home and sitting at a desk again for another eight hours."

"Seven and a half hours, after which you do, maybe, two hours of homework at most? And don't you have swim practice?" Indya corrected.

"Canceled. And that's still approximately ten hours of sitting on my butt." She leaned in close, tapping her mother's leg as she drove. "Do you know what that does to your circulation?"

"Sin vergüenza," Indya said, trying and failing to hold back her laughter. "I see health class is doing you a lot of good."

"Best class ever." Gia leaned back, snuggling into the bucket seat with satisfaction. "Aren't you the one who said that if I don't advocate for myself, no one will?"

Indya maneuvered the car into the drop-off zone of Gia's high school. "When I shared that principle with you, I meant for you to apply it toward improving your grades, not manipulating me."

"What's the point of a principle if you can't apply it universally?" Gia checked her lip gloss in the flip-down mirror before gathering up her backpack. "So, can I go?"

"You sure you want to study biology and not law instead? Because you have one hell of a mouth on you, *chiquita*."

Gia tossed her hair over her shoulder in a dramatic gesture that had Indya pulling a face. "You should be persuasive in everything you do, Mom." Gia put her cheek out for a kiss and Indya obliged, reveling in the still baby-soft surface. "I'm going with that being a yes." She beamed and Indya caught a whiff of the fruity flavor of her lip gloss and an aroma that smelled suspiciously like Indya's Bvlgari Rose Goldea perfume. Before Indya could remind her daughter that anyone who was still young enough to spend an obligatory hour sweating in PE had no business using Indya's very expensive products, Gia had already slipped out of the car in her white turtle-conservation-club T-shirt, tucked into a pair of high-waist blue jeans that Indya could never get away with at her age. Her outfit was punctuated by a pair of brand-new Air Jordan Retro 1 high-tops that Trent's parents had insisted on buying her, because they didn't spoil Gia enough as it was. She watched her clever, beautiful, and way-too-spirited daughter bound into school, scooping up her best friend, Miriam Pereira, on the way, before disappearing inside the school.

Indya didn't move until the car behind her gave a tap of the horn. Recognizing the driver as one of the parents of the high school's PTSA, or Parent-Teacher-Student Association, she waved in apology before pulling out of the drop-off lane. Her brain was as useless as the Cream of Wheat and fruit bowl she'd prepared for both her and Gia's breakfast that morning.

There was no sense in playing coy with herself. She knew exactly what was wrong with her and she was not amused. She couldn't get her rescuer out of her mind and it was starting to get on her nerves. It wasn't the first time she'd had a run-in with a handsome stranger. It didn't happen often, but the stars had somehow magically aligned to place someone in Indya's path who she was actually interested in. She rarely gave herself permission to enjoy it, because she didn't often do things with only herself in mind. If she wasn't planning her life around Gia, she was thinking of the hotel and her endless to-do list. She also had to think fifteen steps ahead of her parents, especially her mother, who had a bad habit of making decisions about the hotel before Indya got a chance to act. She understood where the impetus came from—her parents had been running the hotel for decades and that was not a habit they would soon break, even if the work had become too much for them.

Indya slowly blew air out of her lungs, hoping to expel her numerous and varied frustrations along with it. She drove away from the school and onto Beachfront Drive, crossing exactly five traffic lights and the public beach access at Sea Bass Pier before she pulled into the resort's covered parking lot. Alba Beachside Resort was a midsize hotel that provided all the amenities of a larger resort, but scaled to make residents feel like they were staying in a more intimate setting, especially in their extended-stay bungalows. The property had a large pool with attached waterslide, one heated wading pool, a Jacuzzi, canoe rental, kon tiki bar, and beachfront access. Guests were assigned an umbrella and a set of chaise lounges for their personal use for the duration of their stay.

Indya loved the hotel. Growing up, she had spent more time within its walls than at the family home. Her parents had worked tirelessly to make the lodging a warm and welcoming place people would want to return to each year. Indya remembered doing homework in a room reserved just for her. Most of the time, she slept there, waking up to find her parents in the adjoining suite. They often opted to simply stay on property instead of driving home late at night.

The hotel was as much her home as the house she grew up in. That experience, together with her education and her time in Sarasota, had given her everything she needed to not only handle the workload but to attack the mountain of renovations that needed to be made to return the hotel to full capacity. The hurricane had set them back, but she knew this resort and she knew this community. They would land on their feet again.

She smelled the sea before she stepped out of her car. Indya had never known a life away from the coast. Even when she worked in Sarasota, she'd lived in a condo right on the bay. She couldn't imagine not having the endless ocean as the backdrop of her life. She was made for the sun and the sea. It was in her blood, all the way to her ancestors who were from an island where the surf was never more than a stone's throw away.

She made her way up the walk, her sensible Vivaia medium-heeled sandals clacking against the pavement. Cute and practical, they gave her feet the support they needed. But she always kept a pair of sports sandals under her desk in several basic colors in case she had to run around the hotel without straining her arches and ankles. She'd learned early on as the daughter of hotel owners that comfort trumped style, unless you could afford to have both.

She had worked too hard in this life not to look good while she did her job, even if she was sometimes a little overdressed for a hotel like Alba Beachside Resort.

The glass doors that led to the hotel lobby slid open. Jade, the front desk manager, greeted her from behind the reservation counter.

"Good morning." She smiled, looking up from her screen. "Your mom's waiting for you in your office."

Indya frowned, glancing at the wall clock. It was barely seven thirty. "Already?"

Jade gave a wry smile. She'd been with the hotel long enough to know how Indya's parents were, especially her mother. When Oriana Linares showed up at the office before her daughter did, it meant that things were about to get interesting. Indya briefly regretted not booking them for the week-long cruise to Mexico that she'd been checking out a few weeks ago. They wouldn't have gone even if she had. Indya did not get her tendency to overwork from the ether.

"It's gonna be one of those days, isn't it?" Indya muttered.

Jade's only response was a short "Uh-huh" before returning her attention to the screen, where she was preparing the day's check-ins. Indya shook her head and made her way to the back office. There, she was greeted by the sight of Mami at Indya's desk, on Indya's laptop, doing God knows what with Indya's hotel.

"You're late," were Mami's very first words.

"I'm actually not." Indya set her purse inside the top drawer of the wooden filing cabinet. "You know, have you considered retirement?"

Mami bit back a smile before she grew serious again.

Indya's mother was an older version of her, with the same shade of wavy dark hair, but cut in a bob that had been blown out, same caramel-brown skin and amber-colored eyes. The only difference between them was that Mami was petite, while Indya had gotten her height from Papi, a characteristic Gia had inherited as well. "Your father retired after his stroke. I consider myself semi-retired. I can't leave you to do this alone."

"You actually can, Mami. You really, really can." Indya took the chair across from her desk, not even bothering to try to get her mother out of her seat. It had been hers for decades and Indya could only imagine the trauma of having to give up control, even if it was to her daughter, when so much needed to be done. But Papi was effectively out of commission after his stroke and his care fell on Mami. That's why Indya had come back. If only her mother would actually allow her to do her job.

But Indya was feeling a little bratty and was still sore over a recarpeting fiasco involving her mother that she'd had to deal with this week. "Why aren't you in your own office?"

Mami sighed as if she needed the patience of a saint to deal with Indya, which was ironic as hell, because where was the patience Indya needed to endure her? To make things more interesting, Mami's office was right next door to Indya's. Papi spent three mornings per week in physical therapy, during which time Indya's mother came into the hotel to help Indya with paperwork, which Indya deeply appreciated. However, sometimes, like now, her mother forgot that she had appointed Indya the boss and Mami was supposed to be stepping back. "I'm reviewing the job description for facilities manager and I don't have access to personnel files in my office computer. You should have already set up interviews for that position."

Mami didn't have access to personnel records because Indya had informed their tiny IT office to revoke her authorization. There were privacy laws that had to be respected, and her mother didn't need that information to do her job. Indya counted backward from five before answering. "I have three candidates already lined up."

Mami stopped typing and folded her hands together in front of her. "I set up an interview for this morning."

Indya sat up. "What do you mean, you set up an interview? With who?"

Mami returned her attention to the computer, her smile bland and distracted. "Magdalena and Ronaldo's son. He just moved into town and is looking for work."

Indya groaned inwardly. She could already see where this was going. "Is he qualified for the job or is this just another classic case of small-town nepotism?"

"Nepotism?" Mami huffed, as if it was the height of absurdity to doubt her on this. "Of course he is qualified! I don't want another Carlos on our hands."

Carlos. The other guy Mami had hired. The one who had run off on them without giving any notice. Qualified, yes, but also as flighty as a seabird. Indya wanted to ask whose fault that was, but she knew it was unfair. Hiring was always tricky. It could just as soon work out as go sour and it wasn't necessarily her mother's fault if that happened, no matter how tempting it was to lay the blame at her feet. "Okay, tell me about him."

Mami's satisfaction was palpable. "He's a very nice young man. Just moved to Soledad Bay to be close to his family. He has experience and a clean record. I know because I did his background check and everything for you.

All you have to do is interview him. He'll be here at eight o'clock."

Indya glanced at the clock. "That's fifteen minutes from now!"

Mami smiled. "Not my fault you were running late."

Indya threw her hands up in the air. "How can I be late when I drop Gia off at this time every morning? Are you kidding me?" There was nothing Indya loved more on an early morning than a hefty dose of gaslighting, Latino style.

"Don't be so dramatic." Mami gave a decisive, final tap to her keyboard before taking to her feet. She had even dressed for the part, wearing slacks with a loose, light-weight, button-down blouse in deference to the hot weather. "Here's a copy of his résumé."

"Not sticking around for the interview, are you?" Indya complained, taking the folder from her. Conducting the meeting was the least her mother could do, but there was no sense trying to convey this to her.

"Me? No, I'm semi-retired now, remember? Anyway, your father has a doctor's appointment this morning. Just a routine checkup, but his doctor is always so slow. I know you can handle this part."

Indya was sure the pulsing vein in her temple was the size of a centipede. "You're only semi-retired when it's convenient for you."

"At my age, it's my prerogative to choose when retirement is convenient for me." Mami's smile was a bright, triumphant one. She tapped Indya's shoulder, her manicure glinting in the early sunlight. "I have faith in you."

"No, you actually don't, or you wouldn't have gotten involved to begin with."

"Nonsense. I'm just trying to help you out." Mami rounded the desk, avoiding a flabbergasted Indya, who still could not believe the audacity of the woman who had given birth to her. "You could stand to be a little more grateful for the help."

"I don't need anyone's help!" Indya practically shouted.

Her mother patted her cheek, the floral aroma of her favorite perfume wafting up from her wrists. "Everyone needs help sometimes, *mijita*."

Indya opened her mouth to respond to that, but the phone on her desk buzzed. She reached over to pick it up. "Indya Linares."

Jade's voice, crisp and professional, came over the phone. "I have a guest who says it is urgent that she speak to you."

Indya groaned, staring daggers at the now-empty doorway where her mother, her own personal Loki, had disappeared. It was too early in the morning for this. She sighed, resigned that it really was going to be one of those days.

"On my way."

Chapter Six

Santiago

Santiago entered the soaring lobby of Alba Beachside Resort ten minutes before his scheduled appointment time. The decor was typical of the hotels along Beachfront Drive—wood-paneled walls painted white and hung with oil paintings of seashells and the ocean—but with the palm trees, tropical fruit and ocean blue that complimented the beaches on this part of the coastline. The instrumental cover for Carlos Peña's "Mi Musica" played in low tones in the background, reinforcing a vibe he was accustomed to feeling in South Florida, but never this far north.

Low, pastel blue furniture and reproductions of driftwood and glass knickknacks completed the look. In the far corner stood a water dispenser filled with ice and cut lemons. Next to it, a small Keurig coffee-and-tea bar with every variety of Keurig pods under the sun was arranged on a gorgeous, pale marble, glass-top cabinet. It managed to be both elegant and welcoming at the same time.

He'd checked and rechecked his appearance a dozen times before stepping off his boat that morning. It was more important than ever that this interview went well, given that his mother's reputation was also in play. She had made this happen for him and he couldn't let her down.

The lobby was scattered with guests in various stages of occupancy, some waiting for a valet to bring their cars, others standing patiently in line to check in. Everyone carried the easy air of people who had nothing to worry about because they were on vacation. It was an infectious feeling.

He joined the line to speak to the receptionist, but when he'd given her his name and purpose, an older woman stepped in front of him. She wore a cheerful yellow-and-orange floral beach dress with a matching sun hat, but her flushed skin and pronounced scowl announced that she was anything but cheerful.

"I must speak to Ms. Linares at once! It's an emergency," the older woman barked out with a clipped, German accent.

A pretty, voluptuous Black woman with long, blond braids pulled back to the nape of her neck looked up and smiled with cool professional detachment. "She's on her way, Mrs. Bergeron."

Santiago's ears perked up at the drama. He took a seat on a cream leather sofa, clutching the portfolio that held extra copies of his résumé, and waited. The space he'd been admiring earlier filled with the sound of a voice he thought he would not soon hear again.

"Mrs. Bergeron, how can I help you?"

Santiago flinched, as if he'd been scalded by hot water, before bolting upright, his heart slamming into his chest. Beads of sweat stuck to his overly hot skin, dampening his shirt, which was quickly cooled by the brisk air-conditioning. There, in all her majestic, professional glory, stood the woman he'd rescued three nights ago. She wore a beige and blue, short-sleeved belted dress, endless tan legs sliding into beautiful arched feet that were fitted into matching beige sandals with a small heel. Her long, elegant fingers ended in manicured nails painted with a neutral polish. The same lovely hands that had handled a boat with a strength and expertise that had impressed him.

Mrs. Bergeron's voice penetrated his reverie. "The refrigerator is not working and I'm worried our medicines will spoil."

Santiago heard the woman's words, but he had a hard time processing them. All he could concentrate on was Indya, who hadn't noticed him in the waiting room.

"I'm so sorry, Mrs. Bergeron. You may store your medicine in my office refrigerator. I give you my word that the issue will be resolved before you return from dinner this evening. May I offer you complimentary cocktails for your troubles?"

The older woman, who had arrived vibrating with agitation, visibly calmed down. "Can I use it for the mimosas at brunch this weekend?"

Indya's smile widened. "Yes, you may."

Mrs. Bergeron gave her a shrewd look. "And for my wife as well?"

"And for your wife as well."

Mrs. Bergeron's expression changed, growing comically bright. She had an attractive face that went from stern to amiable with a breathtaking speed that made Santiago think her anger was more theatrical than sincerely felt. "Thank you, *Liebchen*. I'll be back with those meds right away."

With a knowing half smile, Indya watched her guest leave before turning to the young woman who had been working the front desk, and gave her a chin nod in greeting, which she returned with a dimpled smile.

"Your appointment is here," she said.

"Thanks, Jade."

Santiago rose from his seat just as Indya turned toward him. Her face, already poised on the edge of a polite smile, froze, her body going stiff as a sheet of metal. No doubt, like him, she was questioning the veracity of her vision. But unlike him, she recovered more quickly. She cleared her throat before offering her hand for him to shake. "Still English?"

He held her hand with remarkable steadiness, given the somersaults his stomach was performing. It took everything he had to remain outwardly serene. "Still English," he managed to drag out of his dry throat.

He watched her face, the same surprise and recognition hovering at the edges of her professionalism. She was trained not to react to things—an indispensable quality when working with the public. He wanted to stare and stare at her. She was so pretty. But the warmth of her palm registered in Santiago's mind and he realized that he had held her hand for far too long. Releasing it, he let his hand drop to his side.

Indya turned to the woman she'd called Jade, short of breath. "Closed door for thirty minutes."

Jade's eyes flicked between Indya and Santiago, but to her credit, she made no other comment besides "I'll make sure you aren't disturbed."

Indya nodded before glancing back at him, her face stretched with a smile that was warm but polite, the smile of a professional at work and not one of the easy ones she'd given him when they'd met before. "Follow me."

Without looking to see if he was doing what she had asked, she strode down a side hallway to an office with a pale wood desk and matching bookshelves along one wall. She circled behind her desk, a perfect barrier between them.

Being the subject of an interview was already stressful, but being interviewed by Indya, of all people, sent his heart rate into the stratosphere.

Thankfully, just behind her was a large office window, which framed a view of the boardwalk, the wide strip of white sand in low tide, and the frothing tips of sea waves beyond. The familiar sight of the ocean soothed and revitalized him, keeping his heart rate from stampeding away from him. Even in this closed office, with its brisk air-conditioning and mechanical sounds, he caught the familiar salty tang of the sea. He inhaled deeply, imagining the ocean breeze, even as his lungs filled with the biting ice of cooled air. It quelled that shivery tension that had dogged him from the moment she'd taken his hand.

Indya took the seat across from him. "This is a surprise, Santiago."

"It is." He spread his hands in a gesture of helplessness. "Apparently our mothers know each other."

"I told you, Soledad Bay is not a big place. I should have made the connection between the application and your name."

Santiago crossed his legs, fidgeting with the leather portfolio resting on his lap. "I don't expect you to know every Santiago in Soledad Bay."

"There aren't that many, I assure you. In my defense, I never did get your last name."

Indya projected professional neutrality and perfect equanimity, whereas his stomach quivered from encountering this woman once again. It was interfering with his ability to filter his thoughts.

"Do you have a hard copy of your résumé?"

He gave a short nod before sliding a page out from between the leather covers and handing it to her. "Everything in Soledad Bay is still very new to me. How do our families know each other?"

Indya, who had begun skimming the page, lifted her amber eyes to his. "Taste of Caracas is right down the block. It's in the center of the historic downtown area, a section we like to call the Latin Quarter, even though it is only a plaza with several storefronts. All the business owners know each other. Besides your family's supermarket, there's a Cuban bakery, a Puerto Rican restaurant—" she ticked each name off on her fingers "—a Brazilian *churrascaria*, a Colombian café." Indya sat back, chuckling to herself. "Even the diner belongs to a Dominican friend of ours. And if I leave out the taco stand on the beach, Cesar will never make another fish taco for me."

Santiago was enchanted with the variety. "Fish tacos? Are they good?"

Indya nodded. "The best. He is a true artist."

"I will have to try them someday."

"You should." Indya resumed her study of his résumé. "I see you have been working with Atlantic Shores down in Miami for the last year." She continued to read, several minutes vanishing as she made her way down each entry. He waited patiently. She had most likely not had an opportunity to read the document until now, given the suddenness with which the appointment had been made.

She set the paper down on her desk. "I remember from our conversation after your heroic boat rescue that you had just moved up from Miami."

He chuckled at her choice of words. "It was hardly heroic."

"To you, it wasn't. But sleeping out in the open ocean was not how I wanted to spend my Tuesday night." She observed him, her expression shifting. There was something acute and incisive in her gaze now. "Atlantic Shores is a robust franchise. There's one up the coast from here and it does very good business."

"You want to know why I am changing employment," he stated rather than asked.

"I do."

He uncrossed and stretched his legs before recrossing them again. "Atlantic Shores was sold at the beginning of the year. A new management team took over."

"You didn't want to work with the new management?"

"On the contrary. I would have been very happy to work with the new management. But the new management did not want to work with me. Us, actually." Santiago stammered, then cleared his throat to cover his awkwardness. "They brought their own people in and no longer required our services." He folded his hands over his portfolio. "It was enough incentive for me to make a change."

Indya's expression flickered a bit, as if she'd been distracted by something and had returned to herself. "Sounds like a serious incentive."

"The most serious." He smiled, and Indya's eyes went to his mouth. Her gaze flicked away but not before it left behind an achy, longing feeling in his chest.

He chided himself for getting distracted so easily and discreetly inhaled a long, cleansing breath.

"I noticed you owned your own company. I don't think we ever got around to talking about it the other night?"

"You mean the night I heroically rescued you?"

Indya leaned back in her chair, chuckling. "You know, you're very difficult to interview properly." She tapped the table. "Tell me what happened to your company and how you ended up here."

"It's a long story," Santiago said.

"I grew up on telenovelas," Indya quipped. "I like a good, long story."

"If you insist." This was unlike any interview Santiago had ever participated in, but then again, Indya was unlike any potential employer he'd ever met. He was having a hard time seeing her as such, given the way they'd hit it off at the bar. He found it too easy to speak to her, but he had to start fixing in his mind that she might soon be his boss and he would need another approach to her. He had too much riding on this interview to behave with inappropriate familiarity.

"I must begin with my family. My parents moved our family to the US when my sister was young, first to Miami, then here to Soledad Bay. I was very stubborn and stayed behind to be with my then partner and our daughter while trying to keep my business running." He paused, even talking about that time of his life was able to provoke a physical response. "None of that lasted long, not the relationship and most certainly not the business."

"The economics in your country have not been very good lately," Indya offered.

"No, they haven't been, but it didn't help that the co-owner of the business, my supposed best friend, embezzled money, forcing us into bankruptcy."

Indya's eyes grew wide. "Didn't you have any legal recourse?"

Santiago laughed and it came out bitter, which he did not like. He didn't want his anger from that period to keep his life in a stranglehold, and he didn't want Indya to be exposed to it. He needed to accept, learn and move on. "The economic environment is so bad that it is impossible to do any legitimate business. I had to liquidate whatever remained and leave the country."

"That must have been traumatic, having your trust betrayed, losing your business and having to leave your daughter behind." She set aside the résumé, engrossed in his words.

Santiago dipped his head in acknowledgment. "Another error on my part. Because my partner and I aren't married, I could not simply bring my daughter to the US. Even if we had been married, Natasha would never allow herself to be separated from Lisbet. It would have been a cruelty even to suggest it." The memory of his departure from his country threatened to overwhelm him, but he pushed it down. "Instead, I promised Natasha I would bring both of them. When I left, I became very depressed and didn't handle the change very well. I was so angry." He shook his head, regretting that period of his life. "It was not my best moment."

"I know something about anger that comes from disappointment. It can drive you to self-destruction if you let it. I was not…well…after my divorce." She cleared her throat, fixing him with a sympathetic smile that nonetheless felt sincere. "But you're in a better place now?"

"A much better place," he answered. "But only after I made a change for my own well-being and for the sake of the other people in my life who need me. So I left my old life in Miami to come here and start again." He smiled sheepishly, mostly to himself. "I'm sorry, I didn't mean to make things so heavy."

"Don't apologize," She reached across and patted his forearm in a gesture of comfort, only to yank her hand back as if electrified. Her hands were soft and warm to the touch. Wanton images of her hands on his skin flooded his thoughts, which he quickly banished. This was not the time for that. She was being kind and sympathetic, that was all.

"Life isn't always balloons and flowers," Indya said at length.

He shrugged. "*Está pelúo pero.* Here I am. It's been rough, but I'm lucky to have my family to help me."

Indya nodded at this. "You mentioned how difficult it was for you to let your business go."

Santiago shifted again. He wasn't used to sitting so long. "Yes."

"You lived a business owner's greatest fear." Being one herself, it would make sense that she would understand this fear. But he had brought it on himself, a fact his father held against him. "Would you ever consider owning your own enterprise again?"

The question caught Santiago off guard and he answered honestly, "I would, if the opportunity presented itself." Seeing the concern flitter across her face, Santiago was quick to add, "But I would not make any moves without informing my employers. That is not my way."

Indya visibly relaxed, though some tension still lingered in the air. She had not been completely mollified and he hoped it wouldn't jeopardize his chances of being hired.

"Considering how my last handyman left his job, I'm grateful for your honesty. Regardless of what happens here, if I can ever be of help in any way, let me know."

"Thank you." Santiago's voice dropped low and soft. It was an incredibly kind offer from a virtual stranger, and he suspected she was not the kind to make such offers lightly. "I might take you up on it some day."

Her shoulders rose and fell with the deep breath she took, perhaps to steady herself. He couldn't tell. "Please, do. We have to help each other out." She slipped his résumé inside the folder.

"Felt more like a therapy session than an interview."

Indya smiled at this. "Have you been to therapy?"

Santiago grew wistful. "I did, through a nondenominational church I attended in Miami. It helped a lot." He crossed his hands over his thigh. "I used to think keeping things to yourself was good for you, but it's not. Talking about your troubles liberates you. Without intending to, you have helped lighten a load for me."

A flush of pink colored her cheeks. "That's what you get for saving your future employer's life."

"Future employer?" Santiago sat up straighter.

Indya nodded, her eyes falling as if she were suddenly very shy, which captivated him as it had when she'd made the same gesture two nights earlier. "Pending a check on your references, I'd like to make a tentative job offer. I warn you, though. It's trial by fire. The hurricane really left us standing on one leg." She frowned, and he read her worries in the deep lines around her mouth. "Our competitors are almost fully up to capacity, but with my parents' age and the previous facilities manager leaving us, you're going to have your hands full trying to get this place ready in time for the upcoming summer fishing season. Soledad Bay hosts the Salty Fish each June. It kicks off the most lucrative period of the year for the entire community, including us." She sighed. "I wish I could ease you into everything that needs to be done, but time is not on our side. If that's not something you want to deal with, I won't hold it against you."

"The Salty Fish...?"

Indya's face brightened with excitement. "The Salty Fish Deep Sea Competition. People come from all over to compete for the biggest catch, with the possibility of taking home different monetary prizes. It's a pretty big deal and gives the town an important boost in tourism, which translates into dollars. This year is really important since it's the first time that the town is hosting the Salty Fish after

Hurricane Adalis caused so much damage." Indya pointed out the window. "The storm surge nearly reached the hotel. We thought we were going to lose it."

Santiago's heart raced as her words triggered the memory of him closing his shop for the last time. "I'm glad it didn't."

"Me too." Indya smiled. It was wistful and sweet. She said she'd left for Sarasota to make a life for herself and her daughter, most likely driven by her divorce, but it was clear that she loved this place. This obvious fact touched a tender and raw part of him. Owning a business, nurturing it with your own hands to try to make it grow into its fullest potential was a vulnerable experience. Indya was trying to heal her damaged hotel and make it flourish. He had tried and failed, but it felt fundamentally wrong for a tragedy like his to befall someone like Indya Linares.

"I can handle it," he said with a surge of determination that added force to each word. He would not let that happen to her if it was within his power. He had barely been hired, but his commitment was as solid as bedrock. "When would you like me to start?"

Relief washed over Indya's face. He was up to the challenge, but she couldn't have known that yet. "How does Monday sound?"

"It sounds perfect."

Indya abruptly turned and pulled a manila folder out of a filing cabinet. She handed it to Santiago. "This is a packet I put together for the employees about the Salty Fish. It includes its history, the competition schedule and how to register."

"Do many people from Soledad Bay participate?"

Indya nodded. "My parents always put together an Alba Beachside Resort team. I'm thinking of doing the same."

She pulled a sheaf of paper out. "Complete this survey. If you are interested, follow the registration instructions to declare your intent to participate."

Santiago was a solid fisherman and was intrigued by the idea. "Will you be participating?"

Indya looked down at her hands, a sign of nervousness that quickly evaporated under a bold smile. "I did it a few times when I was younger, but I'm still up in the air about whether to enter this year or not. I'm a bit rusty. That's probably why I got stranded out on the Gulf."

He smiled at the thought that she might have intended to practice her deep-sea fishing skills but couldn't do so because her motors had given out. "I'll think about it."

"Please do." She pulled out another sheet of paper, one that looked like a spreadsheet. "I've used the start of June as our target date for getting the hotel ready in time for this year's Salty Fish."

"Thank you," he said. "I will become familiar with it."

Indya smiled her polite smile and offered her hand to him, which he took. Her grip was firm and uncompromising, and he met it with equal firmness, banishing his fixation with the softness of her palm or the curl of those lovely, tan fingers around his. She was his boss now, and he needed to act accordingly. "Until Monday, then."

"Until Monday." She gave his hand a quick squeeze before releasing it. Before he could overthink that squeeze, she'd rounded the desk to open the office door. She walked like a queen down the hall to the open foyer, with her head held high and shoulders pulled back. She'd moved similarly out on the boat, even in casual clothes and with her hair tied back.

She walked past Jade, who was tapping away at her computer. The glass doors that led to the outside slid open, letting in the sunlight of a still-early morning. Indya turned and stood framed in the doorway. Time slowed to a crawl. Wind whipped through her long dark hair, the faint smell of a spicy floral perfume mixed with the smell of the beach, sunlight reflecting off the gold chain around her neck, suffusing her in a glow of the morning sun.

"Say hello to your mother for me," Indya said.

"Likewise," Santiago answered mechanically, still lost in the way she seemed to reflect everything beautiful about the sea.

With some difficulty, he stepped past her and through the exit, the swish of the closing doors a palpable force behind him. He turned to glance through the glass and saw that she lingered near the door, watching him move away from the hotel. She gave a short nod in acknowledgment before turning toward the front desk and speaking to Jade.

It took all of Santiago's willpower to not stop and stare at her again. He was still astonished at the way fate had brought them together, first on the boat, then at the marina, finally this hotel, in this town of all places. Three coincidences piled on top of each another until he found himself here, in this new reality, employed and embarking on the next step of fulfilling all his objectives. It was exactly what he needed at this very moment of his life.

Chapter Seven

Indya

Indya didn't bother going to her office. She knew herself— she'd simply dwell on every moment of her interactions with Santiago until she'd made herself loopy with overthinking. She couldn't believe that the man who had towed her boat was now working for her as her new facilities manager. What were the chances?

She cringed a little inside when she thought about the interview. It had felt too intimate for a discussion between an owner and a potential employee. But it had been too easy to talk to him, ask questions, even reveal things about herself she had not intended to reveal.

She shifted on her feet, pretending to be interested in the movement of guests in and out of the hotel. She was good at that—masking her feelings, appearing as if she was unbothered when she was very, very bothered by the things that happened in her life.

She returned her attention to Jade, who was neatly stacking the bookings for the afternoon, key cards lined up and ready to be scanned with the appropriate room numbers.

She worked briskly, with the ease of someone who had done this same task for years. "So, Santiago Pereira, the gentleman who showed up this morning, is he our new facilities manager?" she asked, not looking up from her work.

"Yes, ma'am. I think he's going to do well. He has the experience and he was recommended by a good friend of the family."

"Hmm," she said. "He's also kinda hot, that one."

Indya swallowed hard. Jade wasn't wrong. Anyone could see how handsome Santiago was. It wasn't knowledge that only Indya was in possession of. She leaned against the counter, watching Jade as her long brown fingers tipped in blue polish sifted through a stack of new key cards, feigning a nonchalance she did not feel. "Carlos was hot, too."

"Carlos was *cute*. He wasn't hot." Jade's eyes narrowed to slits. Jade and Carlos had been friends. She'd told Indya that he hadn't bothered to call and tell her himself about his plans to stay in California, and how much that had hurt her. "Save us from cute, unreliable handymen."

"I don't know," Indya said thoughtfully. "The hurricane left so much damage behind. I don't blame him for taking a look around, realizing it was more than he wanted to take on, and deciding that running away with the love of his life was a better bet. I just wish he'd given us a little more notice."

Jade pulled a face. "When did you suddenly turn into a romantic?"

Indya snorted. "I'm not. I'm actually being very rational." To Indya, Carlos leaving what was promising to be a thankless, overwhelming job for love and a new start in another state was not the absurd decision people might take it for. People chose love and quality of life all the time. Hadn't she given up a lucrative job and leased out her perfect beach-view condo to be with her parents? "In any case, this one doesn't look like a runner. I know his family and they are upstanding people."

"And he's hotter than a busy skillet at the Waffle House."

Indya's laugh broke out of her as if ripped from her chest by force. "Did you just compare our new handyman to a Waffle House appliance? How is that even a compliment?"

Jade shrugged, tossing her perfectly maintained blond-and-brown extensions over her shoulder. "I used to work at the Waffle House on Grant Avenue when I was a senior in high school. Trust me when I tell you, the analogy is perfect." She stopped her shuffling and turned her enormous gray eyes on Indya. "Just give me the satisfaction of admitting he's as hot as a Waffle House skillet so I can finish preparing today's check-ins in peace, instead of pretending that nothing affects you."

Indya was taken aback. "I don't pretend things don't affect me."

Jade scoffed. "Sis, you walk around here, acting like you can handle everything, you don't need help doing a thing, and there isn't a man who can catch your eye and make you feel weak."

"Hey, okay, Doctor. Go easy on me, will you? You didn't have to go into full psychotherapy mode."

"You're not going to tell me I'm lying."

Indya rewarded her with an exaggerated sigh that dissolved into another laugh. The annoying fact about Jade was that 98 percent of the time, she was right. But if you confessed that, you'd never hear the end of it. Indya decided to take the L on this one. "Fine. He's as hot as a Waffle House skillet. Are you happy now?"

Jade set her papers down, folded her hands over them

and stared directly at Indya. "We are beyond the Waffle House skillet, and you know it."

Indya pushed off the counter. Jade was a few years younger than Indya, and had spent the time Indya lived in Sarasota finishing school, earning her degree in hospitality, and learning the ins and outs of hotel management by working in some of the larger resorts. When she came to her Alba Beach Resort in search of a management position, Mami had automatically put her in charge of the front end. Indya hoped to make her the assistant manager when the resort was back at full capacity. She was smart, talented and hardworking. Indya knew that, someday, she would either lose Jade to a corporate hotel chain, where she would have an opportunity to further advance her career, or she'd open her own hotel, but Indya was grateful to have her for as long as she chose to stay.

"I have to be a hard-ass sometimes. It's not like life gave me much of a choice. And now I can't see my parents' hotel go under because of an accident of nature, not after they worked for a lifetime to build it up."

Jade uncrossed her hands and resumed matching the cards with the receipts. "I hear you. But you can allow yourself to indulge in a bit of eye candy. I mean, hell, if I was into men, Santiago could definitely get it."

Indya laughed out loud. "That's a resounding endorsement, coming from you."

"I have impeccable taste." Jade gave her a wink. "You're not allergic to men. You should get on that."

"Give me those," Indya snapped, dragging the papers through the opening in the glass, attempting to evade the question. "You've been alphabetizing the same stack since I got here." It wasn't true. Jade was nearly done and ready to place each one in the small manila envelopes specially prepared for their guests. Indya needed something to distract her from Jade's line of discussion.

Jade kept her iron glare locked on Indya until she relented. "There will be no *getting on that*. Santiago is my employee."

"Technically, you are the owner of this establishment. You make the rules."

Indya pulled a face. "My parents are the owners. And anyway, fraternizing with the employees is a serious lapse in professionalism, whether I'm the owner or not. This is a workplace, not a sex club." She flipped through the pages, quickly ordering them and trying to avoid the images that resulted from putting the words *sex* and *Santiago Pereira* in the same headspace.

"You say it like it's a bad thing," Jade retorted, taking the organized stack from Indya and setting it next to the computer. "It would make for a great sales point. 'Alba Beachside Resort, premier beachfront lodgings and exclusive sex club. Thotties and Hotties, Welcome.' I might consider that when I finally open my own establishment."

"It would definitely be a first in Soledad Bay." It was a fun thought, but the prospect of a distraction in the form of her newest employee to needle her awareness through the day was not one she wanted or needed to add to this particular moment of her life. This hotel required all hands on deck, including her own.

Her daughter, her parents and her business needed her to be on top of her game. She couldn't afford distractions of any kind.

And as Santiago's boss, she had a responsibility to not misuse her authority over him. He was simply not an option, and it was a good idea to keep reminding herself of that.

"At least we can both agree that he's hotter than a Waffle House skillet," Jade said finally.

Indya stepped away, preparing to attack her to-do list for the day. "Yes, we can both agree on that." She waved Jade off, determined to get work done. She was good at using her job to avoid dealing with the more emotionally difficult aspects of life. Fridays were great for that, since check-ins were usually at their highest as people arrived to enjoy a weekend on the beach.

Her phone buzzed, and for a moment, Indya briefly wondered if it was Gia calling her from school. Instead, the notification for her best friend, Nyla, flashed on the lock screen. She swiped the phone to access the message.

Hi, boo. Up for going out to lunch today with me and Rayne?

Indya smiled, shaking her head. Nyla and Rayne were her very best friends from when they were still in diapers. They'd grown up together in the same neighborhood, about a mile inland from the beach, and had gone through elementary, middle and high school together. Rayne was usually in and out of town on sponsored trips as part of her job as a social media advertiser. Nyla, a marine biologist, ran the Sea Turtle Rescue and Education Center and spent most of her time lately on conservation efforts to help rebuild the local beach ecosystem that had been damaged by Hurricane Adalis. She was the sponsor of the high school conservation club, and was one of the few people outside Indya's family with whom she trusted her daughter.

She hated turning them down. Lunch with Nyla and Rayne was exactly what she needed right now.

Busy. Just hired a new employee and I have a ton of paperwork.

The bubble lit up instantly, indicating Nyla was typing
out her response. Indya went to the pool counter and busied
herself stacking pool towels in the cupboards that guests
would request and use throughout the day. Her phone buzzed
again and she paused to read the message.

Too busy for your best girls?

Indya chuckled. You're an instigator and a distraction.
How about next week?

Indya could practically see the smoke coming out of
Nyla's ears. You're kidding me.

I'm not kidding you, Indya answered. You know how
Fridays are. Check-ins are wild.

A vomit emoji showed up, followed by a notification
from Rayne. Nyla had sent it in their group chat and now
Indya found herself having to fend off both women. If you
don't have lunch with us today, we'll just harass you until
you do.

Indya laughed. Harassment would include text messages
full of goofy and inappropriate GIFs. She moved in the direction of her office, texting all the while.

Do what you have to do. Does Tuesday of next week sound
good for both of you?

GIFs showing women crossing their arms and turning
their noses up at her had her laughing into the screen. Her
friends were in peak sassy mode and it felt like such a familiar, comforting place to be. Indya was seriously calcu-

lating what she would have to do to get a few hours off to spend with them, but when she walked into her office and sat down at her computer, she winced at the number of emails waiting for her attention.

I'm going to take that as a yes, she typed out.

God, fine, yes, Tuesday, Rayne answered, ramping up the drama with an exhausted emoji face because it wouldn't be her if she wasn't dramatic in some way.

A stream of thumbs-ups and hearts appeared, which brought a much-needed smile to her face.

Indya picked up Santiago's résumé, examining it again. She was hoping not to dwell on him or his interview, but she couldn't keep her eyes off the words on the page. She decided to fold it and put it in her pocket on the pretense that she would check personal references throughout the day, which she did. She always accomplished what she set out to do. But as the day wore on, the level of distraction that sheaf of paper and the constant reminder of Santiago provoked was more acute than ever.

"Indya."

Indya blinked at the presence of her mother at her office door at the end of the day. *"Sí, Mami."*

"Well, how did it go?"

Indya indicated the seat across from her, which her mother took. "I hired him. You were right. He's very qualified."

"Oh, good. That means I won't have to close off the pool area. He can take care of it."

Indya experienced emotional whiplash. They'd had two sentences' worth of a normal conversation without shock or surprise. Indya should have known even that was too much. "Why were you thinking of closing off the pool area, Mami?"

Her mother, sensing Indya's mood, grew stern. "The pool inspection showed that the slide was due for maintenance so I went ahead and scheduled the repairs. The technicians will work on it Monday afternoon."

Indya closed her eyes and took a deep breath. "And you didn't think to maybe let me know what you were up to?"

"You were busy," she said innocently. "I just wanted to take something off your plate and I've been working with that company for years, so they always prioritize us."

"Mami." Indya rubbed her temples. "I need you to clear those things through me, first."

"Why?" Mami said, her voice growing hard.

Indya stared at her. "What do you mean, why? You did this job before. Why do you think I'd like to be in the loop on things that happen here?"

"*Entiendo,* but I would never turn down help if it was clear I needed it. And you need help."

"I don't need help—"

"*Tú no cambias, mija,*" her mother interjected. "You think that you can do everything by yourself and you won't let anyone help you."

"You are exactly the same way!"

"Am I? Didn't I ask you to come home?"

Indya felt those words land in the middle of her back, between her shoulder blades. Her mom was a competent and proud woman. Indya had not fallen far from that tree, and she knew what it had cost her mother to ask anyone, even her own daughter, for help.

"I'm sorry. Just remember that you have to reach out to me or Santiago, because it's his job now. If you go off and do things without telling him, you are just going to make his job more difficult, and he might not be happy to stay on. You wouldn't want that, would you?"

Mami narrowed her eyes at Indya. "You're not trying to say I made Carlos leave, are you?"

Indya was sure her face reflected her utter confusion. "Where did you get that idea from?"

"Never mind." Mami brushed away Indya's words.

Indya studied her mother for a moment. "You know it's not your fault Carlos left."

Mami sighed deeply, her eyes still fixed on Indya. "Alba Beachside Resort isn't like the big hotel franchises. The people who stay here and the employees who work for us are not anonymous, faceless people. We do everything to make them feel like they are a part of our family." She looked away. "I hired Carlos. I let him stay on the premises when he first moved to Soledad Bay. I knew Chester, his dog. And yet, he left without saying a word."

Indya stood from her chair and rounded the desk to kneel and hug her mother. "I don't think Santiago would do that. His entire family is here and you know them. Carlos didn't leave because of anything we did." Indya shrugged. "He's just young. Sometimes young people can be careless with other people's feelings." She pulled away to look at her mom. "Santiago seems different."

"Yes." Mami patted her hand. "Santiago reminds me of your father when we first met. He was the handyman that your grandfather hired to work at the resort." Her eyes went all dreamy and it brought a smile to Indya's face.

"Was Papi hot?" Indya teased.

"Like a five-alarm fire, *mija*." She smiled. "But I gave him a bit of trouble before I agreed to date him. I loved my independence and I didn't want anyone taking that away from me."

Indya stood, taking a seat at the edge of her desk just

in front of Mami. This was not a new story for Indya. "He promised he wouldn't."

"He *promised* to accept me the way that I was. I just hope you can find someone who will do the same for you. Not like that Trent."

Indya wrinkled her nose. Mami had never liked Trent, and had liked him even less after Indya's marriage fell apart. "I don't know."

"It's not a crime to want company. Honestly, Indya, how long has it been since you've been with anyone?"

"I'm fine, Mami. I have you and Papi, Gia and my friends. Now the hotel. What more do I need?"

Mami shrugged. "Love? Companionship? Sex?"

The last word, coming out of her mother's mouth, was like nails on a chalkboard. "Mami, please!"

At this, her mother rolled her eyes. It would have been funny, but she was rolling her eyes at Indya. "Just think about what I'm saying. You're too young to be so alone, daughter of mine. Promise to think about it?"

"I promise."

"Good. Now pack it up." Mami stood up. "You've been here since too early."

Indya scoffed. "You told me I was running late this morning."

Mami chuckled. "Everyone is late compared to me." She gave her a kiss on the cheek. "Bring Gia by this weekend. I'll make her favorite dessert."

"Tres leches? She will walk to the next town for your cake."

"As she should." Mami blew her a kiss before disappearing down the hall.

Indya sighed and surveyed the work on her desk, all interest in the endless scrolling numbers and receipts lost to the thoughts her mother had put in her mind. The hotel could afford to hire another business manager, but no one was going to run things the way she did. In moments like these, she wished she had someone other than her mother to pick up the slack of her workload, someone who might actually back Indya up when she felt like she was drowning.

Abandoning all pretense of getting anything else done, she picked up her phone to find a message from Nyla, with a silly TikTok video attached showing an octopus in a zoo escaping his enclosure at night to sneak into the exotic-fish aquarium to have a late-night snack before returning before the day guard arrived. Indya couldn't help but smile. She seemed to eat, breathe and live the hotel, but Nyla was just as obsessive about the sea animals she cared for so much, and Rayne about the business she was building from the ground up. Maybe she'd turn their invitation for a lunch date into dinner. Anything was better than staying home and obsessing over her work, and especially over her newest hire.

Chapter Eight

Indya

By the time Monday morning rolled around, Indya had already downed three cups of coffee within thirty minutes of arriving at work, and her office walls were starting to answer her back.

Indya had made sure to get to the hotel earlier than usual. Santiago was starting today, and while heaven knew she had guided more than one employee through the first-day orientation of their new job, Santiago's position had been a critical one to fill. There was so much to do, and loath as she was to admit it, she needed help and she needed it ASAP.

She just hoped he wasn't the type to push back on her authority. With nearly everyone she'd employed in the hotel, she'd had to put her foot down at some point and assert her role as owner and boss. She'd been doing that all her life, even before she'd come back to Soledad Bay. She'd had to do it at the firm she worked at in Sarasota as well. Some people did not take kindly to women in charge.

She kept glancing at the time on her computer. It should

have put her more at ease that Santiago was the person starting his new job as opposed to someone she didn't already know, especially since his reference check confirmed her first impression of him—that he was competent and a good fit for the position. His family was well-known in Soledad Bay. That he had a great personality was a bonus, but not necessary to the job description. And the jury was still out on whether his extreme attractiveness was a blessing or a curse.

There was no excuse for her restlessness, yet here she was, unable to calm down and await his arrival in peace.

She busied herself with checking on the cleaning staff and verifying deliveries for the restaurant before making her way through the endless paperwork that went with running a successful business. However, her edginess wouldn't let her focus on purchase orders and invoices. She decided to go up to the front desk, where Jade was checking in a retired couple who had been returning guests at the Alba Beachside Resort for almost a decade.

Indya tucked her phone into her back pocket and quickly knelt to pick up several pamphlets that had fallen out of the brochure rack. Dusting off her white polo with the hotel logo imprinted on the front and her matching white cotton-linen blend slacks, she turned to see Santiago standing in the middle of the foyer, watching her. His vivid eyes were so dark they seemed to spear her through to the core, pinning her to the spot. She steadied her hammering heart and gave him the warmest smile she could muster. The restlessness she had experienced since she woke that morning morphed into another kind of tension with his warm and welcoming return smile.

"Santiago." She offered her hand, peering up into his handsome features before taking in the rest of him. He wore a pair of khakis and a white, button-down dress shirt that hinted at the prominent definition of his muscles. Indya swallowed hard, grateful that her hotel had a particular dress code for employees because she wouldn't be able to concentrate if he came to work dressed like that every day. She'd never get immune to him.

"Good to see you," Indya added politely.

Santiago dipped his head in acknowledgment. *"Igualmente."*

"Oh, *Español*. Are you feeling a little adventurous today?"

Santiago chuckled. "It's never a good idea to be too dogmatic."

"Dogmatic. You have a larger vocabulary than most natives."

"That's what happens when you read the English dictionary in your free time."

Indya, who had been prepared to move him toward her office, froze at this. "The dictionary?"

Santiago scratched the back of his neck, his body radiating sheepishness. "When I first came to this country, I was convinced that I needed to know as many words as possible to make a good impression on people. Every time I saw a word I didn't know, I looked it up in my online dictionary. I began to study them and use them in conversation but quickly discovered people only use a fraction of those words in real life." He spread his hands, indicating himself. "It was cheaper than a language course."

Indya had to inhale very slowly and deliberately. The sound of his voice lilted in her ears like a melody. His face belied a fierce, rugged beauty, with its high cheekbones, square jaw, and eyes warm enough to fall into. But his voice was as delicate as seafoam and the contrast set her heart racing.

"That…is…the wildest thing I've ever heard."

Santiago shrugged. "I am a wild man."

Indya snorted. "A wild man with his Dictionary.com." She indicated with a wave of her hand that he should follow her to her office. She shouldn't be so charmed by his appearance and dry sense of humor. He was here to work for her and she had to keep that firmly in mind.

She opened the door and strode inside. Picking up a generic boutique bag that sat on her desk, she turned and handed it to him. "For you."

He accepted it with a quizzical expression before opening the bag and pulling out the contents. Inside were five sky blue polos and two pale peach T-shirts, each emblazoned with his first name and the hotel logo. Indya had ordered the colors according to those he selected when completing the information on his application, but the pale peach T-shirts were her own addition, because she had been certain the color would suit him.

"I had them done on Friday after I verified the last of your references." She pointed at the clothes. "Your former employers had nothing but good things to say about you. Consider today the first day of your two-week trial period. Welcome to the Alba Beachside Resort family."

Santiago held up one of the polos. Even without trying it on, Indya was satisfied that it would fit. "Thank you." He shook it out. "May I?"

Indya considered the question until understanding dawned on her, leaving a track of heat across the top of her cheeks. "Oh, right. Sorry. Use my private bathroom." She pointed at a door with a sign that read Restroom: Employees Only. "You can change in there."

He stepped past her. She caught a whiff of a masculine fragrance. It was woodsy, like an amber-and-oak candle she owned, with hints of something cinnamon-sweet that made Indya's mouth water as if she hadn't just eaten breakfast. It took her back to that night he'd rescued her, to the way he'd smelled and sounded—

Indya nearly tripped over her own feet in her attempt to escape into the foyer and away from the ridiculously gorgeous man, who at this very moment, was most likely shirtless in her office, all hard lines of muscles and firm, smooth skin inked over by the elaborate, deep green vines and pink-red flowers of his sleeve tattoo.

Indya stepped out to the ice water dispenser, rich orange slices floating in crystalline ice cubes, and served herself a cup of water that she downed in two gulps before pouring another. She watched the condensation slide down the sides of the dispenser and drip onto the cloth underneath, placed just for that purpose. Her reaction had been fierce, sudden and unexpected. She was going to work with the man—she hadn't given her hormones permission to come out and play.

She tossed the paper cup into the recycle bin. She was a smart professional who knew how to act around attractive people in a work environment. She hadn't just crawled out of the primordial soup.

Indya returned to the office, suitably self-chastised. A moment later, Santiago stepped out of the bathroom wearing one of the peach polos. She experienced a pang of satisfaction that he had chosen to try it out—with his coloring, he was stunning. But this wasn't a fashion show, and she'd already overstepped by ordering extra clothes to begin with. She wasn't a wife or a girlfriend or anyone who was entitled to make those decisions for him. And she was not entitled to ogle him, like she was doing now.

She'd have to be extra careful to keep her impulses in check when it came to him.

He folded his own shirt neatly and tucked it inside the bag with the other polos Indya had given him before glancing up at her. It took Indya a few moments to register that the next move was on her.

"Does it fit you?" she said, her voice airy, a little breathless.

"Perfectly." He swept a hand over his body, a movement •
she followed like a cat tracking a bird.

"Everyone wears their shirts on-site. You have enough for one week, but if you need more, let me know. There are other colors as well." Great. Now she was rambling. She cleared her throat and looked away, stretching across her desk to the radio stand, where several empty charging docks were lined up in a neat row. She picked up a radio and handed it to him. "You know how to use one of these?"

Santiago pressed the button, static bursting through the speaker. He adjusted the volume and clipped it to his belt. "Yes."

Indya bit the inside of her cheek, to focus. "Make sure you put it on the stand at the end of each shift so it will be fully charged for the next one." She pulled a laminated map from the folder and handed it to him. "Hold on to that until you understand where everything is." She moved past him, avoiding direct contact with his skin so she didn't combust on the spot. "Let's take a tour, shall we?"

Indya used a similar map to guide Santiago and help her concentrate on the objective at hand, which was to introduce him to the layout of the hotel. It wasn't too complicated— they had a total of fifty rooms spread out over four floors. There were four buildings shaped like a horseshoe around the common area—tiki bar, pool, slide, Jacuzzi and recreation building—that all led to the beach via a wooden board-walk. In addition, there were ten independent bungalows fitted for long-term rental closer to the beach. After decades in the Linares family's care, the trees that had survived the storm were full and lush, offering shade to significant parts of the pool area. Palm trees soared, trim and tall, over the boardwalk, and thick patches of saw grass, wax myrtle and sea grape lined the path that took them directly to the deep blue Gulf waters. Only a cluster of overturned trees, their bold roots soaring into the air, gave any overt indication of the terrible storm that had passed through.

Santiago paused at the boardwalk, visibly breathing in the air as they looked out over the ocean. Indya stopped talking and looked out over the vista before them. She sensed what Santiago might be feeling—she'd experienced so many moments of awe at the sea as a lifelong resident of Soledad Bay. No matter how busy or distracted Indya was, there was always a moment when she had to stop and take in the immensity of the ocean, etching the salt and iodine into her soul, and letting it grow roots there. Indya imag-ined populations of Sirenas and mermen from the stories of her childhood, calling those waves home, and could al-most believe, as her ancestors had, that they owed some of their native blood to those mythical beings.

Santiago opened his mouth to say something but shut it, leaving her curious. She wanted to know what he was thinking so she could learn and understand him. But that was beyond the scope of what they were doing here. Indya was affected by him, but that wasn't his fault. She owed him the courtesy of professionalism and respect.

She drew herself to her full height just as he came out of his reverie and turned his attention to her.

"Let's meet your team, then I'll take you to your work

area," Indya said in clear, decisive English, more for her own benefit than for his. Santiago followed her to Facilities Management, a separate building where his team had been instructed to wait for them.

Introductions to the coworkers on shift took only a few minutes. Santiago had six people on his team at any given time, as well as a list of local contractors who specialized in the larger maintenance that couldn't be handled in-house. Santiago's focus would be on creating and maintaining workflow, ensuring coverage by staff, keeping track of scheduled maintenance and making purchases necessary for keeping the hotel running optimally. Heba, a half Colombian, half Palestinian woman who spoke Arabic and Spanish but whose English wasn't perfect, was one of their best handy people and would work closely with Santiago. Santiago was a tall man, packed with well-developed muscles, but he had a way of making himself smaller and less imposing, which helped the rest of the team relax during their introductions.

Afterward, Indya took him on a tour of the facility. In the corner of the largest workroom sat a golf cart plugged into the electrical outlet. There were shelves up to the ceiling, covered in tools and liquids that had been placed there without any real rhyme or reason. Indya had tried her best to organize everything in advance of Santiago's arrival, but Carlos had worked in that room for years, and seemed to have made every effort to render the space as chaotic and indecipherable as possible to everyone but himself.

"Carlos was not the most organized person in the world," Indya began as Santiago quietly took in the large work space. "We've been trying to get things under control after he left, but I've been too busy doing his job in addition to mine." Indya dragged a heavy, battered red toolbox from under the large workbench in the center of the room. "Whatever you need should be in here somewhere. Heba will help you, as well as your team. They've been here longer and can help you find things, but if something is missing, don't hesitate to order it. One of the things that makes our resort competitive against some of the bigger franchises here is that we are quick to accommodate our guests with whatever reasonable needs they might have."

"Sorry, you were doing the handiwork?" Santiago asked.

Indya stopped her rummaging to stare at him, nerves bristling at his words. She had zero tolerance for machismo or toxic masculinity in her life. "Why the surprise? Because I'm a woman?"

Santiago's face changed. "No, because you are the boss," he retorted simply.

The scowl on Indya's face melted away and she felt instant shame. There was a lot she could say about Santiago, but he had never struck her as that brand of Neanderthal. "Sorry, I just deal with stupid assumptions all the time because I'm Latina and a woman, so I'm quick to bare my claws."

Santiago effortlessly lifted the red toolbox that had felt like a ton in Indya's hands, and set it on the bench between them. "I understand. You forget that my mother is a business woman in this community as well."

"I could never forget that." She looked around the workroom, something wistful settling over her. "Both my grandfather and my father were the facilities managers in their time."

"The business belongs to your father's side of the family?" Santiago asked.

"Oh no," Indya chuckled. "My grandmother bought the hotel with money from her inheritance. She married my grandfather after he became the handyman at the time. By the time my mother inherited it, the hotel had become a resort. She ended up marrying my father who was the facilities manager. Kind of a trend in my family." Indya looked away from Santiago's penetrating gaze, realizing with growing mortification what her words implied.

"Anyway," she said quickly, hoping a little verbal vomit might cover up her earlier words. "Growing up, I always kept my father company while he worked. I wouldn't leave him alone, but he never minded me being there, even though I'm sure I got in the way." She ran a finger over the lid of the toolbox, coming away with a brown-red dusting of rust. "This belonged to him when he was still working."

Santiago stared at her as if he were following a movie or a play. "I didn't know all of this."

Indya shrugged, smiling at the dented, rusty thing. "How could you?" She laughed quietly. "He taught me everything I know about taking care of the property, including how to fix common things, like a toilet, which by the way, I did twice this weekend. I scheduled repairs for the septic tank this week and Mami did you the favor of scheduling pool maintenance this afternoon." She just couldn't stop herself from rambling. She opened the toolbox, rifling inside. "Anyway, I'm trying to teach Gia as well, but she's more interested in science experiments than hospitality."

Santiago gave a wistful smile that was both tender and disarming on someone as physically imposing as he was. "Miriam wouldn't come near this maintenance room, even if you paid her. She would rather be building her own computer. My parents aren't even considering leaving the supermarket in her hands. She's just not interested."

She leaned against the worktable, drumming the surface.

"I'd love for Gia to take over the hotel, but I also want her to live her own life."

"They have to make their own way. There's nothing that parents can do about that except to accept them for who they are and support their choices," Santiago answered quietly, stepping away to survey the scaffolds. Indya suspected there were layers beneath his words, folds of meaning she wanted to uncrease. "I've been gone for a good part of Miriam's life, so I am trying to be her friend, offer her guidance but not parent her. She already has two parents, and they take the job very seriously."

"She's a lucky girl," Indya said quietly. "Gia has her grandfathers, who are both lovely, but I was an only child with no brothers, so she sometimes misses having more positive male role models."

"What about her father?"

Indya scratched at a spot on the table, chagrined to find that she'd chipped the paint on her manicure. "Trent is a committed father. He loves her and would do anything for her. But his values are not quite aligned to mine, and sometimes, there is conflict when it comes to raising Gia." She slid her eyes away as she asked the next question. "Is it the same between you and your ex?"

Santiago's eyes widened slightly, but his answer was calm and measured, as all his words were. "We agree on most things when it comes to Lisbet, and where we differ, I mostly defer to her. She is with her all the time and knows her better than I do." He put his hands deep in his pants pockets. "I have the belief that if there is anyone who has Lisbet's best interests at heart, it is Natasha."

Natasha. Her name sounded lovely on Santiago's lips, as did everything else he said. She'd been lulled, as much by his words as by the way he spoke each one. She could listen to him speak for days. Imagine having a partner who had faith in her decisions, who trusted that their child was in the best possible hands and didn't question every decision she made.

"Natasha sounds amazing." Indya snapped shut the lid of the toolbox with more vigor than she'd intended. The rusted red metal clanged loudly in the space. "I was hoping to keep this hotel in the family for a few more generations," she added, trying to break the odd mood that had fallen over her. "We'll have to see how things go." Indya had more than enough time to think about the problem of who would inherit this place.

"That's all you can do," Santiago said, bemused.

"Right. So, everything in this room is at your disposal. Again, if you need anything at all, you tell me and I'll get it. Don't be shy about this. I have many repeat customers and I want to keep them coming back, and the hurricane has put this whole town on shaky ground. I don't want to see Soledad Bay turn into a sleepy beach town because businesses were not able to rebuild what was ruined." Indya put her hands on her hips, hoping the gesture made her sound more confident than she felt. "Alba Beachside Resort offers something that is difficult to find in some of the larger hotels along the strip."

He turned away from where he'd been studying a wood sander, curls of fiber still trapped in its metal joints. "And that is…?"

"The feeling of finding a home away from home."

A smile tugged at Santiago's serious expression. "That feeling keeps people coming back."

He reached to take the box, but she didn't release it right away. She spoke from a sudden well of deepest sincerity. "I hope you find a home away from home here as well."

His expression softened and there was real gratitude in his eyes. God, she wondered if he knew how easy his emotions were to read on his face, how incredibly vulnerable that made him appear. How heady that was combined with his strength and easy personality.

"Thank you," he said finally.

"I told you. We have to help each other. Here." Indya gave him another small smile before handing over an iPad she'd been carrying that held the outstanding repair projects and the stream of customer tickets for maintenance requests. "Maintenance tickets come through on our online system. Be sure to clear the tickets as soon as you begin the work so your team isn't running around, tracking down jobs that have already been done. You said you were familiar with this software suite?"

Santiago held the tablet firmly in his hand. "We used it at my last job."

"Good." Indya moved to the door. "Hopefully, you have everything you need to know, and what you don't have, we'll get for you." She turned to see that he was wearing a placid, almost pleased expression and Indya decided contentment looked almost as good on him as the peach-colored T-shirt. "Now, get to work before your boss comes after you."

"Sí, señora," Santiago said, an imperceptible tug at the corners of his lips hinting at humor held in check.

"No, not *señora*," Indya protested.

"Do you prefer *jefa*? Boss?"

"Just Indya."

"Very well, Indya." He said it in such a deadpan way, she wasn't sure if he was joking or not. He could mask his feelings quite well when he wanted to, after all.

She gave a quick wave and turned away as quickly as she could before he roped her in with that low-key, unselfconscious charm that she had no business succumbing to. This was her place of business, her family's legacy. What she'd said earlier hadn't been just hyperbole. For many years, this had been her home. She remembered a little brown girl in pigtails, running around the property, discovering every secret place and making each her own. This hotel was more than just a vehicle for earning income. She loved it, with all its quirks and imperfections, which was a good thing, because the hurricane had added to the scars of the place. Memories were everywhere and clung to her like sticky spiderwebs.

The radio buzzed, then went silent. Indya nearly turned around to check on Santiago on the pretense that the aborted radio call might have been his, but the excuse was a flimsy one. He might have been testing the radio for all she knew. If he needed her, he'd reach out to her. Indya walked down the corridor and left Santiago to his work.

Chapter Nine

Santiago

He fired up the truck and pulled out of the parking lot, determined to run a few errands related to the ongoing repairs to his family's supermarket and not dwell endlessly on his new boss. He had a short schedule today, given that Indya had asked him to focus on familiarizing himself with his work environment. It had been generous of her to let him ease into his position, given how much needed to be done.

Tackling his to-do list would calm the excitement of his new job, and his new boss. He imagined every iteration of her—boat captain, drinking partner, employer, woman—and each one was as compelling as the others. Santiago had so much going on, so many loose ends to braid together into a life that could accommodate his daughter, that he didn't need this additional distraction, but she was the most pleasant one to dwell on.

She was his boss. He just had to remember that and maybe he could get over this attraction.

He'd focus on completing the renovation of his boat, and helping his parents with their repairs. His time on the

Aragona was temporary—he would lease an apartment as soon as he was stable in his new work—but he loved that cruiser, loved taking her out and dropping a few hopeful lines off her stern. He dreamed of taking Lisbet on trips up and down the shore, in addition to all the plans he had for her in Soledad Bay.

By the time he was done, he was relieved to see that it was time for Lisbet to be released from school. The school day was shorter in Venezuela than in the US—five hours versus the seven and a half his sister, Miriam, spent in school. He was grateful because he didn't think he could wait another minute to give her a call and share the good news. His entire attention would be pinned on Lisbet and not a certain boss of his at a resort on the sea. As soon as he pulled into the parking lot of the marina, he found her contact and called her. Natasha had at first resisted giving a ten-year-old her own cell phone, but after he agreed to allow Lisbet to have one with only their numbers and those of her closest relatives, and no internet access, Natasha had finally relented.

"Papá!" came his daughter's excited voice over the line and Santiago felt a thousand bands of longing wrap around his chest.

"Bebe," he said fondly in Spanish, calling forth the image of her full, round cheeks, and dark hair curling over them in hues of soft brown. "How was school today?"

"Good." She giggled. "Lupe brought a lizard to school today and everyone screamed when he escaped into the classroom. Señora Rios finally caught it, but by then, the hour was finished."

Santiago laughed at the image of a class lesson erupting into chaos because of a tiny amphibian. "Was the teacher upset?"

"So mad! Lupe got an afternoon detention because of it."

"Her parents will not be happy. I think you said they were strict."

He could hear the way her voice grew serious at this. "Yes. She said she will be grounded because the school called her mother."

Santiago remembered his own antics in school, the number of times his knuckles were rapped with a ruler by his teachers, and the further punishment he got from his parents when he got home. Luckily, his daughter lived in an age where teachers did not use physical punishment as discipline, something he would not have been able to endure, living so far away from her.

"Guess what?" he said, deftly changing topics. "I got a new job."

"Really!" she shouted then repeated his news to someone off-line, probably Natasha. They were inseparable, the two of them, especially after both of Natasha's parents passed away and her only sister had moved to Florida about the time Santiago's parents had relocated. "Does that mean we can come to visit?"

His heart swelled with the thought of having his daughter with him. "I promised it would be your birthday gift."

She squealed in excitement, the phone thudding a few times before there was a shuffle and his daughter's voice came back on. "Sorry. I dropped the phone."

Santiago laughed. "That's okay. I hope you have a case on it."

"It's a Barbie one and it's so pretty Papá. I'll show you when I come."

"Promise?"

"Promise." She paused. He heard voices talking in the

background before Lisbet returned. "Mamá asked if you wanted to speak to her?"

"Of course I do." When they had first broken up, things were understandably tense for several months. Natasha initiated the breakup, but eventually, he understood that it had been for the best. They had outgrown each other as romantic partners, but they made damned good friends and co-parents.

"*Hola*, Santiago," Natasha's voice came on the line, the familiarity of it both soothing and aching to him. It reminded him of home, but also of his daughter, who he missed desperately. "Congratulations! It didn't take you long at all."

"Thanks to Mamá, who knows the owner of the resort. It's a management position." He described the job and the benefits. "It will be good for us."

"I had no doubts. You always find a way." One of the things Santiago had always appreciated was the faith Natasha had always shown in him, and that hadn't ended when they broke up.

"Hopefully, we'll be on target to have you both come in July."

Natasha laughed at this. "I still can't believe she is calling the entire month of July her birthday month. Where does she get these ideas?"

"She might not have the internet, but her friends talk. It's a popular idea here, too."

"And here I was, restricting my fun to only one day. I have been missing out," Natasha teased.

"It's never too late to start," Santiago responded.

"*Oye,*" Natasha said, her voice changing, growing quieter. "You okay out there? Are you taking care of yourself? How is your father?"

Santiago groaned. "Still mortally offended with me for existing."

"Nooooo." Natasha drew the word out between laughter. "I don't think it's that extreme."

"It feels like it," Santiago said, adding, "I can't help but think he might calm down when Lisbet comes."

"Well, we'll be there soon, God willing. Then he can start behaving again."

"Let's hope." Santiago paused before adding, "And you take care of yourself and Lisbet. I can't wait to see you both."

"I know, Santi. We'll talk tomorrow."

When she hung up, a sense of being lost descended on him. He missed being surrounded by people who knew him well, from the very beginning, even. He felt like he was always starting over, putting his best foot forward, trying to get people to notice him, to form a certain opinion of him. Natasha knew him better than even his own parents in some things, and it made him aware of how much energy he expended, always being the new guy in a new place.

Before he tucked his phone in his pocket and locked up the truck, he called his mother. He couldn't let the day go by without telling his mother the good news about his job.

Getting released from his previous job had been a blow to Santiago. While he would always prefer owning his own business to working for someone else, this new position provided a decent and consistent income with good benefits. It could lead to other side jobs, which would give him the extra funds needed to bring Lisbet and her mother to the US to live with him even more quickly and allow him to give his daughter a good life.

He couldn't deny the additional bonus of working with Indya. She was the most interesting person he'd met since coming to this country. And quite possibly, the prettiest as well.

The next few days at work were uneventful, disaster-wise. He had a good staff who was willing to help him out. They covered calls for routine maintenance while he learned how things worked.

Indya appeared and disappeared, depending on where her responsibilities took her. She was not overly familiar with him but she wasn't unfriendly, either. Just a perfectly annoying business neutral. He didn't want to examine why her impeccable professionalism put him off so much. He wanted the Indya who laughed easily while throwing back beer, who bantered with her friend and bad-mouthed a cat who had decided she was not worth her attention. Anything but this professional automaton.

He pulled into the small parking lot behind the super-market after his last day of work for the week, to check the progress on repairs. It felt like more of the same—all he had talked about this week was what to schedule, how to budget it, how to make sure none of the routine mainte-nance fell by the wayside. But the work here at the super-market wasn't going to do itself. Inspectors were coming in soon, and his parents needed to pass with flying colors.

He shut off his truck and collected his phone, taking care not to leave anything visible that would encourage someone to break into his car—an old habit from when he lived in Caracas—and made his way inside. His family lived in a house a few blocks away, with a sprawling yard overhung by tropical plants and fruit trees. But they spent most of their time in the supermarket, and when Santiago wasn't working on the boat or out and about, this is where he came to spend time with them.

"Mamá?" he called out as he walked through the back entrance of the store.

"Hijo," she answered, waving him over to where she worked, organizing the rolls of bread for sandwiches. She'd refilled the hot case with *pancitos*, *rellenos*, *arepas* and *boñuelos* that warmed under the heating element. The refrigerator held cakes in different varieties and a freshly made *quesillo* that was bathed in thick caramel. Santiago had a terrible sweet tooth and ached to try a slice.

Instead, he bent to give his small mother a kiss on the cheek.

"¿Cómo te fue esta semana?"

"This week went really well," Santiago answered. "Everyone has been helpful."

She clapped her hands and threw her arms around his shoulders. *"Bien hecho, mi niño.* I told you that you would like working with Indya Linares. She has a good reputation. Hardworking and serious. She would never throw her employees away like they did at your other job."

"Mamá, I've told you a dozen times. The owners did not throw us away. They sold the hotel. It was the new management who didn't want us."

"New management, old management. Who cares? I still blame them," she retorted, her face suddenly fierce. "The way these companies treat their employees, it's amazing there aren't strikes every day."

Santiago laughed. His mother was still getting used to working in a different cultural and economic environment, even after all these years. "It's different here. If people do not like their job, they do not protest. They just quit and find a new job."

"And that's why these companies get away with whatever they want."

"Okay, *rebelde*," Santiago chuckled. "Not everybody will have their own business the way you do." Santiago stared at her with exaggerated concentration. "You should actually be thinking of retiring soon."

"I'm too young!" She swatted his words away. "And anyway, I want to see you married and working at something you like. Your sister is still in high school, and I have a feeling that one is going to take a long time to settle down. Until at least one of you is in a stable situation, I'm not going anywhere."

"No pressure." Santiago shook his head.

His mother shrugged, as if guilting children into marriage and stability was perfectly well-adjusted behavior. "It's for your own good."

"Right, because it has nothing to do with the fact that you wouldn't know what to do with free time, would it?" Mamá had been working all her life and she seemed bent on continuing to do so until she couldn't physically manage it anymore.

"I could find a lot to do." She ticked off each item on her finger. "I could get a makeover, go on a cruise, take English classes, practice playing the guitar—"

Santiago laughed at her. "You play the guitar?"

She paused, looking almost affronted. "And why does that surprise you? I am a very musical person."

That was partly true. His mother loved music and listened to it all the time. But she was not particularly endowed with a gift for it, if her singing voice was any indication.

A rustling from the storage room at the back of the store reminded Santiago of why he was there. He took a deep breath. "I'm going to go check on Papá."

His mother gave him a sympathetic smile. "Just remember that everything he does comes from a place of love, even if he doesn't know how to show it."

Santiago nodded before making his way to the back. He pushed through the metal door to find his father, large and imposing, carrying a stack of boxes. Santiago raced to help him, removing the top two boxes from the precarious stack Papá was carrying. He had done construction work for a good part of his life, until his age caught up with him, making his overused muscles ache and his joints creak.

Santiago followed his father, putting down the boxes where he indicated.

"Santiago," he said, as if he were forcing his name out.

"Papá." Anxiety began in his stomach, clenching its way up his chest, the way it once did when he was young and knew he would receive a reckoning for his bad behavior. Except he felt this way with Papá each time he was in his presence, ever since he could remember, and more so after the last few years of his life. His father handed him his set of tools.

"Trabajamos, no?"
Let's get to work, no?

Santiago nodded, starting in on the remaining drywall. They worked quietly, mostly companionably, though Santiago never felt completely at ease in his father's presence. The last time he'd sensed any kind of camaraderie with his father was the year before Santiago opened his business. The work itself hadn't upset his father as much as the lack of security it represented and how none of it resembled what he had studied in school. Santiago missed his father's pride in him.

"Y el nuevo trabajo?" his father asked, out of the clear blue.

Santiago cleared his throat. "The new job is great. I'm learning their way of doing things."

His father's jaw was clenched as he sawed through a piece of wood. When he was done, he said, "Oriana Linares and her husband, Fermín, own the hotel, but her daughter runs it now that her parents are too old to do it. She's a good daughter, that one."

Santiago sensed the subtext of his father's criticism but let it go. "I was hired by Indya."

Papá nodded, acknowledging that. "They are an upstanding family. But be careful," he said, wagging his finger at Santiago. "You represent our family here in Soledad Bay now. They have done you a great kindness by giving you a job. Do not embarrass us."

Santiago wanted to retort, *And when had he ever embarrassed his family?* But Papá had never approved of one decision in his life. Not the decision to open his own company, not his decision to move in with a pregnant Natasha without getting married. And he had been especially scathing when he lost the company he'd so strongly advised him against opening. When everything fell apart, it felt like his failures only confirmed what his father believed about him—that he was rebellious and unreliable and would only continue to fail. He was the kind to keep score and there was no way of knowing how long he would hold Santiago's mistakes against him.

"I know how to work, Papá. I'm not going to be irresponsible," Santiago retorted, keeping his anger under control by the thinnest of threads because of the ingrained respect he had been raised to have for his father.

"*Bien*, because we have worked a long time to build up a good reputation here. Your mother is a woman who everyone looks up to. And your sister is known as a good student at the high school. Don't bring shame on us."

Santiago swallowed down the bile that burned his way

up his throat at Papá's words. All he wanted was to redeem himself in his father's eyes, but sometimes he believed his father refused to see anything redeeming in him.

Santiago packed up the tool he'd been given. "I think Mamá needs some help."

His father shrugged instead of saying goodbye, which served only to motivate Santiago to get out of there more quickly. There was nothing he enjoyed more than to be reminded of his father's low opinion of him.

When he stepped through the door, he was greeted by a familiar voice coming from the front of the store.

"Hello," Miriam called from beyond the counter. Santiago hurried toward the sound, eager to be away from his father and with his sister instead, who was, besides Lisbet, the person who meant the most to him in the world.

"Miriam, *mi niña*." Mamá greeted her with a kiss. She stood taller than their mother, with wavy dark hair that she had set in a flawless French braid. Everything about her, from her large brown eyes to her skin that was so similar to his—a pretty deep-gold that reminded him of their mother—hinted at the endless possibilities that only the young could exude. Like the world was waiting for her to crack it open and fish out the endless pearls that waited for her inside. He remembered that time in his life, when everything seemed to be within his grasp, every dream attainable. He missed that feeling.

"¿Que tal, hija?" his Mamá said to the girl who had walked in behind Miriam. *"¿Como está tu Mamá y abuelita?"*

In Santiago's hurry to get away from his father, he hadn't properly registered the girl's presence. She was taller than his little sister, with perfectly styled wavy hair, sun-kissed tan skin and distinct, angular features that struck Santiago as vaguely familiar.

"Mami's good, thank you, and so is Abuela," she answered in impeccable Spanish and he remembered Indya's words about not wanting her daughter to be monolingual. This must be Gia.

"Tell her I said hello," Mamá practically sang before pausing to glance at the clock. "It's earlier than usual. Did school let out already?"

Gia's eyes flicked toward Miriam before answering, "No. I just happened to be faster than usual getting here today."

"You were not!" Miriam retorted, affecting a pout that Santiago was too embarrassed to admit he always gave in to.

"I won," Gia answered. "Because I was faster than you."

Miriam shrugged, then smiled even more broadly at her mother, whose features had darkened significantly since they'd started talking. Mamá had that look on her face that meant she was not having any of their nonsense. Santiago leaned against the counter, entertained by the exchange. "What did I tell you about racing your bikes downtown, with all those people who don't know how to drive?"

"It was my fault, *señora*," Gia interjected. "I challenged her and then beat her. I regret having done that."

"You have no regrets," Miriam shot back before catching herself and giving her mother that winning smile again. "*Sí*, Mamá. We're very sorry. We won't do it again."

"You can charm the skin off a snake," Mamá huffed. "Santiago." She turned to him. "This is Indya's daughter, Gia. Gia, this is Santiago, my son and Miriam's older brother. Your mother just hired him to work at the hotel."

Gia extended a hand politely, which he shook gently before releasing. Gia was the spitting image of her mother, same glowing tan skin, same wavy hair, though much lighter in color, and large, wide-set brown eyes, slightly angled up at the corners. Even with the similarity in appearance to her mother, Gia also reminded Santiago of his sister, with whom she was apparently close enough to race with across the small town of Soledad Bay. He felt a sudden surge of protectiveness toward both girls.

"A pleasure. Miriam talks about you all the time," Gia said.

Miriam's face grew dark. "No, I don't."

Gia pulled a face, effectively destroying her perfectly well-mannered-girl facade. "Can you spell hero worship?"

"Snitch," Miriam murmured.

Santiago laughed, flattered and warmed by his sister's obvious affection for him. "You don't have to be ashamed. I'm worth worshipping."

Miriam rolled her eyes and groaned.

Turning back to his mother, Gia asked, "Can Miriam come to the boardwalk with me? We're meeting a few friends to hang out and get some ice cream."

"Are you racing each other there again?" Mamá asked with disapproval, even as she packed a paper bag full of treats. Gia's bank card was in hand but Mamá brushed it away. It was clear they'd done this many times before.

"No, *señora*. I don't want to make her feel bad by beating her again."

Santiago bit back a laugh, especially when his sister hurled a murderous glare at her. "You didn't beat me," she retorted, pouting again even though she was well past the age where pouts should be effective.

Santiago switched briefly to English. "I can put the bikes in the back of the truck and drop you both off."

Miriam shook her head, a glint of mischief in her eye. "No, we'll get there on our own."

Santiago was 100 percent certain Miriam would not let this win stand, given how competitive she was.

"Mamá?" he asked, looking at her meaningfully.

She crossed her arms. "Santiago is right. You cannot be trusted. Put your bikes in the back of the truck. He will take you downtown." Miriam began to protest, but Mamá put her finger up to silence her. "Another word and I'll have Santiago take Gia to her mother and you can go directly upstairs to do your homework."

Miriam made a strangled sound. Gia, who was the picture of calm, gave Mamá a smile that had Miriam rolling her eyes. "Yes, Señora Pereira."

Santiago caught Miriam's eye roll but wisely kept his mouth shut.

"Vamos," Santiago said, waving to the girls to follow him out. "Bikes in the back."

"What's the point?" Miriam said after she'd pushed past the glass doors, glaring at the truck as if it had done something to her.

"Don't worry," Gia said soothingly. "I'll get Mom to bring you home later."

"What about your bike?" Miriam asked.

"I'll drop yours off at the house," Santiago said to his sister. "And I'll leave Gia's at the hotel. We'll let her mother decide what she wants to do with it."

Gia cheered. "The hotel is right next to downtown! Just leave her backpack, too, so we can work on our projects together. Thank you!"

"Of course," he said, securing both bikes in the bed of his truck. The girls clambered in behind him and they quickly traversed the half mile it took to get to the public beach. They barely said goodbye before they were out, Gia's backpack abandoned in the truck, a casualty of her rush.

Santiago turned the truck around and drove to the hotel's employee parking lot.

A quivering sensation bloomed in his belly the closer he got to Indya's office. As he cleared the bright halls and impeccably clean floor to the main lobby, he fully expected to have to search for Indya. So he was not prepared to find her standing before him, conversing with a couple at the front of the hotel.

When her eyes fell on him, she stopped mid sentence. People moved around her, the sound of voices scooped up and magnified by the vaulted ceiling of the foyer, but she might as well have been alone, for all he had eyes for anyone else.

She blinked, gave him a smile, and everything fell back into alignment. Exchanging a few last words with the couple she'd been speaking with, she moved in his direction.

"Santiago. Do you like your job so much that you couldn't stay away?"

He liked her more than enough to keep coming back, but she didn't need to know that. She looked as impeccable as when he'd first seen her that morning, as if she wasn't in the late hours of her workday.

"I had the pleasure of meeting your daughter today. She was with my little sister."

Indya's eyes widened. "Yes, she is!" A series of light bulbs seemed to go off in her head. "My daughter is very good friends with your sister. I had no idea when we first met."

"I only discovered this fact this afternoon, when I met Gia at my mother's supermarket. She had just been racing Miriam on their bikes and both were on their way to meet friends downtown."

Indya frowned, a furrow appearing above her nose that

he wanted to smooth away. Seeing her worried look provoked a instinctive need to do something about it. "Racing, huh? She knows better. I've warned her a hundred times not to do that."

Santiago nodded. "My mother warned them of the same."

"Can't say I don't get it, though. I grew up in this hotel and we did more than a few dangerous things in my day. But the town was smaller and there was much less car traffic then."

"They are in the downtown area now, but I have the girls' bikes and backpacks in my truck. I thought it might be easier if I brought everything here to you." He remembered that she drove the equivalent of a toy car and added, "Or I can drop Gia's things off at your house, if you have no way to get the bike home."

Indya mulled it over. "I can take care of it. But thank you for the offer." She shifted on her feet. "And for taking care of them."

Santiago warmed from the praise. "It was either that or they would have had to face another lecture from my mother."

Indya laughed and he liked the sound of that, too. It sounded right coming out of her lovely, soft mouth. "I hope the girls were grateful."

"As grateful as fourteen-year-olds can be."

Indya's smile deepened and Santiago was officially out to sea. He reigned in the burble of giddiness in his chest at her small but constant attentions. He hadn't felt so charmed and undone since he was a young man.

"Come." She waved at him to follow her. "I'll take her things off your hands and you'll get to see another part of the hotel you haven't seen before."

Santiago raised an eyebrow but said nothing more as she led the way down the corridor.

Chapter Ten

Santiago

After tying Gia's bike to a covered bike rack close to his work area, Santiago followed Indya to the hotel corridor that was near her business office. Indya carried Gia's backpack and Santiago carried Miriam's. Santiago tried not to stare at the soft sway of her hips under her slacks or the tiny waist that, paired with her thick thighs, turned the curves of her body into a dangerous invitation to touch. Santiago had to take a deep breath—the booming of his heart threatened to drown out his thoughts.

It's only the backpack, he huffed out in his mind. *No other reason to be so out of breath.*

"This is where you will find Gia and Miriam if they aren't out on the plaza," Indya said, using her magnetic card to open Room 188. She stepped inside, setting Gia's bag on the luggage rack. Santiago did the same thing, the door slamming shut behind him.

The room was not small—it was an L-shaped suite with a sitting area, a partially equipped kitchen, and two full-size beds. A standard beachfront room, but it had been personalized with posters, a colorful, rainbow duvet, turtle-themed lamps, and an already-too-messy study area piled with books and papers. Fairy lights framed the generic hotel painting above the bed.

"They come here after school when I have to work late, which is often," Indya continued. "They study here, and sometimes have dinner in the restaurant across the lobby." Santiago opened his mouth to say something about the costs of the meals, but Indya anticipated him and stopped him from talking. "They're best friends. My mother always said, where one eats, so can two. I won't hear a word about Miriam paying for anything. Your mother is just as kind when Gia comes over to stay with Miriam."

He took in the room again before letting his eyes settle on Indya. "Seems like you worked everything out. Why are you telling me this?"

Indya stepped toward the sliding glass door and out onto the patio. A gust of refreshing salt air rushed through the room. "If you're working and you ever worry about Miriam, you can just come here and see her." Indya turned away from the view. "I know you are very close to her."

Santiago made his way to where she stood, reveling in the wind that swept through his hair. "How do you know I am very close to her?"

Indya darted a quick glance in his direction before turning her face away. "It's logical. She's your sister."

"I've been away a long time." Santiago internally quaked under a new realization. "Maybe you've been asking about me?"

Indya pushed away from the railing, which overlooked a carpet of tropical vegetation that melted into steep sand dunes. "What if I did? You're my newest employee. Of course I'm going to want to know about you."

"Fair enough," Santiago said, backing away before the clear evidence that she had done more than simply ask about an employee, enjoying the wild thrill that it gave him. "Thank you for the offer."

Indya turned back to lean on the railing of the balcony. "I'd never get between family."

Her ferocity both captivated and intrigued him. "It's a nice system you have here."

Indya frowned. "What do you mean?"

"This," he indicated with a chin nod in the direction of the hotel room. "The teenage years are hard for them and they can get rebellious." He knew for a fact that he had. "But Gia seems perfectly happy."

"She knows how to get what she wants." Indya's smile grew soft and tender, and it occurred to Santiago that telling a parent that their children appeared happy would be the highest compliment. "I think kids get rebellious because they want more freedom than they can handle. This arrangement makes her think she's independent, but I can still keep a close eye on her." She looked down at her manicure, fussing with a chipped nail. "Though I have to admit. Owning a hotel makes that a little easier." She crossed her arms to study him. "Your parents do the same for Miriam."

He had to acknowledge that this was true. "They did that with me as well, but in Venezuela, where there were so many more 'interesting'—" he air quoted the word "—things to do in the streets than here. I always found a reason to rebel. No room at the back of an office or shop was enough to keep me from getting into trouble."

"The system wasn't Santiago-proof." Indya laughed. At his sheepish expression, she changed tack. "How is your daughter?"

His mood instantly brightened at her interest in Lisbet.

"We spoke yesterday. She's doing well in school. I'm hoping to bring her to visit me for her birthday."

Indya brightened. "That's wonderful!! When is her birthday?"

"July. Just a few months away."

"School will be out by then. Maybe we can get her, Gia and Miriam together and take them out on the boat. Does Lisbet like sailing?"

Santiago's stomach gave a flip at Indya remembering Lisbet's name. It was such a small thing, but it meant everything to him. "She's my daughter. Of course she loves sailing."

"Silly me. I should have guessed." She put her face up to the wind and he was captivated by her profile, the smooth line of her chin and the column of her neck. He discreetly inhaled and took in her perfume, an expensive floral blend that he had already come to associate with her.

It was as if he had been plunged under a sea wave. His head swayed from the intensity. He wanted to reach out, scoop up an armful of her and press her close. It was overwhelming and painfully inappropriate. She was his boss, and it had not yet been a week since he'd started working for her.

He had to bury any of those kinds of impulses relating to Indya and he had to do it instantly. He visualized the stack of forms at home for the next round of paperwork for his daughter and her mother to come to the US.

Straightening under his resolve, Santiago turned to Indya, pulling her out of her own reverie. "Thank you for this. I am grateful for the care you have given Miriam."

"As I am grateful to your parents for taking care of Gia." She stopped his retreat with a hand on his arm. "It's what we do. Help each other out. Especially after the hurricane."

He dipped his head in acknowledgement before moving toward the hotel room door, Indya following close behind. Her presence was even more intense in the confined space of the suite and he moved quickly to step into the corridor.

He needed to get out on the open beach, breathe in the fresh sea air and get his thoughts in order again. "Thanks again. I know the way."

Indya looked confused but only said, "Yeah, sure. Okay." She lingered a moment, her eyes raking over his face, and it was like a creeping sunburn across his skin every place they landed. "See you tomorrow?"

"Bright and early," he said, repressing the dangerously infernal urge to dip his head down and sample the sensuous softness of her lips against his own.

He had gone downhill in a precipitous way.

Thankfully, she turned, throwing a last glance at him over her shoulder, and made her way down the hallway that would take her to the lobby and her office beyond.

Santiago raked a hand over his face. He needed to get out of there and center himself again. As he drove home, he concluded that it had been the confined space of the hotel room that had worked on his imagination, together with her perfume, her smooth skin and soft, voluptuous curves—

It would pass. He would go to work with the intention to avoid as much contact with Indya as possible until his hands no longer itched to wrap themselves around her waist.

Except the thing about good intentions is that they had nothing to do with what life chose to deliver.

Santiago learned Indya's habits as the weeks passed. Some he was not privy to, with his responsibilities taking him all over the property. But some he picked up easily, like how she had the same precise morning routine from which she rarely deviated. She took her coffee at the same time every day, and in exactly the same way. She always walked the property at the beginning of her shift, taking each building in the exact same order. He imagined, from her mostly organized space, that Indya was a creature of routines. He wasn't going out of his way to keep track of her, at least that was what he told himself.

And true to her habits, she appeared on location nearly each and every time he or someone on his team took a call.

"It's like she got so used to stepping in and covering for Carlos that it's almost automatic for her," Heba confided in him after nearly a month of him being on the job. It was the longest conversation she'd ever held with him up until then. Perhaps she'd finally decided that he was worth trusting. Santiago had been in his office when Heba arrived with the full intention of unleashing her frustrations on him. She'd returned from yet another call that Indya had flagged, indicating she'd gotten to the job first. Instead of a toolbox, Heba wore a belt that hitched on her generous hips, stocked with her tools. She was a big, strong woman, and Santiago had quickly come to respect her. "It's gotten to where she doesn't even notice that she's doing it anymore."

"I mentioned it to her a few weeks ago and thought it was getting better, but she's back to showing up for calls when she's on site," Santiago observed as he flipped through the call log.

"That's because she's as stubborn as a mule," she said in desperation. "She's always so concerned about appearing professional, but she doesn't realize that by stepping in all the time, she makes the rest of us look incompetent."

"I'll talk to her about it again, but this time, I'll show her the number of calls she's taken. She may need evidence to convince her," Santiago said, knowing that this was some-thing he, as a manager, should approach.

"Thank you," Heba answered. She had moved up from housekeeping to land a position in facilities management, which paid better. It might have even been a test of his management abilities, but also his level of commitment to the job, because Heba considered Alba Beachside Resort to be more than just her workplace. Indya managed to make the staff feel important and at home, much as she had done with her repeat customers.

Still, this was a delicate matter. He checked the well-worn calendar that was slowly moving them closer to the Salty Fish and concluded that it was inefficient for their boss to be doing manual repairs when there were more than enough staff to get it all done. He'd been avoiding her for reasons he could only confess to himself, but he had to engage her on this. He just needed to wait for the right moment.

The opportunity came a few hours later, when a new ticket for a repair came through. Santiago quickly flagged it as In Progress and headed to the bungalow in question. He had carefully memorized the names of each guest as per hotel procedure and recognized the surname on the request as the Bergerons. Ana and Mae Bergeron were a retired, married couple who flew down from Canada each spring and spent two months in one of the long-term rent-als. Each bungalow was actually a suite that included a full kitchen, two or three bedrooms, and two bathrooms. They were reserved for guests who were booking fifteen days or more. Indya's time and effort spent fostering relationships and creating a homelike environment had paid off with a stable and devoted collection of return customers, and the Bergerons were two of those customers.

Santiago knocked on the door of their bungalow, a cozy whitewashed building with a small terra-cotta walk-up. It was surrounded by Florida oak hung heavy with Spanish moss and cactus flowers that bloomed in a bed of sea ivy.

The door flew open on the second knock. "Mrs. Bergeron?"

An older woman with dark brown hair tied up in a bun and wisps of gray hair streaked throughout answered, "Come in, come in." She stepped aside and he entered the corridor, where the woman who'd been upset about the broken refrigeration on the day of his interview stood. Her blond hair was now tinted purple and styled into a perfect bob that just reached past her jawline.

Santiago hadn't had a chance to visit all the units, though he was working his way methodically through each one, noting any undiscovered damages or repairs that needed to be completed. But it was slow work, even with him delegating calls like this to his team. He wasn't sure how the previous manager had gotten to everything and suspected he actually hadn't, judging from the preliminary results of his review.

"Hello, I'm Santiago. We got a call?"

"Santiago," the dark-haired woman said cheerfully. "I've never seen you before. You must be new."

"I am. I'm the new Facilities Manager, at your service."

"Wonderful! Well, come in," the blonde woman said from over the first woman's shoulder. Free of irritation, her German accent was clear as crystal and lilting in its cadence. "I'm Ana and this is Mae. We've been coming here for nearly a decade so we know everyone, and you, my dear, are a fresh face."

"Yes, we've known Indya's parents from before she moved from Sarasota to help them with the hotel. A good daughter and a lovely lady," Mae continued, her accent giving her Canadian origins away.

"Um, yes. She is," Santiago stammered. "I'll get to work on that sink."

"Of course," Ana said, indicating the bathroom, then thinking better of it. "You probably know where everything is."

"Yes." Santiago made an effort to give her his most winning smile. "Thank you."

Santiago walked inside the bathroom, surveying the space to find the valve he needed. He had confirmed that the hot water heater outside the unit was functioning and, with a wrench, proceeded to test the valves. The turns were tight and Santiago couldn't help but wonder when these sinks had last been looked at. Taking out his oil can, he sprayed the calcified metal and added it to his follow-up list.

After replacing the washers, and satisfied at the steam that wafted up from the hot water that now flowed from the faucet, he barely registered the knock on the door that reverberated through the bungalow. Santiago only paid it half a mind until he heard a familiar voice make its way down the hall.

"Mrs. Bergeron, did you call for service?" Indya asked.

"Why, yes, dear. But you've already sent someone," Mae answered. Santiago straightened from his work and turned to step out into the hallway when Indya appeared at the door.

"You're here?" she asked, a little breathlessly.

"Yes, ma'am," Santiago said, taking immense satisfaction at the annoyance crossing her face.

"I thought I told you not to call me *ma'am*," Indya huffed.

"And I thought you hired me to do a job, but you keep trying to do it yourself," Santiago retorted.

"I'm not trying to do your job!" Indya pointed at the iPad. "You didn't flag the task to let the system know you picked it up. And I didn't want to inconvenience the Bergerons with yet another repair. So I picked it up when I saw no one else had."

Santiago frowned. "I did flag it." He took out his iPad and swiped at the screen. "See?"

Indya leaned in close to look down at his device, her perfume seizing him by the throat and not letting go. The only word he could think of was *expensive*.

When she looked up at him, barely a sliver of space separated their noses. Their breaths seemed suspended and nothing moved, except the wind and the sea beyond their walls. Indya's eyes flicked down, lingering on his lips before lifting them up to hold his gaze in an implacable grip. Perhaps distracted, she slowly licked her lips.

"I—I could have sworn it was unflagged," she whispered, the words spoken as if exhaled. As if she barely had any oxygen left to form even the shortest sounds. She looked like she was swaying on her feet.

Santiago pulled back. "You have to start letting me— my team—do our work. You have enough to do with the management of the property."

Indya looked chastened but also determined. "Yes, but you're new and there's so much—"

"I'm not that new anymore." Santiago's gaze was fixed on the frown on her cherry-red lips. He wanted to reach across and wipe away that frown with a kiss. Indya's eyes glittered, blown wide with some inscrutable emotion. She was such a temptation. All he'd have to do was tip his head forward—

"Excuse me," came the melodic German accent that

made them fly apart as if they'd been shocked with electricity. "I made coffee. Would you care to join us?"

Indya came to attention like a rubber band that had snapped back into place. Mae, who stood behind Indya, looked from her to Santiago, her expression sly and knowing.

"I should get back to the office." She straightened, already mostly recovered, and turned to Ana. "Mrs. Bergeron. Mrs. Bergeron," she acknowledged Mae as well. "You are in capable hands with Santiago."

Indya dipped her head in greeting. Both women walked her to the door, and Santiago desperately wanted to follow Indya, mostly on the pretext of talking to her about this baffling habit of hers but also because he was half-drunk on her proximity and the desire that had pulsed so brightly between them.

He was too easily affected by her, and it should have been something he could control. It was the one aspect of his work that he hadn't figured out yet.

When he was done with his repairs, he stepped into the living room of the bungalow to let the Bergerons know that the sink was fixed.

"Don't run away so soon," Ana said, indicating the stool at the kitchen island that divided the white-and-blue painted living room from the kitchen. "You've earned yourself a break."

"I have to—" Santiago began but was cut off by Mae, who stood between him and freedom.

"If you're worried about Indya, she'll be fine. We'll put in a word for you."

"Now, that's a strong-willed woman right there," Ana said, setting down the freshly poured mug of coffee and sliding it to where he should sit at the island.

Santiago glanced at his iPad, which thankfully held no notifications for repair requests, and relented, taking the seat. "She's, um." He gripped the handle of the mug tightly, words still a challenge when Indya's aroma still clung to his nose.

"Doesn't it take one to know one, though, *Schätzchen*?" Mae winked at Ana, setting down a tray with cream and sugar and spice cookies. "How do you take your coffee?"

"Coffee and cream," he answered, watching her pour the ingredients into his mug. She left a silver hotel-issue spoon inside, which he used to stir everything together. Santiago, who had a passionate love affair with coffee, inhaled deeply. "This smells good. Thank you."

"It's a South American blend," Ana said, and Santiago smiled into his coffee. South America was a huge continent, and Venezuela exported very little coffee, but it was the gesture that counted.

"You're very kind," he said, sipping the coffee.

"So, you're new to the hotel," Mae said, taking the stool next to him while Ana hovered across from him. He looked from one woman to the other, expecting a spotlight to suddenly shine on his face. "What's your story?"

Santiago looked to the door, as if it held the key to his salvation. But there was no saving him. The Bergerons were not going to let him escape without getting some useful information out of him and he prepared himself for the onslaught.

"I'm not sure where to start," he said sincerely.

Mae smiled at Ana. "Tell us everything."

Chapter Eleven

Indya

Indya escaped the Bergerons' bungalow and went straight to her office, where she shut the door and sagged against it. Her fingers flew up to her lips, the heat of Santiago's breath still warm against the tender skin. It was true that she'd been running around, picking up calls for things she thought she could quickly handle, partly for the sake of efficiency and partly because, as embarrassing as it was to admit it, the hotel still needed so much work. Also the time disappearing on the calendar gave her so much anxiety, the only way she knew how to manage it was to get out there and get her own hands dirty. Her parents had given Carlos too much control over the renovations and they'd been left stranded. Now she was afraid to make the mistake again by handing over total responsibility to Santiago for it all.

She was starting to have nightmares about never recovering again if the hotel couldn't be ready in time for the biggest fishing event of the year.

But selfishly, she had to acknowledge that if she slowed

down, even for a moment, Santiago would appear in her thoughts like a fever.

Of course, when he showed up to do his job, as he'd always done so far, she went and did stupid stuff like nearly kissing him in a guest bathroom, with the two biggest gossips on the planet within hearing range.

It would have been so much easier if Santiago had been a little more irresponsible, the way Carlos had been, or a little more dismissive, like her ex, Trent. She was familiar with the kind of people who let her down and had the tools to handle them.

Santiago was too earnest, too competent, too *beautiful* to put out of her mind.

It had been over a month since Santiago had started working at the hotel, exceeding her every expectation of him. She didn't know when admiration had turned to wanting, but whenever it happened, she had no time for any of that. She was too aware of the clock ticking on her hotel, aware of the sectioned-off areas, the still partially functioning facilities, the avalanche of tiny repairs that were getting done but maybe a bit too slowly for her own taste.

She glanced at her phone. Gia should be out of school by now. She thought about Nyla and Rayne, who had been texting her regularly, trying to corner her for another girl's brunch or even a night out. Indya needed something, but a girl's afternoon wasn't quite it.

She fired off a text to Nyla, asking if she could pick Gia up and keep her at her place until Indya got back that evening. She usually let Gia stay with Nyla when she went out on the boat on a school night, especially when she had too much homework. Nyla was a marine biologist and she often took Gia with her when she checked on the turtle nets during nesting season. Gia was blessed to have adults she could bond with over her particular interests.

She tried not to think too hard about the last time she'd gone out on the *Gia Marie*. She'd met Santiago, and even then, she'd been attracted to him. That's where all her troubles had been compounded.

Her phone pinged almost immediately.

Sure, hon. She can come home with me right after The Turtle Warriors meeting.

Indya had forgotten that the high school conservation club Nyla sponsored was meeting after school. Do you mind bringing her to the house to get her things?

No problem. I got this. Enjoy your spin out on the water. And be careful!

Indya sank into her office chair. Nyla knew her so well. Of course she'd guessed that Indya needed a bit of alone time on the *Gia Marie*. Nyla spent a good part of her life at sea and Gia loved going out on the surf with her friends. But Indya needed the sun, air and water for her sanity. Especially when she'd come *this close* to kissing Santiago. It was completely unacceptable for her to go around kissing her employees. Obviously, the stress was getting to her.

She slipped out of her office, only slowing down to let Jade know that she was heading out, and dipped in to quickly change her clothes in Gia's room.

She drove up to the marina, stopping by the office on the way to her slip.

"*Amiga!* You're never here on Thursday. Too close to the check-in rush."

Why did all her friends have to know her so well? "Jade's got it. I just…need an afternoon spin."

Wil wagged a finger at her. "Rough day, huh? Needed to break up the stress. I get it." They chuckled. "Just be careful out there. Don't need you getting stranded again."

Indya threw up her hands in exasperation. "Are you going to remind me of that for the rest of my life?"

"Only every time you go out."

"Listen," Indya said around a laugh. Leave it to this maniac to make her feel better. "Engine's on point, the fuel is the best I could buy. I'm pretty sure I'll be alright for a few hours."

Wil gave her a once-over. "If you say so. Load up the ice. I'll take a look at the engines one more time."

Indya opened her mouth to protest, but Wil cut her off. "You would think you'd learned your lesson that time you got stranded out on the Gulf, young lady." They mumbled something that sounded like, "Always out on that boat alone."

"Do you have all your gear?" Wil called out more loudly when Indya had loaded the last of her tackle box and fishing rods.

"Yes, Mommy," Indya answered. "Promise, I finished all my chores."

"You better have," Wil said, throwing their arms around Indya. "Take care of yourself out there!"

"You know I always do."

Indya prepared to start up the motor and ease out of the slip. She wasn't planning on going very far this time, perhaps troll along Apalachicola Bay for a few miles, take in the sunset and try her luck by casting a line. She should be able to purge Santiago from her mind by filling it with the soothing sounds of the sea. Plunged deep in her thoughts, she was caught off guard by Wil shouting, *"¡Hermano!"*

Wil didn't have a brother. Confused, Indya looked out past the fishing boat and caught sight of a figure a few slips down from hers. Her heart plummeted. Even if she hadn't recognized the *Aragona*, she would know Santiago's broad back and tapered waist anywhere. He was unmistakable.

She had already untied her ropes and started the engines, but she couldn't leave now without acknowledging him. Not with Wil flagging him down like a long-lost sailor. When he'd turned around completely to face her, her breath caught. He was radiant, his tan skin sharp against the stark white of his T-shirt. His legs were unreal, muscled and defined but not bulky. His musculature came from hard work and athleticism, making him big but not brutish. Already her mouth had gone dry and they had yet to make eye contact.

Recognition washed over his features, and for a moment, he only stared before raising his hand to wave at Wil. His eyes visibly swept the ship until they landed on Indya. He tipped his head forward in greeting before good manners forced her to respond, though all she wanted was to power the engines to full throttle and escape, even if that was the worst thing to do in such a narrow space. She waved back and shouted, *"Hola, Santiago!"*

He took that for the invitation she had intended but hoped he wouldn't accept, striding up the dock in long, unhurried strides. Even the way he moved was strong, but sinuous, as if he had secured the agreement of every single muscle in his body to move without awkwardness or uncertainty. The way he did his work—with a quiet confidence that made her believe he could do just about anything. Indya wasn't used to feeling that sense of dependability toward anyone other than her parents and very best friends, and that, more than his beautiful appearance, was the trap she kept wanting to fall into.

"Santi!" Wil said, hurrying over to greet him. "Did the hotel let everyone out at the same time?"

"I'm not sure. I left at my normal time. Some others snuck out without telling anyone," he said, casting a meaningful glance in Indya's direction.

"I did not sneak out," Indya muttered under her breath. She fixed a friendly smile on her face and waved at him from the captain's deck.

"Your engines sound good."

"Fuel," she blurted out. At his confused expression, she clarified, "I put good fuel in her."

He nodded at this. "That's good to know. Going up the bay?"

Indya indicated the deep blue sky. "Just for a couple of hours. Wanted to see what I could catch." She gave his outfit a chin nod. "What about you?"

He gave her another meaningful look that she didn't want to interpret too deeply. "I was going to do the same thing."

"Well." Wil clapped his hands, startling Indya. She'd forgotten he was still standing there. "I've heard Santi's very good at fishing."

"Santi?" Indya asked.

Santiago pointed at himself. "My nickname."

Wil continued. "You should go out together. That way, Santi won't be terrified of sinking his ship and losing his every last worldly possession, and you, sis, don't have to be out on the bay alone." They smiled with great self-satisfaction.

"Oh, I don't know," Indya started but Santiago—*Santi!*— interrupted.

"I'm not terrified of sinking my ship," Santiago protested.

Wil gave him a long, mordant look. "That's not what you said the other night when you stopped by the bar for a few shots."

Santiago's face flushed a soft pink. "I only mentioned that it was a possibility, not that I was afraid."

"Same thing. Indya, what do you think? Grand idea, eh?" Wil was practically rubbing their hands together. They were up to something and Indya was not amused.

"Well—"

"I'd love to come with you, if you'll have me."

Indya's heart galloped double-time in her chest. The sky was clear blue beyond, the utter absence of clouds and the still air that was the bane of all sailboats creating the perfect conditions for casting a line in deep water. His gaze was just as clear and direct. He wasn't offering out of politeness, but from a genuine, mysterious desire to accompany her out on the boat. There was no hesitation, and that was even more disconcerting than if he had politely declined.

"Well, my motor's already running," Indya said, shoring up her courage. Continuing to make a fuss about things would be insulting at this point and she was never one to back down from anything or anyone. "I have bait, tackle and snacks. All you have to do is bring your rods."

A knowing smile pulled at the edge of his lips and Indya would have given a million dollars at that moment to hear what he thought he knew. He gave Indya one last, long look, as if coming to some conclusion before asking, "Should I bring a few beers, too?"

"Only if you don't like Medalla. I have a case in the cabin."

"I love Medalla."

"Good."

"Great!" Wil clapped his hands, far too invested, in Indya's opinion, in this outcome. "Now I won't get another ulcer, worrying about you out there alone."

"I'll just get a few things," Santiago said, jogging down the main deck back to his craft. Indya didn't realize her breath was coming in pants until she hopped down toward the engines and lowered them to idling. This was not at all how she'd intended her afternoon to go, but apparently, it was what Wil had been maneuvering toward since the moment Santiago showed up.

"Wilfredo!" she called. They were stowing the extra lines away in one of the communal storage bins situated throughout the marina.

They froze. Indya rarely used their Christian name.

"Indya?" They turned, speaking carefully.

"What in the barnacle-bottom ship was all that about?"

Wil's eyebrows sailed slowly up their forehead, the picture of innocence. "I just don't want you to go out there alone."

"I've been out on this bay at least twice after I was stranded at sea, and you didn't toss every Tom, Dick and Harry at me to keep me company when I sailed out."

They made a small squeaking sound, as if they were afraid she might throttle them. She wanted to, that was undeniable. But she would never actually do that.

"Santi's not every Tom, Dick and Harry, *amiga*."

"Don't *amiga* me," Indya snapped. "What's your game?"

Wil approached her boat, hopping onto the stern. They gave a quick look around before leaning toward Indya. "Okay, okay. Listen, Santi came out the other night to shoot the bull and throw back a few." They leaned in closer. "Indya, he likes you."

"Oh pffft," Indya scoffed. "I'm his boss, Wil. That's not how it is between us."

"Aw, come on, girl. Haven't you ever heard of a work-place romance?"

"Wil," she whisper-shouted when a glint of sun reflecting off the metal of Santi's—*Santiago's*—cruiser showed him moving off his boat. Soon, he'd be on hers. "I'm the boss. I'm not going to get it on with my employee. It's unethical."

"Unethical?" Wil laughed, a little too loud for Indya's taste. "You're not some pervy guy shoving his hand up somebody's skirt. You are a beautiful—" they waved their hand over her "—talented, magnificent woman who has a sexy thing pining at her feet. Lord, me, when?" Wil looked up at the sky as if it was going to open up and grant them their wish on the spot.

"He's coming," Indya whispered. Santiago was only a few slips away. "Stop talking."

"Do you know he's four years younger than you?" They meowed and Indya felt her soul leave her body. "Live your cougar dreams, sister."

"Get off my boat." Indya pointed at the deck, her barely repressed laugh belying the sharpness of her words.

"I love you, too," they said, loud enough for Santiago to hear. They dropped their voice again when they added, "Have fun." They left a swift kiss on her cheek, then leaped down onto the deck.

Indya stood, absolutely dumbfounded by her friend's audacity.

She gave Santiago a weak smile as he boarded her vessel. "There's some space for your tackle box and rods." She indicated where he could place his things before racing off to where the life vests were stowed. She tried to process what Wil had said and found that, despite her numerous reservations, deep down inside, she knew they were right. Santiago did like her as more than just his boss. That meant he must have felt the pull of their near kiss earlier today. She couldn't have been alone in that.

She wasn't sure whether it was better if she had been alone in that or not.

When feelings got the best of her, work was her go-to. She pulled out an extra life vest from the storage compartment and adjusted the fishing rod holders to accommodate his before clearing a space for his supplies in the sideboard stowage.

He set down his things and Indya handed him a vest.

"What is this?" he asked.

"A life vest," Indya answered.

"I see that." He furrowed his brow. "I don't usually use one."

Indya thought back to the afternoon they'd met. He had not been wearing a life vest then. That was unacceptable. "Well, on my vessel, you have to wear it. Captain's regulations."

Santiago looked from her to the vest with skepticism before slowly donning it. "I forgot how bossy you were outside of work, too."

"Well, this bossy woman doesn't take safety lightly," Indya retorted.

He snapped the belts closed, the vest a bit snug around his broad body, despite being the largest one she owned. "It interferes with my ability to swim."

Indya felt like she was talking to Gia, which was unexpected. "You're not supposed to swim in it. You're supposed to float in it, especially if you are unconscious, and therefore stay alive."

He gave a *harrumph* sound that she'd never heard before and found shockingly adorable. "Listen, our chef makes the best sandwiches in Soledad Bay, though please, don't tell Efrain that. He will get very offended."

"Efrain?"

Indya, who was putting on her own vest, paused in her work. "The owner of the Puerto Rican restaurant. Haven't you been there yet?"

"My boss keeps me too busy," Santiago deadpanned.

Indya pulled a face. "Seriously? You came on my boat to complain?"

"Never."

Indya rolled her eyes. "Well, you have to go. They are incredible. However, I happen to have a pile of sandwiches from our restaurant in my cooler. You wouldn't want to lose out on a chance to try them just because of a life jacket and your ego, would you?"

A half smile appeared on Santiago's face. "Okay, okay, you've persuaded me." He smoothed the front of the bright orange-and-violet design. "It's stylish, at least."

"Gia chose them," Indya said. "She's in an all-about-fashion stage of her life. 'Why be practical when you can be an icon?' Her words, not mine."

"I have to agree with her," Santiago said. "Should I?" He pointed at the captain's deck, and the extra seating for passengers who wanted to keep the captain company.

She'd be navigating with Santiago right next to her. Santiago, who Wil said liked her. She was sure even Gia would be able to manage this situation better than she could.

"Yes. Please take a seat, sir. We're heading out." Indya reached for the dock line that lay sprawled across the deck where she'd haphazardly tossed it, but Santiago had anticipated her. He gently took the rope from her, giving her a small smile to head off any protests.

"Thank you for allowing me to accompany you. I was missing the sea," he said in a low soothing tone. Here, alone with him, she could not escape the effect of his voice, the way it curled around her in warm, lilting tones.

"I was looking for a little escape, too," Indya said, letting him take the rope from her. There was no way to tell him that she had been escaping from him, and anyway, it didn't really matter. She was taking her distraction with her out to the open sea.

He deftly wound up the rope and set it inside the compartment on the sideboard for that purpose. Santiago might not have appreciated the safety benefits derived from a life vest, but clearly he understood the importance of not leaving loose rope all over the deck.

Indya hopped onto the bridge, powering up the boat. "Ever been out past the bay?"

He stepped into the bridge beside her, settling into the plush white seat next to the captain's chair. He pulled down the brim of his cap, casting his eyes and half his face into shadow. "I haven't had many chances to explore. I took a short drive south last week."

Indya wished she could pull his hat off. All she could see were his full lips and strong chin, but his eyes were a mystery to her. "In that case, you're in for a treat."

She forced herself to focus on steering the boat, while Santiago's attention seemed resolutely fixed on the water speeding by.

Chapter Twelve

Indya

Weekday boat traffic was light—most people worked nine-to-five and were at home at this time of the day, preparing dinner or tending to their families. Indya was grateful for this. The ocean belonged to her, glittering diamond bright under the cloudless blue sky.

The departure was predictably rough as they cleared the waves at the break lines, cutting into deeper water. Their town was located at the entrance of the bay, where the Gulf currents rounding the outcropping emptied into a basin of calm waters, their gentle rhythms making the beaches popular for families and retirees. Surf-worthy waters were located just a few miles south of them, where the waves rushed uniformly up the uninterrupted beachline. The warm wind whipped by as the *Gia Marie* sliced through the water, carving her own path through the placid surface of the Gulf. Santiago took it all in with his quiet intensity, and despite the tense awareness Indya had felt earlier, his company was soothing and undemanding, allowing her to find the calm and stillness she always sought from her excursions.

Indya glanced over to him. "How is Lisbet?"

Santiago looked away from where he was watching the waves. "She is doing well." He gazed ahead, nodding as if to himself. "I speak to her and her mother every day after she comes out of school. I sometimes talk to them more than to the people who live in the same country as I do."

"I really admire that you are on such good terms with your ex," Indya blurted out before thinking the better of it. Why should she care about his relationship with his ex? Attempting to make her interest sound casual, she pretended to check the coordinates on her fish-finder.

Indya felt his eyes on her, but she continued to work as if what she'd said had been inconsequential.

"Thank you. We are close friends, even if we are not together. It is important for us to have a good relationship for Lisbet's sake."

Indya bit the side of her cheek so hard, she tasted iron. She couldn't help the surge of resentment that climbed into her heart at his words. *It's not jealousy*, she scolded herself.

Santiago had managed to find a way to get along well with the mother of his daughter, despite no longer being with her or even residing in the same country. What was so wrong with Indya that Trent couldn't have done the same with her?

Nothing! she scolded herself. Her daughter was perfect and Indya was giving them both a good life. But the words echoed in a hollow space inside her, the part of her that she was constantly trying to heal.

"Thank you for always asking about her," he said, so quietly the wind almost carried away his words. "I was just thinking of her." Santiago's voice pulled her away from the edge of her dark thoughts. He stared out at the waters parting before the sharp beam of the vessel. "She would love taking a ride on this boat. She has always loved the sea."

Indya smiled. "Like her father, if I remember correctly."

Santiago laughed, a sound so rare, Indya had to catch her breath. "Very much like her father. And she loves to read about animals, especially lizards for some reason." He shook his head and the image brought back her own memories of one of Gia's many obsessions.

"Maybe it's the idea that they are like small dinosaurs? I know that's why Gia used to love them. Now she's moved on to sea animals. Turtles are her great passion these days, and it looks like this time, it might stick." As a child, Gia had been curious and indulged a new obsession every other month.

Indya caught Santiago's wistful expression and wished she could do something to ease his obvious longing for his daughter. "Sea turtle season just started. When she comes to visit, Gia would be happy to show them to her. They are the focus of Gia's school club."

"You mean, the conservation club?"

"Yes." Indya smiled, turning the boat slightly away from the shoreline. "They're called The Turtle Warriors."

"They sound fierce."

"Oh, you have no idea," Indya said. "They can be passionate about their cause. I love that for her." Indya grew thoughtful. "Indifference is a disease."

She felt Santiago's eyes on her for several long moments before he said, "I would be grateful if Gia shared her passion with Lisbet. Thank you."

His thanks warmed her to her toes, the lilt of his voice like a siren's song, drawing her in.

A glance over at him revealed the happy expression on his face. She liked seeing him happy. It looked good on him. The realization seized Indya with a powerful emotion that almost carried her away. Thankfully, something off starboard caught her attention.

"Santi!" Indya called out over the roar of the engines. She pointed out at the sea. "Look!"

There, in the placid blue of the Gulf, was a family of dolphins cavorting in the waves. Indya scanned her location, found that they were close to one of the barrier islands, which promised less turbulent waters for fishing than the opening of the bay, and cut her engine speed. Maneuvering the boat leeward of the closest island, she allowed it to coast parallel to the small group of sea creatures, reducing the chance that they could be harmed by the small propellers of the outboard motors. Santiago followed Indya as she descended to the bow where they could see them more clearly.

"They're so beautiful," Indya breathed, the dolphins slicing through the water, then leaping in the air, as if they knew they were being watched.

Santiago had begun a video and recorded their antics, the way the sunlight glinted off their smooth skin, the smile that seemed perpetually etched onto their faces. They filled Indya with a quiet joy that she loved to sink into, a contemplation of how lucky she was to be surrounded by so much beauty. Thankfully, Santiago wasn't needlessly chatty. She could enjoy this moment in the company of someone who understood the value of silence.

Santiago continued to film them until they finally swam too far out to be seen.

"Lisbet will love this," he said as he tapped away, no doubt forwarding the video to his daughter. Her heart squeezed at the way his daughter was always first and foremost on his mind, much as Gia was the reason for every decision Indya made in her life.

"They usually don't frolic out this late in the day," Indya said. "They like the cooler temperatures in the morning."

"Then, we are very fortunate," Santiago said. He had turned his cap around and now she could see the beautiful texture of his eyes under the glittering sun, the intensity with which he watched her. "We are both at the mercy of fate, you and I."

"When it comes to each other, it seems we are," Indya answered truthfully.

The soft undulations of water rocked their legs back and forth with the movement of the boat. Without warning, a particularly strong wave crashed against the side. Indya yelped, her hands flying out, finding nothing but air. She felt the acceleration as she fell backward, anticipating the hard contact when she inevitably crashed onto the floor of the deck.

A strong arm caught her around the waist, pulling her upright. Indya slammed against a hard mass of muscle, the shock of salt and cologne, and the musky smell of a man making her head swim. Indya gasped for air—she'd had the wind knocked out of her—and felt the matching hammering of another heart under her hands, which gripped the front of Santiago's T-shirt.

"Oh god," she panted, catching her breath after her near fall. Santiago's proximity confounded her, steadying her while at the same time sparking every nerve ending to life. She was powerful and brittle all at once, as strong as the pylons that kept the marina in place, but soft and slippery as wet sand.

Santiago's voice surrounded her, a cocoon of melodic strength that was palpable in her ears. *"¿Estás bien?"*

She could only nod. She released his T-shirt, only to splay her palms across his chest. The magnetic pull she felt earlier that day wound itself around her, squeezing her, drawing her toward Santiago. His back to the sun, he cast a cool shadow that blocked the worst of its rays. His eyes, steeped in green-brown intensity, focused on her and it seared her worse than a sunburn.

He pushed a loose curl behind her ear, his fingertip blazing a path of heat along her skin.

"Seguro?" he prodded, that same hand dragging its burning embers down her back to steady her further.

"I'm sure." She slowly straightened, finding strength in her legs again. As gently as he'd captured her, he let her go, arms falling to his side.

Indya's throat was dry as sandpaper. "How about that beer?" She walked away without hearing his answer to pick up two beers from the cooler before the rush of emotions overwhelmed her. She was on fire as she hadn't been in a very long time. The blast of air from the ice locker was a welcome relief from the heat in her veins, but it still burned deep in her belly. Desire was a distant memory—she didn't remember when she had ever felt it so powerfully. But here she was, ready to take an ice bath, anything to find relief.

When she returned, Santiago was preparing his rod. He was stunning in his precise strength, the way he threaded his line through the pole loops and handled the hooks. The weather was unreal at this hour of the day—slanted sunlight that no longer held its midday bite, and a soft breeze that carried occasional droplets of sea spray from the waves sloshing into the side of the boat. But all Indya could see was Santiago, glowing bronze and bright in the sunlight, a trap she was having a hard time not falling into.

She uncapped the beer, passing one to him, ignoring the way the smell of sunblock wafted off his slick, well-defined arms. His tattoo seemed to dance for her, daring her to touch it again.

But she stepped away instead to pick up a bag of shrimp she had planned on using as bait. "This should be enough for the both of us."

Santiago looked at the bag, then at her face, before his gaze flitted away. "Are you trying to catch pompano?"

She nodded. "Or red snapper, if I'm lucky."

He handed back the bait. "Thank you. I brought chicken liver. I was hoping to catch catfish."

Indya wrinkled her nose. "Ew?"

Santiago's expression was genuinely confused. "You don't like fried sea catfish?"

"My father always warned me away from it. Said you needed to know how to prepare it or it would taste horrible." Indya picked up her rod, working the hook onto the end of the line.

Santiago chuckled and Indya couldn't help staring at him. Laughter transformed him, made him appear less intense. He still had something brooding about him, but it lost its edge when he smiled. "I happen to know how." He cut excess line from his rod before sliding it into the rod holder. "Someday, I will make it for you. I can change your mind about it."

Words clogged tightly in Indya's throat. They couldn't... It simply wasn't something she could allow herself, was it? She remembered Wil's words, that Santiago liked her. There was real heat between them, she felt it even now, simmering in the background. Searching for some escape, she found it in the gentle tugging of one of her fishing lines. She had to turn away before she said or did something incredibly stupid.

"I'm going to bait my weapon," she said before stepping away to nestle her deep-sea fishing rod in the holder, hoping the monotony of tending her rods would cure her of this unbearable anticipation.

Indya tried her best to bring down her emotional turmoil by focusing on the sea. Once the actual fishing got underway, she was relieved to find that Santiago's company turned quiet and competent. He helped her when her line became knotted, and tended to his own lines with a serene precision that soothed Indya. He was just as happy exchanging the occasional comment as he was with accepting her silences. There was a special understanding among anglers, a complicity that allowed those necessary silences to bloom and spread between them, and Indya found that in Santiago over the next few hours. So much of fishing was simply learning to get accustomed to long stretches of being alone, until that habit became a need the angler couldn't live without. It was even more important than the fishing itself.

They slowly filled the ice locker with the fish they caught, returning those that were too small or outside regulation back to the sea. In addition to pompano, they caught whiting, snook, and even the red snapper that Indya had hoped for, while Santiago scored a few of his beloved catfish. They took pictures of their largest catches, making sure that one of them stood next to each fish to provide a sense of scale.

They gutted their fish at the cutting board Indya had set up, quick to rinse and dispose of everything to keep from smelling any more like fish than they already did, before setting their cleaned and wrapped catches in the ice locker.

On a particularly large catch, Santiago took out a pair of metal-mesh, cut-resistant gloves, and held a sharp knife.

Indya moved to search for her own gloves, but Santiago put a metal-sheathed hand over hers.

"Don't worry," he said. "I can do it."

"I know, but I can—"

"I have it." Santiago smiled softly. "Let me take care of…of it."

The thrill that raced through Indya was so strong, she shivered as if winter had blasted across the prow of the ship. She did everything alone, or she was always in the thick of things. Santiago would not let her just carry everything, and it both excited her and left her exposed, something soft and raw in her that wanted, *needed*, to find cover.

When he was done and her feelings had subsided, she asked, "Have you considered competing in the Salty Fish?"

Santiago paused in hosing down the deck. "I haven't."

"Well, you should. You're very good." She collected scraps of cloth and other things she'd have to wash in fresh water when she got home.

"So are you. Have you registered a team yet?"

Indya thought about the handful of times she'd competed. She used to fish much more regularly when she lived in Sarasota and together with her father when she came to Soledad Bay before he had his stroke. "I will, but I don't know if I should personally participate. I'm not as good as I once was."

"I think you should not underestimate yourself, Señora Linares," he said, chuckling at the look she gave him.

"If I did go out, I'd need a crew, at least one other person, if only to stabilize the boat and help bring in fish when the catch gets big."

Santiago nodded thoughtfully. "I will be your crew."

Indya paused. "I wasn't actually planning to enter. Not with all the work that is still left to do in the hotel."

"It will get done," Santiago said with a solemnity that left very little room for doubt.

"Santiago, I—"

He stepped close to her. "I think we could make a good team."

Indya's heart gave another lurch, stealing her breath, making her sway on her feet even more than the waves buffeting the boat. "A great fishing team," she said, feeling the need to clarify, to throw up every boundary she could muster, because Santiago was overrunning every single one. And she was going to let him if she didn't take precautions.

Santiago nodded. "Yes, that, too."

Indya bit her lip hard enough to bruise. She needed to get this thing under control before she caved. The sun lay at a gentler angle, the sea whipped up by sweet winds and a rising tide. And Indya was a tiny thing battered by forces both inside and out that were proving ever more difficult to resist.

"I need your number," she blurted out.

Confusion raced over Santiago's features. "Don't you have it?"

"I—Yes, I do." Indya stepped away, creating much-needed space between them. "But I don't have it on my own cellphone. I want to send the pictures I took." She pulled it out of her pocket. Indya was protective of who she gave her personal number to, but it felt different from other times in her life when she had felt an overwhelming need to keep her work and home life separate. An impulse she should still feel.

He removed his gloves and reached for his phone, slow to unlock it, as if she'd caught him entirely off guard. "Here." She took it from him, typing in her number before handing it back to him. "Now you can call me anytime."

His eyes flashed at her words. "Anytime?"

She felt sheepish and unbearably shy. "Y-yes," she stuttered out, rushing off toward the captain's deck and away from his all-too-knowing gaze. "Anytime."

Indya drew up the anchor while Santiago made quick work of gutting the remaining fish. By the time Santiago climbed onto the deck, Indya was already calculating their return trip. When she'd turned over the engines and set the boat into motion, he said, "I'd like to organize a cookout to make the fish. I have a grill in storage that is large enough to smoke the giant red snapper I caught. We can invite the girls, too. I know Miriam likes my catfish."

Indya, who had been steering, froze, her face growing rosier than it already was under the effects of the sun. How did an outing meant to get away from thoughts of Santiago turn into a multiday Santiago extravaganza?

"A cookout? Like a barbecue?"

"Yes, on the boat. Except…with fish."

"Like a fish fry," Indya corrected gently.

"It could include that, too." Santiago smiled.

As much as she was kicking and screaming internally, a significant part of her wanted to organize something with Santiago. She wanted to see him eat a meal from her hands, or better yet, help her make it. She wanted to hear him tell her how good everything tasted. She wanted so many things she shouldn't, and that desire moved like the tides through her.

Would it really be that bad to give in?

Her resolve was weaker than wet papier-mâché.

"When we get back, we'll check everyone's schedule," she answered, placing a hand on Santiago's arm, which was a giant mistake, because his skin was a soft, warm layer over hard muscle and it was wholly irresistible. "Let's get rid of this fish together."

Santiago's smile went softer, as if he were offering it to

her, alone, and no one else. "Only if you let me help you cook it."

Indya thought her knees were going to give out. Was he setting out to fulfill every single one of her fantasies? Him in her kitchen? Him in an apron? Him in *nothing but an apron*?

Indya almost let out a squeal at the vision that manifested in her mind's eye, blinding the path of water in front of her. Thank god she was steering a boat through the Gulf waters and not a car down Ocean Avenue or she would have run into someone by now. She was sure that having Santiago in the kitchen with her was going to be no help at all.

She pulled her hand away from his arm before she had other, wicked thoughts. "My paella is to die for. We can make a feast out of it."

"I would like that. Thank you," Santiago said quietly. Indya found herself facing down his penetrating gaze head on. She was far more aware of Santiago than she had been on their journey into the bay. He was so close, she could sense the rise and fall of his chest.

Santiago's proximity to her was dizzying. Intoxicating. She wanted to run her hands up his chest, feel the warmth of skin and bone beneath the palms of her hand. Taste the salt and sea on his skin. "It's what friends do." She paused, the heat that simmered through her making her reckless. "Are we friends, Santiago?"

How had she let that question fall out of her mouth? Her throat had gone dry and her skin was pulled so taut, she was sure she could peel it off and crawl out of it. Her heart was tight, her breath short, and everything, everything strained to reach out to him and pull him down for a kiss.

He surprised her when his hand came up to her cheek, cupping it gently. "Indya, I'm anything you want me to be."

"Santiago, I—"

He closed the distance between them, the boat and the wind and the ocean all but forgotten. His lips were a whisper of heat against hers, soft where they pressed, his power held in check by the gentleness he possessed in equal measure to his strength. Indya whimpered. He pulled back, watching her with eyes heavy and far darker than they had any business being out in the still bright light of the late afternoon sun.

It wasn't enough. His lips, his taste, that kiss, was not going to be enough.

She set the boat's engine to low, turned fully in her chair and leaned in. Where his kiss had been soft, a request for permission more than a demand, hers had purpose. She wound her arms around his neck and pulled him in, the press of their lips insistent and growing more so with each moment. Wil said Santiago liked her. Santiago had done nothing to convince her otherwise. If he wanted her to stop, he only had to let her know and she'd respect that. She would put up those boundaries between employee and employer once more, never to be bypassed again.

She tilted her head, opened her lips, and he fell into them like rushing surf spinning down the vortex of a water spout. His tongue was soft and strong, tasting with a frenzy that was absent in everything else he did. He was methodical, quiet and measured, but his mouth on hers, something else was unlocked and he was devouring her without mercy.

When they pulled apart, her mind was reeling and her breath was gone. She had plunged, headfirst, into the deepest, darkest waters and now that she was coming up for air, she was blinded by all the light that surrounded them.

"Indya?" Santiago's words cut across the fog and disorientation. *"Estás bien?"*

Was she fine? No, she wasn't. She wasn't sure which way was up. "Maybe?"

Santiago searched her face, as if checking for an injury. "Want me to drive?"

"No," she scoffed, wiping her lips with one knuckle before turning to take the wheel. "I've got this under control."

"I know you do. You always do." He placed a hand over hers, the one that rested on the throttle, keeping her from getting the boat out of idle. "But sometimes, it's okay to let go of control and allow others to take over."

It felt like a variation of what everyone else always said to her, but coming from Santiago, it hit differently. She could bring the boat back in. She'd done it a million times. But what if she let go of control this once, and let him take care of this?

She got up out of her seat, freeing it for Santiago, who slid over into it. Before she could round the console to get to the other side, Santiago pulled her down onto his lap, giving her another kiss that left her heart racing and her lungs empty. When he'd kissed her so thoroughly she didn't have the legs anymore to get upright, he carefully lifted her and settled her down next to him.

Indya was a tall, curvy woman. But being manhandled by Santiago was probably the sexiest thing she'd ever experienced.

The trip home was significantly more subdued. Indya was turned listless by the sun, the water and Santiago's kisses. Sunset made everything more peaceful, and the sweet lethargy of exhaustion started to set in. Santiago drove confidently, checking his devices with the ease of practice, while Indya watched the waves rush by, pointing out things along the coast line that caught her attention every now and again. It was hard for Indya to find that peace they'd had before their kiss, but she still felt lulled by the solidity that radiated from Santiago.

Chapter Thirteen

Santiago

They returned to the marina just as the sunset plunged the world into darkness. When Santiago maneuvered the boat into the slip and shut off the engine, it was all Santiago could do to not reach over, settle Indya on his lap and kiss her until the sun came back out again.

Wil had manipulated the situation, based on the too-easy banter they'd shared the other night, to get Santiago on a boat alone with Indya. But Santiago had wanted to discuss Indya's stepping in to do everyone's work. He had not intended to make out with his boss.

He had not intended on kissing her and never wanting to stop.

It was a complicated situation to have a romantic interest in your boss, a complication Santiago didn't really need, given his goals for the hotel and Soledad Bay in general. He had his family, his job and his daughter to think about. It was no small decision to take such risks when his future and that of his daughter depended on everything going well.

There was not much to be done for it now, he supposed, because the omelet was already cooked. They'd simply have to make the most of this situation, no matter how it turned out.

When he'd stepped off the bridge, he found Indya on the marina's dock, tying the lines of the *Gia Marie* to the pylons. He moved over to lend her a hand, which she accepted with a small smile.

Her skin was sun-kissed, despite her hat and sunblock, making her appear radiant. He had sensed so much from her—interest and companionship, but also desire—in their shared kisses. He could not have mistaken it. He had touched her and her body had responded to him. It had been a revelation and now he looked at her with new eyes. He had almost anticipated her refusal, because she would always be a proud woman, but at least physically, Indya Linares was not indifferent to him.

"I have a cooler you can use to transport your fish to your ice locker," Indya said when they'd stepped back onto her boat, predictably returning to being all business. She fussed with the rods, the tackle boxes, hands flying as she gathered their things together. Her focus on everything except him. Santiago captured one of her hands, still in motion, and held it fast between his own. She stopped her frenetic movements, her breath coming in pants.

"Hey," he said, looking her over. The energy was crackling off her skin. *"Estas bien?"*

She closed her eyes, taking in a deep, steadying breath. *"Sí,* I think so."

"Me allegro." He reached out to capture the same wayward curl that was too short for her ponytail, threading it behind her ear. "Nothing happened tonight. Everything is good between us, okay?"

A crease appeared between her eyebrows and Santiago hurried to explain before she got the wrong idea about what he was trying to say. "Not that kissing you was nothing. It was something. A very big something." He squeezed the hand he held. "But we're still good. And nothing else ever has to happen again if you don't want it to."

Indya looked out over the marina, wind whipping her hair, including that stray curl. She turned back, swiping it behind her ear. "It's been a while, you know?"

"I know. It is the same for me."

Indya nodded. The sun had completed its descent and only deck lights and a few stars illuminated the darkness. "There's the whole work situation."

"We don't have to take this to work. In fact, I would prefer it if we didn't." He brought her hand up to his lips, running them across her knuckles, reveling in the soft strength, how such long, delicate fingers were so quick to do even the roughest work. "No one here is in a hurry."

He looked up to watch Indya's gaze fixed on him. There was interest but also uncertainty, which was something he rarely saw from her. The afternoon had purified his feelings, making them clear to him. Now he simply felt good, hopeful even, if also a bit uneasy for wanting things he wasn't entirely sure he could ever have. But he sensed that what happened on that boat had not had the same clarifying effect on Indya. If he pushed her too hard, she might throw up those professional walls she used to keep everything around her in place, and he would end up losing out on his chance to be with her.

He let her hand go, stepping away from her. "Good night, Indya. And thank you again. I haven't had such a good day in a very long time."

Indya dropped her eyes, an uncharacteristic moment of softness and vulnerability for someone who seemed able to carry the world in one hand. "It was good for me, too. I wouldn't have had such a good haul without you."

"We could always try our luck with the Salty Fish," Santiago answered, the feeling of excitement bubbling up in his chest. Fishing was his passion, and to share that passion with someone like Indya didn't seem like it could be real.

Indya's shifted on her feet. "I haven't given up on putting together a team. See you at work tomorrow?"

"I hope so," Santiago answered. She had sidestepped his comment on the Salty Fish and there was a wariness in her eyes that shot him through with acute anxiety, but her expression had also brightened at his suggestion about the competition. Despite the surprising events of the afternoon, she'd clearly had a good time as well. Pleasure radiated from her. She indicated the cooler with his fish inside, which he easily hoisted over his shoulder, tackle box and rods in his other hand.

"Good night, Santiago." She hesitated before standing on her tiptoes and leaving a chaste kiss on his cheek. He experienced physical pain at watching her walk away and not being able to do anything about it, especially now that he knew she responded to him as much as he did to her. But she was choosing distance for now and that was something he had to accept. His life was full anyway, with work and the supermarket and preparing his life to welcome Lisbet and her mother with him.

At least, that's what he repeated to himself as he carried the cooler to his boat and situated his fish in his ice locker. He knew sleep would elude him and not even the prospect of Wil's company was enough to soothe him.

Santiago spent the following days immersing himself in his work. When his mother called to tell Santiago that he had received a letter from the Venezuelan consulate, sent to his mother's house, his entire focus fell there. Both Natasha and Lisbet's immigration interview appointments had been assigned a date. Santiago didn't bother waiting until his workday was over to call Natasha with the news.

"I was just going to call you!" Natasha said. "We have our interview in June. If this goes well, we will be there for Lisbet's birthday."

"Have you told Lisbet yet?" Santiago asked, eager to experience his daughter's enthusiasm when she heard they'd be seeing each other again soon.

"No," Natasha said. "I think it is better to wait until we are closer to the date in case something falls through. I wouldn't have told her about our plans at all, but someone I know has no self-control."

Santiago grinned. "I couldn't help myself."

Her laugh came, husky and warm over the airwaves. "You're as bad as she is." She grew quieter. "Things are so bad here. If it wasn't for Mami's inheritance, and the money you and your family send each month, we would be struggling a lot harder than we are now. You know teachers get paid next to nothing."

Natasha rarely shared this side of things, always emphasizing how well they were doing, assuring him that Lisbet was thriving. But he knew how things were on the ground. He watched the news. He had friends who did not filter the truth the way he knew Natasha did sometimes to keep him from worrying.

"I'm counting down the days," Santiago said. "It's nice here. You and Lisbet will love it."

A shuffle in the background as she moved papers around on her desk. She was a teacher in the same school Lisbet studied in, and Santiago had called her during her planning time.

"I know we will. Thank you. For everything."

"She's my daughter and you are my friend. There's nothing to thank me for."

Natasha paused before speaking again, her voice thick with emotion. "I know you are doing your best and I am so grateful to you. I would never leave my aunt and cousins if I didn't have to, but for Lisbet's future, I will do anything."

"I know, Natasha. The same is for me. I promise," he said with fierce determination. "You will have a good life here."

Natasha sniffled, but her voice was steadier. "I know we will try. My students will be here soon. Talk to you later?"

"Same time, same place," Santiago said, trying to lighten the mood. When Natasha signed off, he leaned his forehead into his hands. It was just a matter of time now, but even the idea that Natasha and Lisbet might be suffering in any capacity made him lightheaded with powerlessness. Natasha never complained, never gave any indication of the severity of their situation, but he knew, and knowing made the wait excruciating. The months couldn't pass quickly enough.

Indya avoided him for the next week. If he saw her from far away, she would magically disappear, no doubt relying on her superior knowledge of the ins and outs of the hotel to help her move about. She still surprised his team when she picked up repair calls, but she had gotten better about it since their conversation. Yet somehow, none of those intersected with his. It was clear as daylight that those lack of interactions were by design.

He missed her, and he did not like this turn of events.

He had promised her space, but he was a weak man when it came to her. He had been working on a report summarizing his survey of the property, which gave a more realistic picture of what remained to be accomplished. Banal as it was, he had needed a plan for himself to move forward, and this had fulfilled that need. He was going to simply email it to her and wait for her feedback, but the desire to see her was too great and this game of avoidance had gone on long enough. He'd been hired to do a job. He could not in good conscience procrastinate.

He collected his things and went to Indya's office, where

her door stood ajar, and prepared to knock. Inside, she sat at her desk, staring intently at the screen. She wore practical pants and a mint green polo with the hotel's logo on it. Her makeup was simple, without added embellishments, making her look just a bit paler, a bit more tired.

The ocean beyond was burbling under the soft oranges of a setting sun. He was on a later shift today and wouldn't leave until after the sun had set. He was grateful for the strength that the constant presence of the sea gave him.

He knocked on her door, startling her from whatever held her attention so firmly fixed.

"Santiago." Rolling her shoulders, she indicated the chair in front of her desk, a silent invitation to take a seat. He accepted, sinking into the soft leather. Her eyes flicked quickly over his body but just as quickly settled on his face. "How can I help you?"

He tried not to be put off by her ultra professional demeanor, the way her smile seemed stapled crookedly on her face.

He cracked his neck, trying to bring his thoughts back to the purpose of his visit and not to her non-expression. He unlocked the iPad screen he'd perched on his lap. "I finished the report that I told you about some time ago." Santiago's eyes lingered briefly on the smooth expanse of her skin through the V-neck of her polo, the long column of her divine neck that was made for his lips. The undulations of muscle and sinew in her forearms, each laced by gold bracelets. He tore his gaze away and scrolled the desktop on his iPad to find the file. "I summarized a survey of what remains to be done on the premises, prioritizing each task by its impact on guests and fitting it onto a timeline."

Indya's hand came to rest on the column of her neck, as if she were rubbing the heat of his gaze into her skin. She took the device from him with the other, flashing him a quick smile before she turned her attention to the screen. Her long lashes fluttered as she read through the report and he was captivated by the movement, like tiny butterfly wings caressing the tops of her cheeks.

She did not scan the document, but studied it carefully, asking questions to clarify points. Besides her beauty, Santiago was impressed by her sharp mind, the way she drew quick connections between types of damage, able to identify which were a remnant from the storm, and which were simple wear and tear. She knew her hotel, and the environment within which it functioned better than anyone, even though it had not yet been six months since she herself had returned to Soledad Bay.

"This is very thorough," she praised, scrolling through the last of his findings. "Are you saying everything will get done—"

"Well before the Salty Fish begins," he finished. "That timeline takes into account allotted man hours for each member of my team, including a recommendation for overtime in some cases."

She looked at the timeline again. "This is very encouraging."

Santiago nodded. "It does not allot any man-hour contribution by you. It assumes that you will not be participating in handiwork and tickets issued by the system."

Indya brightened. "That means I can speed things up by helping where I can."

"Or," Santiago said carefully, "you could leave the maintenance to your very competent staff."

A furrow appeared between her eyebrows. "Why?"

Santiago prepared himself for resistance. "I'm not the owner of the hotel, so I will not presume to tell you what to do—"

"Good."

Santiago was flustered by her clipped tone, but he pushed on. "It helps the staff if we can get those maintenance calls organized and scheduled without…surprises that cause us to make double visits and interrupt guests unnecessarily, throwing everyone off. Instead of helping, it sets us back."

Her eyes remained fixed on him. Indya's wheels were visibly turning as she processed what he said. Santiago sighed. "Again it is your hotel. Your staff will work around any circumstances and find a way to get it all done, but it is easier if there are no surprises as we work."

Indya continued to consider him. Santiago waited, until he suspected she might never say another word again.

"I'll go now." Santiago stood to leave.

He was on his feet and turning to leave when Indya's voice froze him in place.

"Santiago."

He paused. "Yes?"

Indya stood as well, rounding the desk to stand across from him. "Thank you for doing this." She twisted her fingers together. "I didn't mean to sound harsh before. And I'm sorry I've been a bit…distant…these last few days."

Santiago sighed. He hated that she'd disappeared ever since their time on the boat together. "I meant it when I said that no one is in a hurry."

"I know." She shook her head as if confused about what to say. "It's work, mostly, and I don't handle stress very well."

Santiago didn't bother to hide his surprise. "That is not the image you project."

"I know how to hide it when I'm struggling. To look like I have things under control when I really don't. I actually experience a lot of anxiety and I compulsively run around, doing things that I could easily delegate. It's a manifestation of that." She picked up the iPad he'd left on her desk. "This helps me. It's a plan and I can work with plans."

"I like plans, too," Santiago said. "I work better when I have a clear objective. But Indya, it's why you hired me. To do things like this." He pointed at the iPad. "I know what I'm doing and I hope you will learn to trust my work."

"I do. And every day, I trust you more." Indya set the iPad back down on the table. "I'm so sorry if I ever gave you the impression that I didn't."

Her words stoked something fiery in him. Santiago could not turn away from this woman, or deny how absolutely compelling authority looked on her, and how much better her trust felt. He'd never realized that, of all the things he might find attractive about a woman, her ability to do her job well would be the one that set his blood on fire the most. But Santiago was coming to understand that when you were attracted to someone, you were attracted to everything about them, even the least romantic parts.

And he wanted to do this for her. He wanted to come through and show that he could be trusted with things that mattered the most to her—in this case, her hotel.

"It's okay," he answered. She looked drained and he knew the stress was getting to her. He wanted to ask her about things between them, but that wasn't the conversation they needed to have at this moment.

He stepped closer to her and spread his arms. "May I?"

Indya looked up from tracing the grain of her wooden desk, a panicked expression on her face. "A kiss?"

"I was offering a hug, but I'll take a kiss, if you're offering."

Indya's face split into a grin, the first unguarded smile of the visit, and it melted all tension in her heart. "A hug, it is."

He wrapped his arms around her, careful to hold her but not to overwhelm her. Even that contact released an anxiety that had been twisted tight inside him, replacing it with something sensuous and warm.

"This is nice," he offered sincerely, breathing in the scent of her soft, wavy hair.

"I missed it." She pulled away and tilted her head up to look at him. "Everyone tells me that I'm not good at asking for help, but I'm trying to learn."

"It's my job, of course, but I am always happy to help. You don't even have to ask."

"You do more than your job. I admit, I was nervous about hiring you because I wasn't sure if it would work out. But now, I have no regrets." Her gaze held his and it was forged of so much more than the words she was sharing, especially when she switched into Spanish. *"Ningún arrepentimiento."*

No regrets.

All mechanical noises seemed to recede, except for the waves crashing on the shore, a sound that always played in the background, like a soundtrack on loop. Or maybe it was the cacophonous rush of blood through his veins that drowned out the world. Her words were pointed and he refused to believe that she hadn't meant them to be so.

"Yo, tampoco, me arrepiento."

I have no regrets, either.

Indya's gaze intensified, and Santiago felt himself being reeled in, falling into her gravitational pull. As he leaned toward her, his phone, tucked into the pocket of his khakis, buzzed insistently. The vibration slowly pulled them apart.

"Someone wants you," she said, pointing toward the sound.

Santiago gave her a sheepish grin as he pulled the phone out, swiping the notification on his screen. "It's a reminder to collect the key to my rental house from the real estate agency's lockbox. I signed a lease."

Indya beamed, pure excitement written across her face. "Congratulations! When did that happen?"

He waved his hand, as if it were not important. "During the days you were avoiding me."

She crossed her arms. "I was not avoiding you."

Santiago raised an eyebrow but said no more, tucking the phone back in his pocket. "It needs a little work." He had negotiated to do the home improvements in exchange for a reduction in rent. "Not much, but it will be ready by the time Lisbet comes."

Indya took out her cell, glancing at the screen. "Good thing our shifts are nearly over."

Santiago pinched his lip. "What a coincidence."

Running a finger along her office desk again, Indya said, almost casually, "Yes, funny how that worked out."

She was responsible for approving the master schedule each week, and his shifts consistently coincided with her own.

Santiago was suddenly loath to let her get away. "Do you want to see my new home?"

Indya's face split into that wide, playful grin again, that she'd been withholding all week, the one he loved to see. "Do you want to show me?"

"Very much."

She hesitated before quickly gathering up her keys. "Gia is with my mother this afternoon, so I have a little time." She stood at the door as if the appointment was hers and he was the one keeping her. "Ready?"

Santiago was getting emotional whiplash. He'd come in to speak to her about one thing and found himself in a completely different scenario that he could not have foreseen. But as he walked alongside Indya to the employee car park and his truck, he didn't question it. They had promised not to bring any of this to work, and he was more than happy to get her away from her office if it meant spending time with her.

Chapter Fourteen

Indya

Indya could barely believe how quickly she'd given in to being with Santiago when she'd done such a thorough job of avoiding him for days. She'd hoped that, with time, the impulse to be in his presence and to spend as much time as she could with him would dissipate.

She was wrong and she'd caved like a house of cards at the first opportunity.

Now she was a passenger in Santiago's truck, questioning her life decisions and vacillating between excitement and mortification at how flimsy her resolve had turned out to be.

There was no question of Santiago driving, but Indya had a hard time just being a passenger, always responsible for getting herself and Gia to places. As she settled into her seat, she experienced the weirdness of feeling like she was being chauffeured around. She was used to being in control, even of the wheel, and now, as Santiago pulled out of the parking lot, she did her best to not let the anxiety get the best of her and turn her into a backseat driver. She focused on the truck instead. Like everything else associated with Santiago, she found it immaculate and well-maintained, if much plainer than her accessory-packed Audi. Indya shifted on the overly warm leather-and-polyester seat, which was slowly cooling down with the ice-cold air-conditioning blowing through the cabin.

"Thank you for inviting me to come along," she began, trying her best to ignore the traffic, and keep herself from scrutinizing Santiago's driving decisions. "I needed to get out of there."

"When you are busy, you are more serious than usual," Santiago said, adjusting the air just as Indya was beginning to feel too cold. It was uncanny, since she hadn't complained out loud.

"You know how it is," Indya said, wincing when Santiago seemed to come to a stop too suddenly behind a supply truck. Santiago's vision quickly flicked to her before he returned his attention to the road. "At work, I'm a different version of myself. Work Indya is great, because she get things done."

"I know Work Indya very well." Santiago reached over to take her hand, threading their fingers together.

"Everyone does." She glanced down at their hands, locked in an intimacy that made her very nearly blush. She resisted the urge to grab the dashboard when Santiago changed lanes without using his signal light. She squeezed his hand instead. "But when I'm not being Mom Indya or Daughter Indya, sometimes Work Indya likes to take over everything, and while it is an important part of who I am, I have to be careful that it doesn't turn into my entire personality."

"I think that's true for everyone to some degree. We are not the same person in every situation. We change ourselves to fit the expectation." When she inhaled sharply at a car cutting in front of them, Santiago squeezed her fingers, his warm hand a powerful, grounding force.

"Then, you understand," she said, turning her attention to his profile, which was perfectly cut against the world that sped by beyond the truck's window. She would ignore everything else but him. "All this to say, it's a habit to become her, because I need her. She gets so much done, but sometimes, I have to fight to create space for the other part of me that likes to laugh and fish and simply be happy."

Trent hadn't liked the sum total of her parts, afraid some imbalance would make her too frivolous, too unfocused on the things he thought that mattered. He wanted a version of her that conformed to his strict ideas of womanhood, ones that Indya couldn't satisfy.

"You're afraid I will not like these other parts of you," Santiago said.

"Perhaps," she said, glancing out the window again and happy to find they'd turned onto a side street with little traffic. She felt far too exposed and regretted bringing up this topic of conversation to begin with.

Santiago brought her fingers to his lips, pulling her attention away from the trees that sped by. "If we are being completely honest, I like every version of you. Even Work Indya, who can be very demanding." She snorted at this, her breath catching when he left kisses on her knuckles. "You don't have to hide anything from me."

An irrational relief swelled through Indya's chest. They could just be words, but they meant something to her. She leaned in, leaving a kiss on his cheek. "Thank you."

It was his turn to flush a fresh pink. With only one hand, he somehow managed to maneuver the truck onto a driveway before parking next to a large Florida oak hung thick with Spanish moss.

"See? I got you here in one piece." He grinned at her.

Indya released his hand to cover her face. "I'm not used to being a passenger."

"I figured as much." He got out of the truck and rounded to open her door. "I hope someday, you will get used to it."

The implication that he might be driving her around in the future triggered a dozen conflicting uncertainties, but his gallantry made it hard for her to dwell on any of them.

A pale blue stilt house rose before them. The bottom floor had an open plan, with enough space for a car and a half-enclosed work room. They took a flight of stairs that led up to the second floor, which had a screened in, wraparound balcony. There was ample space for patio furniture and a table.

"I love stilt houses," Indya said while they took the stairs.

"It's very cute inside as well, though it needs a bit of work," Santiago said, opening the screen door to let Indya inside. A lockbox hung on the doorknob, which Santiago reached for. After punching in a code, the box opened, revealing the house keys that Santiago used to unlock the front door.

"After you." He swept a hand to usher her in.

Indya stepped past him, taking in the space inside. It was an open floor plan, with a kitchen counter that curved into a breakfast bar, dividing the main living space from the kitchen. The bedrooms were down a corridor that ended with French doors emptying back out onto the balcony. Santiago described the plans he had for the space, the colors he would choose, especially for the three bedrooms—one for Lisbet, one for him and a guest room.

"Natasha has a sister close by who will be helping her get established. They only have to clear the immigration interview before they can finally come."

"So close," Indya said, though she had no idea what the

process entailed. Her powerful desire to see him happy made it almost a given in her mind. If nothing else went well in the world except for this, she would be overjoyed on his behalf.

He showed Indya his bedroom on the other side of the corridor. The city park was visible across the street. Two blocks farther was the public beach access, beyond which lay the sea.

"I see what you meant about the view," Indya said, watching the waves in the distance. "An accident of location."

"A happy accident. Lisbet's room has the same view." His face went wistful and Indya imagined him thinking of his daughter, perhaps playing on the balcony in the warm breeze, looking up every now and then to see the ocean just over the railing.

Indya placed a hand on his arm. "You are a good man, do you know that?"

His face went a warm pink that spread to his neck. For the second time in one day, Indya had made him blush and she was rather proud of herself.

"Thank you. But I haven't always been the wisest."

She placed her hand, light and delicate, on his chest. "You're allowed to be unwise every now and then."

Santiago turned toward her, gathering up her hand in his larger one. He held it fast, his warmth enveloping her. He was so big and strong, but he never made her feel crowded or suffocated. The power that radiated from him was tempered with kindness and human decency, the kind of power that created space and didn't crowd anyone out.

"You make me feel good about myself," he said in a voice that had gone low and gravelly with emotion. Indya was slowly getting drunk on the sound.

"You of all people shouldn't have any doubts about what you're worth."

Santiago gave a small gasp. Without warning, he brought

her knuckles to his lips, brushing the briefest of contacts over the skin he found there, before lifting his eyes to gaze into hers. There was that warmth she couldn't turn away from, but also a sharper need piercing through them. She panted, her chest rising and falling with the rhythm of a hunger that echoed its beat in his pounding heart beneath her palm. He had caught her out too quickly, had not given her time to reassemble the armor she used to keep her feelings and thoughts intact, leaving her exposed by his small gesture. This version of herself was her most vulnerable and needy, and she hadn't given access to that part of her to anyone in a very long time.

"Mi reina," he whispered.

My queen.

Her sharp intake of breath was the only sound she registered for several long moments.

"You shouldn't call your boss that. It's not appropriate," she whispered at length, her voice as thin and frail as the sea breeze falling apart among the blades of saw grass.

"I shouldn't." He gazed at her with naked hunger and she could not barricade her mind against images of them, splayed out in abandon against each other like two unclenched fists. "But that's what you are to me."

She huffed in disbelief, but she was not displeased. No one had ever seen her that way before, but it didn't feel like an exaggeration when he said those things to her.

She slid her free hand up his shoulder, fingers buried deep in his hair. She dragged him down, to press his thick, flushed lips against hers. She didn't care about taking it slow, kissing him with a ferocity that forced him to take a step back. Her desperation to taste him disheveled his hair and his clothes. She pressed her body against his, feeling every inch of him in one hard, burning line against her body. Until now, she had been holding herself back, dampening her own reactions for reasons tied up with ideas of who she had to be. But now she was in his arms, mouth fused to his, trapping him to her by all her passions come undone.

Finally, at long last, they pulled apart. His eyes were wide and glassy, his lips glistening and pink. His polo had come untucked and his hair—she couldn't help but giggle, which blew away all the intensity of the last few moments like a strong wind. She chuckled as she used her fingers to bring some semblance of order back to his curls.

"You look like someone electrocuted you," she said between laughs, shocking herself with this new and easy familiarity.

He playfully shook the curls out. "I feel electrified."

God, Indya felt so good. She didn't want any of this to end.

"What are you doing Saturday night?" she blurted out, her nerves gathering in her stomach, twisting uncontrollably.

Santiago stepped back to adjust his polo, which had come untucked on one side. "I have no plans. The renovations on the supermarket are done."

Relief flooded her. He'd given hours of his free time to helping his parents repair the damage to their business caused by the hurricane. She fussed with his polo, which it didn't need, but touching him calmed her. "You mentioned a fish dinner at one point."

He tilted his head, confusion giving way to recollection. "Yes, I did."

She shrugged as if she weren't dying inside. "I have an excellent grill that I'd love to fire up."

"Do you?" He considered her more closely, as if trying to determine if she was serious.

"I'm inviting you to dinner at my place," she said more explicitly. She dropped her eyes, feeling unbearably shy. "If you would like."

He gripped her gently by the shoulders, drawing her eyes back up to his face. "Of course I would like to come for dinner. I can bring fish."

"*I'll* bring the fish. You bring something to go with it. Anything you want."

He visibly swallowed. "And the girls?"

Indya paused, confused. "The girls?"

He drew his hands down her arms until they rested on her elbows. "When we talked about it, we mentioned having the girls over."

Indya toyed with one of the buttons of his polo. "Santiago, I'm inviting you over for a date." She leaned closer to his ear. "As in, you come alone."

"Oh. *Oh*," he stammered. *"Muy bien, muy bien."*

"Is it?" she asked quietly. "Is it okay?"

"Dios mío, mujer. Sí," he laughed, drawing her in close, his hug this time warmhearted, despite the low burning fire in Indya's belly. "Wholeheartedly, one hundred percent yes."

Indya chuckled at that. They let each other go, awareness of the time rushing at her. "Want to show me anything else?"

He opened his mouth to say something, but evidently thought better of it. He cleared his throat and said, "No, you've seen everything."

"Not everything…yet." Indya stretched up to press a soft kiss on his lips before taking him by the hand, which had grown clammy. His sweet nervousness quelled hers somewhat as she did the familiar thing—took charge and led them out of the house. They'd have a date on Saturday and Indya grew lightheaded at the idea of the path she was embarking on with him.

Chapter Fifteen

Santiago

Santiago could not have imagined when he walked into Indya's office earlier during his shift that his day would end with Indya, wrapped in a passionate kiss in his future home, her presence like a benediction on that space.

He hadn't wanted to let her go. He seemed to be feeling this way often lately.

He'd have to find a way to make sure that her leaving him would always be a "see you later," and never a goodbye.

Santiago and Indya parted ways in the car park, Indya to make a few last-minute calls before putting an end to her workday, leaving Santiago to track down Miriam, having promised her a ride home after studying with Gia. They were in Gia's room, Indya's mother keeping an eye on them, taking advantage of a home health aide's biweekly visit to stay with her husband to help Indya with the hotel's paperwork.

He messaged Miriam on the way to Gia's room. Santiago questioned how much time two teenagers with a heavy dose of spring fever were going to get done, but he was happy to leave the parenting to his mother when it came to Miriam. Santiago felt like a teenager himself after his meeting with Indya. He kept thinking about their time alone this coming weekend, and experienced a level of excitement he hadn't known in a very long time.

Forcing himself to focus, he arrived outside the girl's room, hearing shouts and giggles even before he'd reached the door. That didn't sound at all like two people doing homework. *"Ven*, Miriam," he said from outside the door. "It's late and Mamá is waiting for you."

"Un momento," she spoke in a singsong, followed by another round of giggles. The door flew open and Miriam appeared, cheeks flushed pink and backpack slung half-open over her shoulder. *"Hola hermano!"* she said cheerfully.

"Why do I feel like you two were busy planning a crime?" He poked his head around his sister and saw Gia, already in her pajamas, waving from inside.

"Are you going to be okay alone?" he asked.

"Abuela is still here somewhere and Mom texted to say she was on her way down. She had to finish up something in the office." Gia looked at Miriam and they dissolved into giggles again.

"Okay, okay, the silly is at maximum here. Good night, Gia."

"Good night, Santiago. Miriam." On the last syllable of Miriam's name, Gia erupted into another round of laughter that she smothered with a pillow.

"Dios mío," Santiago muttered, chuckling to himself when he closed the door. He took Miriam's backpack as they walked to his truck. "I hope, in the middle of all those giggles, you got your homework done." At her suddenly guilty expression, he paused. "You did finish your project, didn't you?"

"Well…" Miriam shrugged sheepishly.

Santiago sighed. "Wasn't that the whole point of being here? Why didn't you just go straight home after school if you knew you weren't going to get it done?"

"Because!" Miriam whined as they neared his truck. "I didn't want to miss out on a chance to hang out with my best friend."

"But you see her every day. You're practically fused to each other's hips." The beep of the fob unlocking the truck doors cut through the night.

Miriam climbed inside. "It never feels like enough time. Plus you got to spend time with Ms. Indya. That's a good thing, right?"

He pulled the truck out of the parking lot, putting it in gear and maneuvering into the gentle traffic of Beachfront Drive. "I see her every day, too."

"School and work are not the same. Plus, it's good to be friends with your boss. It contributes to a positive work environment, in my opinion." Miriam punctuated the last sentence with a wag of her forefinger.

Santiago laughed at his sister. He'd noticed this persuasive quality in Gia as well. This generation was a little too clever for his taste. "So you were thinking of me all this time, *chiquita*? Is that it?"

Miriam gave him the most beatific smile she could muster. "I would make any sacrifice for my favorite brother."

"Ya, ya, ya!" he said around a howl of laughter. "Enough smooth talk. You're too much." He grew serious. "Now I'm going to drop you off, and as quietly as possible to not wake Papá, I want you to go directly to your room and finish your homework. You want to play? You have to pay."

"Yes, sir!" she said with an exaggerated salute. Santiago chuckled again as he pulled into the driveway of his parents' house. He had been ambushed on all sides by women tonight, and each one was more audacious and clever than the other. If everything went according to plan, soon Lisbet would be here, too, and he imagined Miriam would train her to be just as clever as she was.

Santiago couldn't wait.

A small light from inside his parents' house was visible through the otherwise darkened kitchen window. Santiago got out of the truck to walk his sister to the door.

"Lend me your phone light," Miriam said, flipping through her keys. Santiago had just located the app on his phone when the door opened. His mother stood in the doorway, pink rollers on the ends of her hair matching the pink housedress and slippers she wore.

"¡Finalmente!" she said, giving Miriam and Santiago a kiss each before letting them both come inside. "It's later than usual."

"I had work to finish," Santiago said. "I apologize."

"No te preocupes. I'm happy to see you working so hard for the Linares." Mamá herded them into the kitchen, handing each a mug of milk and honey she'd been warming on the stove. Santiago remembered when he was young and drinking a cup each night before going to bed, how soothing and relaxed it had made him feel.

Miriam's eyes lit up before she took a long sip, emptying the cup in one impressive swallow. Mamá, who had been looking on in astonishment at the way her daughter drained her mug, took it from Miriam.

She tugged one of Miriam's soft curls. "I'll rinse your mug. You go upstairs and get ready for bed, okay?"

Santiago gave Miriam a pointed look, to which she smiled. "Yes, *Mamá.* And then I'm going to read a little bit before I fall asleep." She returned Santiago's stare with a pleading expression that he simply was unable to resist. He sighed, giving a barely perceptible nod that only Miriam could see.

She hugged her big brother tightly and whispered, *"Gracias,"* in his ear.

"Good night, *chiquita*."

She bounded up the stairs, phone already in hand, no doubt to text Gia.

"And put that phone away, too!" her mother said to her retreating back. "You're going to go blind, always looking at that thing."

Miriam shoved the phone into her pants pocket.

When Miriam was upstairs, Santiago turned to his mother. "Papá?"

She switched to speaking Spanish. "He's in bed. You know how he is. When he sleeps, he doesn't hear anything."

Santiago nodded, both relieved and disappointed. He loved his father and was happy to see him, but he could make Santiago feel like he was three inches tall. "Tell him that I said hello. I'll stop by the supermarket tomorrow."

"Wait, *mi amor*," Mamá said when he started for the door. "I was talking to Oriana, Indya's mother, this afternoon. She stopped by the supermarket to pick up a few things. She said you've been doing really well at your job and that they are so happy with you."

"Me allegro," he said, sincerely pleased that they were satisfied with his work. "Would you mind telling Papá what she said, too?"

"Yes," she said, her smile faltering. Maybe she had told him, but in usual form, he was not impressed. "Anyway, we never got to properly thank them. I invited Indya and her family to dinner on Saturday."

Santiago thought of the promised cookout, and the sudden surge of disappointment at the prospect of not being able to spend that time with Indya was more dramatic than he anticipated. "I have plans."

"Well, cancel them," Mamá said without hesitation.

"What do you mean, cancel them? Mamá, I'm a thirty-year-old man. As grateful as I am to them for having hired me, you have to talk with me before you make plans like this."

Mamá huffed, her pink rollers bobbing with her response. "Well, it's too late. Oriana and I already agreed and she will tell Indya as well."

"Indya is not going to appreciate having her plans ruined, either."

"How do you know what plans Indya has this Saturday?" She eyed him carefully and Santiago realized he had committed a fatal error.

"She mentioned that she was busy this weekend." He scrubbed at his chin. "It's been some time since I started working at the hotel. Why are you thinking about doing this now?"

Mamá pinched her lip, suddenly uneasy. "Your father wanted to make sure things would…work out with you."

Santiago smarted from those words. "You mean, Papá was afraid I'd do something to ruin this."

"Santi," she whispered. "You know I don't think that way about you."

"But he does," he said, more curtly than he'd intended. "I'm grateful to the Linares for giving me a chance, and I am grateful to you for recommending me. But they are not performing a charity. I work hard for them and I know what I'm doing." His father's lack of faith in him was exhausting.

"I never said you didn't. But people wouldn't have known

that until you showed them. And you did." Mamá placed a hand on his cheek. "We are so proud of you."

"You are so proud of me. Papá was hedging his bets." He stepped past her and moved toward the door, his stomach burning with disappointment and shame, even though he'd done nothing to earn those feelings. He was infuriated at how his father could still make him feel this way even as an adult.

"Santi, please." She reached the door with a speed that shocked him. "Your father had to leave Venezuela even though he did everything he was supposed to do. He got an education, he worked hard and he never took anything from anyone. And for a long time, he felt like a failure. Sometimes I think he projects this onto you. But he loves you." She placed a hand on his rigid arm. "We both do."

"I know I have your love. What I need is your respect."

"You have it." At his unconvinced expression, she pushed on. "Just do this one thing. For me. You won't regret it."

Somehow, Santiago wasn't too sure about that. But he couldn't continue to rely on the goodwill his parents had built up in Soledad Bay to get him ahead. It was good for him to make an impression based on who he was and what he could do, not just because of his family's reputation. Thanking the people who were responsible for helping him out wasn't such a bad move at all.

He'd had his heart set on spending an uninterrupted dinner with Indya…and maybe more. But he had to relent on this. There would be other nights, other opportunities. If there weren't, he would create them.

"Okay, but next time, please consult with me before you make plans that involve me. I'm not sitting at home, staring at the phone. I have my own life, too. *¿Entiendes?*"

"Entiendo." Mamá smiled sweetly. "I'll try. We are set in our ways. It's very hard for us to change."

Santiago gave her an answering smile. "Don't worry. I have faith in you." In his father, maybe not so much.

He wished his mother a good-night and was inside his truck and on the road in minutes. The events of this evening had given him emotional whiplash, and he was eager to get home and get into bed before anything else happened. He was fairly flexible and understood where his mother was coming from. From what he knew about Indya so far, she was not going to be happy having her time dictated to her, but it was a fait accompli by their families, and like most things that had to do with families, it was something they would simply have to resign themselves to.

At least Indya would be there.

But that didn't stop him from thinking about all the things they could have done together when they were alone.

Chapter Sixteen

Indya

Indya had been on such a high when she got back on the premises after spending the afternoon with Santiago. It had been a revelation to listen to his dreams and ambitions for his life with Lisbet, and she could have listened to him for a terrifyingly long time, more time than she thought she'd ever spare a person.

So she was not prepared for her mother's ambush when she stepped into her office. When her mother filled her in on her intentions for the very night Indya had planned to have dinner with Santiago, her cloud of contentment evaporated.

"I can't believe you did it again. No matter how many times I tell you to not make plans without consulting me, you do it anyway." Indya was resisting with great difficulty the urge to launch a stack of files against the wall, if only because she'd be the one to clean up the mess afterward.

"Magdalena wanted to do something and was afraid she'd waited too long. It's just one Saturday, Indya," her mother answered.

"It's really nice of her. It truly is. But if you had asked her to wait until you consulted with me, you would have gotten what you wanted out of this without making your daughter feel like an infant."

"Indya—" she started in that same, dismissive way.

"Mami!" Indya shouted, shocking her mother into silence. She regretted it instantly, especially when her mother seemed to wilt into her office chair. Indya never raised her voice to her parents. She hadn't been raised that way. But Indya's emotions were burning hot. It was more than the disappointment of having her heart set on spending an evening with Santiago and discovering she would not. "I've done everything you've asked me to do. I uprooted my life as well as your granddaughter's to come here and do the right thing by this hotel."

"I never wanted you to—"

"I'm not done, yet," Indya said quietly, but just as firmly. "I don't regret coming back to Soledad Bay. This is my home, and believe it or not, I was ready. I just needed an excuse to make the change." Indya sank into the chair across from her mother, utterly defeated. "But I'm tired, Mami." Indya felt her nose itch and she knew she was a few more sniffles away from tears. "I can do anything, handle anything, but not if you keep putting your shoulder against me and pushing."

Mami rested a hand over her neck, watching Indya with a mournful expression. "Aye, *mijita*. Everything I do is with the idea to make your life easier. To help you."

"It doesn't help me, Mami." Indya dabbed at the corner of her eyes, trying to stem the flood of tears that wanted to fall—tears of stress and frustration, whose reprieve she'd only found when she was with Santiago in his new house. "And before you tell me that I can't control everything, I already know that. But I can't wake up every day, terrified of what new surprises you have waiting for me. It's a layer of stress that I don't need."

Indya bit her lip, staring out the window instead of at her mother. She heard her mother shuffle out of Indya's office chair and move toward her. Soon, her mother was in front of her, in much the same position that Indya had been when they had had a similar conversation only a few weeks ago.

"I'm sorry," she said, taking Indya's hand and holding it. "Sometimes I feel so guilty about making you leave your job and your life down south to be here with us." Indya turned to see her mother's pained expression and moved to protest, but her mother pushed on. "Between the habit of running this place and wanting so much to help you, I forget that you have your own life to manage as well. I don't mean to be disrespectful. It is because you do so much, my beautiful, capable girl." She ran her fingers through Indya's hair, catching on tiny knots that quickly unraveled under her stroke.

"I'm trying to be capable, Mami. But it's a lot."

Mami gave her such a sweet smile, it brought Indya to the edge of tears. "You're right. Let's make a deal. From now on, I will consult with you on anything relating to the hotel, no matter how small or insignificant it appears to me."

Indya rested her hand on her mother's, where it was still toying with her curls. "I'd like that."

"However," her mother's voice grew sterner. "You have to promise that you will let me help you."

"I do—"

"You don't, *mijita*. And it's my fault. I was terrible about asking for help, but I had your father who knew when to step in and carry the load. You've never had that, even when you were married to Trent. Especially when you were married to Trent." Her mother shook her head at the mention of his name. "You don't know what it means. But you have to learn to let people help you."

Indya nodded. "If you do this, it would already be a big help."

Mami reached across to leave a kiss on Indya's forehead. "I am sorry about this weekend."

"It's fine," Indya said, waving her words away. Talking with her mother had gone a long way toward softening her irritation about Saturday night and making her feel lighter about things in general. "Knowing Magdalena, she will have already started to prepare dinner the moment the decision was made. Let's let it go for now. But next time, please…"

"Te lo prometo," her mother said, crossing her heart to seal her promise.

Indya leaned forward and hugged her mother. "Thank you. For everything."

Her mother hugged her back even harder. "No, my love. I am grateful for you, my sweet, overworked girl."

Indya laughed, even as she wondered at the intensity of her disappointment over canceling her dinner with Santiago.

Indya drove Gia early to school, pulling into the parent parking lot before the drop-off line became too long. Gia was weighed down by a box of supplies that held her contribution to the hydroponic garden project. Indya had been following her work on the class's social media, and had cleared her schedule for the presentation of completed projects only a week away, which Gia couldn't stop talking about. She had invited her father and both sets of grand-parents to attend as well.

"We even have a dress code. Anyone wearing sneakers, jeans, shorts or other casual clothes won't be allowed to come inside." Gia huffed as she gathered her things. Indya shut off the car and rounded the trunk in time to help Gia with her box.

"That's because when you are in the work world, you can't simply wear what you want. You have to adhere to company policy."

"Not if I own my own business, like you do."

"And yet I still dress appropriately. The impression you make on people is the first step in every business relation-ship."

Gia shrugged her backpack on, taking the box from her mother. "I don't have to worry. I'm stylish all the time."

"You need help with this?" Indya asked.

Gia shook her head. "I got it." She jutted her cheek out for her mother to kiss. "See you later."

"Bye, baby girl." She watched as Gia walked quickly to the school entrance, grateful that her daughter was thriv-ing at her new school. She remembered Santiago's com-ment that Gia looked like a happy girl and how much that had meant to Indya.

Her stomach was a jar full of butterflies at the thought of him, especially given that he was her next stop. She headed in the direction of the marina. She was on her way to see Santiago. It was important to make him understand that this weekend was the result of their parent's collusion and not because it was something she had planned or ac-tively wanted.

Indya really, *really* wanted to spend time alone with Santiago and figure out what she was feeling. It had been

building up in her for some time, which was why she'd
stayed away from him. She knew herself. She needed to
find her certainty. Once she did, her only recourse was to
take action. That's how she was made.

Mami and Santiago's mother had become the proverbial
wrenches in her well-oiled plan and she was not amused.

Upon her approach to the marina, her phone vibrated
with an incoming text. She parked the car, leaving the motor
and the air running, and read the message. It was from
Rayne.

We are giving you a reminder that you will be kidnapped
for lunch on Friday.

She smiled at her best friend's antics, which instantly
took the edge off her irritation. Such polite kidnappers.

Her phone buzzed again. You're a little too slippery for
our taste.

Indya answered, I'm a busy woman. Best to make a reservation when you want to see me.

This is your reservation. Friday. You, me and Nyla. Lunch.
Shopping. Cocktails.

Indya laughed to herself. That's a packed schedule.

The most. It's a date?

It's a date.

A GIF of a dancing bear shouting Yay! appeared in her
next message.

Indya shook her head, tucking her phone into the back

pocket of her cutoff jean shorts. Her rainbow-themed tank top was both slimming and cool, and her designer sandals gave her all the support she needed. Spider veins were a thing in her family and she was doing her best to avoid getting those.

She glanced toward the marina office and paused. She didn't want Wil to see her. After their little confession the last time they'd been here, she didn't want to give them any ammunition with which to tease her. They'd talk, but it would have to be another day.

She snuck in, dodging the restaurant and the shop before slipping behind the giant wooden columns holding up the carved sign announcing Sunset Marina. She strode down the main deck, her knitted orange bag bouncing out a rhythm against her thigh. When she'd found Santiago's slip on the far end, several slips down from hers, she leaped easily onto the deck and knocked on the door.

It occurred to her that Santiago could be running errands and it would be a good idea to text him, now that she had his phone number. She hadn't exactly been thinking clearly, especially with her silly besties texting her so early in the morning.

She raised her fist again to knock when she remembered that it was still stupid early in the morning, especially for Santiago, who also had the second shift today, and dropped her hand. She was a mess. That's what she was.

She made to sneak off, in the hopes he was sleeping, or even better, wasn't home, when the cabin door opened. There, in all his half-sleeping glory, stood Santiago, rubbing his bleary eyes. His hair stood on end, his face had the rough stubble of a morning beard and his chest—

Santos de la tierra y de los cielos, he was shirtless, his broad, work-chiseled pectorals and abdomen fully on display.

Santiago's hair was a light brown that turned bronze in the sun, a sprinkling of his polychromatic curls nestled in the center of his pecs. They turned into a trickle of hair down a line that disappeared into a pair of gray sweatpants hanging low around his waist like the man candy that he was.

Indya's hand came slowly over her mouth. She was as parched as the Sahara at midday.

"Santi," she whispered. "I…didn't mean to wake you."

"Indya," he said sleepily. "That's the second time you call me Santi."

Indya slowly dropped her hand. "It is? I don't remember the first time."

"On the boat." He smiled and it was brighter than the Florida sun. "When you saw the dolphins. I think you were so surprised, you said it without thinking."

"That must be it." Indya wasn't thinking at this moment, either. She was completely bedazzled by him. Who woke up looking that good in the morning? "Do you mind me calling you that?"

His plump lips curled into a sly smile. "You could call me *perro* and I would come."

Indya recovered herself but only somewhat. "I'm not calling you *dog.*"

"Your choice. Would you like to come inside?" Santiago said. "I can make you coffee."

Indya scooped the remainder of her composure off the ground. "Not if I just woke you up. I can come back later."

"I'm already awake," he said. *"Ven."*

Santiago stepped aside, steadying Indya by her elbow as she descended the stairs into the cabin of his cruiser. The boat shifted softly beneath their feet, a swaying presence that caressed them as they moved. Indya was used to treacherous footing on a boat. If she was disorientated, it was because of Santiago's partially clothed proximity to her.

"Give me one moment while I wash up and get a T-shirt on."

She wanted to protest and tell him he was fine just the way he was, but Indya knew that impulse was not coming from a selfless place.

"Can I take a look around?" she asked.

Santiago took a look around himself. "There's not much to see, but please, go ahead."

He retreated to the bow of the cabin. Santiago didn't know that Indya's interests in boats extended far beyond using them to get to her favorite fishing spot. She was also curious about the dimensions and capabilities of each type of craft. Unlike most boats the same size as Indya's, the *Aragona*'s extra length was reflected in a more compartmentalized living area, instead of typical boat designs with cramped quarters in the smallest possible square footage.

The compact, tidy interior had clearly been refurbished, belying the boat's advanced age. Inside, the windows had been resealed and the wood trim freshly varnished. Even the kitchen appliances gleamed, having been either replaced or restored.

"It's beautiful," she called out, running her fingertips along the wood and brass, limned in gold from the sun that snuck in through the yellow-and-orange curtains.

Santiago appeared, freshly washed, wearing a new T-shirt. "It's a work in progress. I bought her for next to nothing two years ago down in Miami. The wood had rotted away from neglect and the electronic system was nonexistent. I had to gut her and rebuild her interior. It helped keep my mind off my troubles. Most of the time." Indicating the rust-colored cushions that matched the curtains and throw rug, he said, "Please have a seat."

"Thank you," she said, surprised by how comfortable the cushion felt.

"Did you renovate this by yourself?" she asked, waving her hand around her.

"Woodworking is a hobby I picked up from my grandfather. That hobby turned into the small business I ran in Caracas." He turned away to prepare coffee in a small Moka pot. "At least, until Jose."

"The one who embezzled from your company?"

Santiago looked up from his work. "Yes." He lit the tiny butane stove, pulling a container of milk from the fridge and pouring some into a small saucepan. "That, on top of a national financial crisis and weak governance, led to my personal economic catastrophe."

"I'm sorry," Indya said.

Santiago took out two wide-bottomed mugs, made for boats, and placed them on top of two felt coasters on the table.

"Don't be. I'm not angry anymore. Good things are waiting for me." He cast a long glance in her direction before returning to his work. The familiar smell of brewing coffee, together with the sizzle of water that escaped the seam, no matter how new the pot or how tightly it was closed, filled the cabin. "So, you like my work?"

Indya accepted the subject change. "It's very well done," she said, sweeping her hands over the soft, orange fabric that coincidentally matched the accents on her multicolored T-shirt. She purposely ignored the way his eyes flit over her generous bosom or her long legs, revealed by the cut-off jeans. She hadn't worn them for him. Not at all. "You should have brought pictures of the boat to the interview. I wouldn't have even checked your references."

He took the seat across from her, handing her a cup of coffee. "Yes, you would have. You would not overlook such a protocol even if Michelangelo Buonarroti had applied for the position."

"You're probably right." She sipped her coffee. It was the perfect combination of sweet and creamy, just the way she liked it.

After taking another sip, Indya asked, "How do you know how I take my coffee?"

Santiago's mug, which was hovering close to his lips, paused, but only infinitesimally. He shrugged nonchalantly. "I pay attention."

Indya sipped the coffee again, enjoying the warmth and the kick that it gave her. "What else did you observe about me?"

Santiago hummed. "Well, you always match your pedicure and manicure."

"That's standard for anyone. What else?"

Santiago smiled. "You won't eat ham on your pizza, but you will eat pineapple, as if you could have one without the other. So strange." He shook his head, as if he couldn't believe her.

Indya set her mug down. "That was very judgmental."

"I was judging you."

"Hey!" She tapped the top of his arm lightly, which was like hitting a tree trunk. "I did not come all the way here to be judged."

"Okay, okay," he laughed, capturing her hand. Instead of letting it go, he brought her fingers to his lips and kissed each one. Every joint in Indya's body evaporated, leaving behind a useless collection of limbs that were not allied to each other.

"What else?" she whispered.

He folded her fingers over his fist, brushing them with his lips, leaving them hypersensitive to his featherlight touch. "Hmm? Oh." He lifted his head from his ministrations. "Gia is always the first thing on your mind when you make a decision, you adore your mother, though you wish she would listen to you better, and you hide all your insecurities away because if you reveal them, you think that people will not care about you anymore."

Each word felt like another layer of her being peeled away, exposing the softest parts of her to sunlight. "Santiago, I—"

He took her other hand, holding them both in his large, powerful ones that knew how to take care of things. Of people. Knew how to take care of her.

"It's a lie, you know. The people who really care for you will do so whether you are weak or strong."

"Do you care for me, Santi?" Indya asked, his nickname slipping out like a prayer.

Santiago slid in close to her, putting an arm around her shoulders. She shivered from the contact. "More than anything."

He drew her in closer, his finger resting under her chin, heat spreading from the place where he touched her. "You are like a queen to me, Indya. *Una reina.* You deserve to be cherished. Worshipped." He dipped his head down, his lips sweeping over hers. When he pulled back, he asked, "Would you let me?"

She bit her bottom lip before releasing it slowly. There was no question of wanting. She'd wanted him since he fished her boat out of the sea. It was everything that would come afterward that had her alarmed. A moment or an age passed, but finally, she said "Yes."

Her heart kicked up a beat that drowned out every other sound, from the sea to the gentle knocking of the boat against the deck. He gazed at her, traced the line of her jaw with his thumb, as he cupped her face in his palms.

"¿Estas segura?" he asked.

Was she sure? The only certainty she had was that she was wildly attracted to him, any other rationality flying headlong out the window.

Santiago stared at her lips with eyes that were heavy lidded and hungry.

He leaned in, his breath fanning warmth and desire over her skin. He smelled like the ocean, and the faintest traces of bodywash. When he pressed his lips to hers, they were unbearably soft, like sea mist she could get lost in. He kissed her gently, and she reveled in the tender pressure of that soft skin before he pressed in farther and deeper. Her answer was quick with surrender as her lips fell open under the pressure of his.

She was both fire and ice, heat and goose bumps spreading over her skin when he swept in to claim her mouth. He tasted like toothpaste and coffee, sharp and bold. She eased her arms around his neck, pulling him closer. She wanted him on his knees and at her mercy, putty-soft and pliant in her hands.

When they pulled apart, he said, "You know what I like the most about you?"

Indya shook her head. "No."

He ran the tip of his nose up her neck, and the sensation of being traced and studied, of being slowly, slowly consumed left her lightheaded. *"Hablas como una reina.* You talk like a queen. You don't ask. You say what you want, and expect to get it."

"Not always," she whispered, her fingers curled at the nape of his neck, toying with the baby-soft hairs she found there. "Sometimes I don't know what to ask for."

"With me—" he bit down on the top of her shoulder through the material of her top, pulling a whoosh of surprised sound from her "—with me, you are soft and sweet and uncertain. But you are also strong and determined, y *me encanta*. It makes me want to fall to my knees and worship you."

"Worship?" she purred, tilting her head in silent invitation for him to continue his explorations. "I like when you say that."

Santiago pressed his lips along her neck until he reached her clavicle, flicking his tongue there. He reduced her to a vessel that only held her need for him. But she was aching to be filled up by him, to want and take until they were both satisfied.

She dug her fingers into his hips, pulling him toward her as much as their awkward position could allow. His groans were a sudden hurricane-force wind blowing hot and furious through her. She slid her hands beneath his T-shirt to drag along his skin. Her skin burned so hot, she thought she might melt into the cushion, singe her fingers where she touched him and set them both on fire.

"Worship," she repeated, as if trying out the syllables, rolling them around in her mouth and finding that the taste satisfied her. "Show me."

He stood, pulled her off the sofa and scooped her up into his arms, his powerful legs steadying them against the movement of the boat. "It would be my pleasure, *mi reina*."

Chapter Seventeen

Santiago

Santiago carried her the short distance from the living room to the sunken bedroom, which was a minor miracle, given the cramped space and the way the boat was swaying. He arrived in the constrained space swallowed up by his full-size bed and end table. The room was a triumph of compact comfort, for which he was grateful, so that he could give Indya the pleasure she deserved. Two brass lamps affixed to the wood-paneled wall sparkled in the sunlight that streamed in from the two stern-facing windows. Santiago set Indya down, all long legs and tiny waist. She was also cast in gold, ready to melt into his heat.

He reached past her to close the curtain against curious passersby, leaving the light of a porthole above, the glass too distorted to look through. He removed his clothes with lightning speed, never taking his eyes off Indya as she did the same. She kicked off her sandals, flung her tank top and shorts to the ground before dropping onto the bed to crawl backward along the mattress. She wore a sheer, pink bra and underwear set, the color making her skin look soft and luminous and imminently kissable. That's what he would do. He would kiss every single last inch of her skin until nothing was left undiscovered.

When he freed himself from his boxers, her eyes grew wide.

"Oh god," she said, sitting up to crawl closer to where he still stood at the foot of the bed. Her breasts were firm and round, and her bottom rose and fell as she moved. "You're beautiful."

"Not more than you," he said, running his fingers through her long, dark hair. She lifted her eyes to him, her lips swollen and flushed before she reached up to set them against his jaw, leaving kisses along the skin of his neck and shoulders. Her hands roamed over him, electrifying him, pulling his breath out of his lungs with every touch. Her fingertips grazed him from his hips to his bottom, and down his thighs and calves. He couldn't stop touching her in turn, was desperate to have her, not once, but many times, until she could not remember a time when she had ever been so satisfied. When she set her lips on one nipple and sucked, his brain turned into the consistency of rice pudding, messy and useless for anything but staring at her as she moved.

He squeezed his eyes shut and threw his head back as he let her do what she wanted to him. He was at her mercy, and he gave himself up to her, every inch of skin, presented for her pleasure, from the top of his shoulders to his manhood, straining, hot and burning, beneath her attentions. She pulled him onto the bed, straddling him as she explored his body, alternating her hands and mouth until he was so close, he had to stop her.

"Please," he begged, stemming the tide of his climax as it built like an inferno inside him. He had promised her worship, and this queen, who asked for what she wanted and gave so much in return, deserved more than to have him lose control before he could give her all the pleasure he'd fantasized about. He pulled her gently up to his face and gazed into her desire-blown eyes, her full lips, and kissed her, tasting traces of himself on her tongue, which drove him just a little bit out of his mind.

"Reina," he said when they broke off. "Lay back. Let me take care of you,"

"I thought you were supposed to do what I wanted?" she whined but did as she was told, that acquiescence sending a shock of desire through him. Indya was not a person who easily acquiesced to anyone.

He took her foot, kissed the soft skin of her heel, the hard angle of her ankle bone and the firm swell of her calf. When he kissed the inner fold of her knee, she shivered and didn't stop as he made his way up her inner thigh, his hand tracing a similar path up her other leg. Much as she'd done, he worshipped her, the smell and taste of her intoxicating him. He looked at her from between the cage of her legs, saw her head thrown back with need, a litany of *oh-oh-oh* falling from her lips. When her fingers burrowed in his hair, he busied himself with pulling more of those delicious sounds from her, his own orgasm gathering again at the base of his spine.

She climbed and climbed, the fingers in his hair painful as he kissed and nibbled at her sweetness. And when she came, he was sure there would be patches on his head where hair might never grow back again from where she'd pulled him so hard. He wiped his mouth with the back of his hand, and gripped her thigh as he rummaged in his end table for a condom. He wanted to touch and taste every inch of her skin, but if he didn't have her now, he'd explode, stupefied and confused, and miss the chance to finish with her heat surrounding him.

Dazed and molten, she pulled him close for a kiss. She was all command, pressing his head down to kiss her breasts, which he did, pulling the flimsy material away from the full swells that were revealed, inch by inch. He latched onto her tight, brown peaks, licking and biting until she could barely breathe.

He held the condom in his grip, which she snatched away. She tore the package with her teeth, making a face.

"Ugh, spermicide," she complained as she pushed him back, tossing the offending foil to the side and carefully held the delicate thing in her hand. Santiago laughed at her—wild hair, face twisted in distaste, her bra dangling unhooked and uselessly around her rib cage—and felt something move in his chest. But that was subsumed by her warm hand sliding the condom over him. He hissed, which pulled a curling smile out of her. When Indya had rolled it on, she slapped his hip lightly, leaned back and said, "*Ven*, finish me."

His head was reeling. He was in her hands, a marionette with which she could play whatever games she wanted, and he was there, throwing himself at her feet. He gathered her up, kissing her long and thoroughly, his hands caressing the silk of her skin before he took himself in hand, lined himself up and pushed into her, all wet and hot, the pliant softness of her pulling him in until he was fully sheathed.

Her heel dug into his back where she'd hooked one leg around her waist, the other onto the arm that leveraged him, opening her up for him. His slow rocking turned into something hotter, more insistent. Their bodies knew this dance and took over. Sweat beaded along his back despite the air-conditioning blowing cool air over them. Her fingers scrambled to hold on to him, her eyes squeezed shut against the onslaught.

"Look at me, *reina*. I want to see your eyes when you come."

Her eyes fluttered open, as if she were seeing him for the first time, a feral lust turning the brown of her eyes to a deep black. Her face contorted as her climax shot through her, the endless flutter of her walls pulling him under with her. He chased behind her, endless and pulsing. He had never experienced such a thing in his life, as if his pleasure had been yanked from the most primal part of him, against his will and reason, and sent smashing headlong into hers.

With a last pair of shudders, they slowed to stillness, Santiago's breathing deepening while Indya wore a small smile that oozed satisfaction. He slowly pulled out, searching for his discarded shirt and wiping them both, wrapping up the used condom to dispense with later. Then he slid to the side of her, gathering her up to him, until he was on his back, and she lay, cocooned in his arms, her head snug on his chest.

They remained that way for some time, holding on to each other, their breathing slowing, becoming almost synchronized. Santiago wanted to ask her if she'd enjoyed herself, if this would change anything between them. He couldn't give this up, not now. Possibly not ever, and he needed her to know that. But just as he was ready to make his great confession, he heard a tiny snore from somewhere over his heart. He chuckled to himself, pulling a quilt from the bottom of the bed, covering them, and decided to settle in for a much-needed nap as well.

When he next woke, more than an hour had passed. He looked over at Indya, who was stirring as well. He thought of their coffee, left abandoned on the table, and smiled at that tiny domesticity. He envisioned the house he'd leased and dreamed of taking Indya there when the place was renovated, to prepare her a proper breakfast, and make love to her on a proper bed.

"Reina," he said when she blinked awake. "Did you sleep okay?"

She stretched, sinewy and catlike, before she settled back again. "Excellent nap." She turned on her side to face him. He reached out to sweep the hair away from her face.

"You know, I had a legitimate reason for coming here this morning," she said.

Santiago dragged a finger along Indya's shoulders and down her arm, which was conveniently tucked under her marvelous, full breasts. His desire stirred again, but she was talking and he didn't want her to think that's all he wanted from her.

"You mean, besides seducing me?"

Indya's eyes flared. "I did not seduce you."

Santiago chuckled. *"Y esa camisa? Y esos pantalones cortos?"*

Indya blushed so prettily, he wanted to kiss the top of each cheek. "My shirt and my shorts are perfectly decent, thank you very much."

"Bueno, if you say so. If you didn't come to seduce me, what did you come for? Surely, it was not for my accommodations."

"This is a beautiful boat." Indya frowned at him. "Don't talk it down. Boats are very sensitive. They'll make you pay for the insults."

"De acuerdo. Okay. I'm sorry, *Aragona*!"

Indya chuckled before going quiet, as if thinking. Finally, she said, "Sorry about the dinner this Saturday. I really wanted to be alone with you without the entire *familia* present."

Santiago nodded. "It was my mother's idea, after all. I'm not sorry to have the dinner, because I am very grateful to your family for giving me a chance—"

"Please, Santiago, you don't have to—"

"I know you don't expect it, but it's a good thing to do. I cannot depend on my parents to open doors for me. I have to make my own way and show gratitude to those who helped me."

"Yes, it's true of course." Indya leaned up on her elbow, resting her head on her hand. "They opened the door for you, but you walked through and did your job. That's all on you."

He thought briefly about his father, who gave him so little credit for his struggles. He pushed him out of his thoughts. He did not want to admit his presence in such a wonderful moment between him and Indya.

"You're right. I can't thank them for everything." He nuzzled her neck and was gratified to feel the shiver that ran over her skin. "There's also you."

"Santiago." She shifted, pressing him away. "It's the same principle. I read your résumé and you were a good match. Nothing more, nothing less. Your talents just happened to align to my needs. You do your job, and that speaks for itself."

"Perhaps, but you gave me a chance and that means something to me and my family," he pressed on, a strange disappointment welling up in him. He wanted something more from her. Working with her was special, and he did not want it reduced to a cold transaction.

"Yes, but you're doing what you were hired to do. There is no need for gratitude." Indya watched his face, and he, who was unable to hide anything, allowed her to read his expression.

"Is that how you see what I do? As a job, and no more?" Santiago felt like he was talking to his father and he didn't like the feeling at all.

"I didn't say that," Indya said. "I meant it as a compliment. You always do what you have to do."

"It's a strange compliment," Santiago said and rolled away from her to the edge of the bed, the taste of Indya turning bitter on his tongue. "You make it sound like anyone can do my job."

"Not anyone, no." Indya sat up. "I'm just saying, if someone else with your résumé had shown up, I would have hired them. You have a skill set and you've done a good job with that skill set. You don't have to thank anyone for that." Indya frowned as she spoke. "Why do I get the feeling like I'm saying something you don't like?"

Santiago rubbed his face. How could he describe what he was feeling right now, that he wasn't talking to his Indya, the one who could be so sweet and affirming, but a version of Indya who sounded too much like his father?

"You sound like you're talking to an employee, not to me."

"You are my employee," Indya said, confusion written across her face.

"Not in bed, I'm not."

"I... I know this." Indya radiated shock. "It wasn't my intention to slip into business mode, but it is a part of who I am and what I do." She swung her legs out of bed, standing stark naked in front of him. "When you have sex with someone, you have sex with every part of them. You don't get to pick and choose which parts you like and which parts you don't. If you talk about work, that's what you get."

Now it was Santiago's turn to be confused. "That's not what I meant to say."

Indya searched the room for her discarded clothing, dressing quickly. "It may not be what you meant to say, but it's what came out of your mouth."

Santiago watched her get dressed and pulled on his own sweatpants. "Why are you leaving?"

"Why?" Indya huffed out. "I already had to deal with an ex-husband who thought the only parts of me that were worth anything were the ones he considered feminine. Everything else should be repressed or ignored. I'm not in the mood for a repeat."

"I'm not picking and choosing," Santiago said, frustration pushing each word out of him. "But maybe Work Indya can stay out of our bed, *si*? What do you think?"

"I'll put in a request, and get back to you in five to ten business days." Indya slid the door of his room open, a particularly strong wave nearly knocking her sideways. Santiago reached for her to keep her from falling, but she sidestepped him, scooping up her bag as she did and was out the door before the boat returned to its easy rocking.

Chapter Eighteen

Indya

Indya spent the next few days sidestepping Santiago again, which wasn't difficult to do because this time she sensed he was doing the same. She fell into her tried-and-true coping mechanism for emotional pain—she got busy, which kept her from dwelling on him or the path they'd traveled that brought them to say those words to each other. Things were going so well that, even now, she was still too stunned to fully appreciate the depth of her disappointment.

Here she had believed that he'd be different from Trent, and in most ways, he was. But on this issue, the one that mattered so much, he was the same as her ex, and that realization hurt. She'd held Santiago to a much higher standard because his behavior until then had made her believe he was worthy of that esteem. Now she was horrified at how badly she'd miscalculated.

But maybe Work Indya can stay out of our bed.

When had Indya ever treated him as less than a person she was incredibly attracted to? It was like déjà vu from the early days of her marriage, from a time of her life she thought she'd worked through. Clearly, that was not the case.

A clatter of footsteps and voices filled the hallway outside her office. Before Indya could make it to her feet, Nyla and Rayne were in her doorway, shrieks and laughter shrinking her office to the size of a dime. Rayne, who was a petite, olive-tinted, half-Greek, half-Colombian woman with curly black hair and more mouth than height stood next to Nyla, a Dominican woman with a tall, graceful frame, her body lean from a lifetime of swimming and deep-sea diving, and skin so dark and radiant, it made Indya mourn her neglected skin-care routine.

"What—" Indya choked out when Rayne rounded the desk and slung her arms around her neck, squeezing her with unexpected strength. "What are you doing here?"

"What do you mean, what are we doing here?" Rayne released her stranglehold on Indya while her voice traveled down the hallway. "We warned you that we were kidnapping you today. Remember? Lunch? Shopping? The works?"

Indya groaned. They had, and up until a few days ago, it had been a treat she'd been looking forward to. Then Santiago happened and she'd lost track of what day of the week it was.

"I hate that I dragged you guys out here, but something came up and I—"

"All I hear is noise," Nyla interrupted. "Come on. Shut down that computer. It's time to eat."

Indya almost protested, but after the way she'd been feeling, she knew she was useless for work. If she sat in that office, she'd get nothing done except overthink every word she'd exchanged with Santiago. Each one had been unexpected, and had hurt. She could either dwell on the memory or do as she'd promised and spend the afternoon with her besties.

She shut down her computer with a flair and grabbed her keys. "You're right, I've been too caught up with things I shouldn't be lately." Rayne clapped with excitement, her tiny crop top above a pair of cream-colored joggers a little too short for the maneuver, while Nyla beamed, her strapless, bright yellow jumper molding prettily to her gorgeously long body.

Indya followed her ladies out of the office, pausing to speak to Jade. "I'll be out for about a couple of hours. Can you hold the fort?"

"'Can I hold the fort?' she asks. Please, Indya, I *am* the fort." She shooed her away with both hands. "Get on out of here. I'll take care of Gia when she comes back from school. Santiago's here, too. We got this."

"Santiago?" Rayne asked, always sniffing around like a damned shark in bloody waters.

"He's the new facilities manager I was telling you about."

Indya made a show of looking at her watch, a vintage Piaget Dancer she'd picked up at auction. "It's only twelve thirty. I'll be back long before she's released."

"I hope not," Jade retorted, turning to Rayne and Nyla. "Please keep her out. She needs to interact with people who are not her customers or her employees."

Indya's first thought was that Santiago wasn't just her employee, but that did not exactly contradict Jade's assessment.

"Yes, ma'am!" Rayne exclaimed while Nyla quietly fist-bumped Jade, who she'd dated for a short period in high school and was now good friends with. "We'll take her down to Miami Beach and feed her mimosas under the sun before dropping her off on your front curb sometime tomorrow afternoon."

"Don't do that," Indya complained, pointing at the clock. "I'll be back in one hour."

Jade gave Indya a *Bitch, you thought* look before waving them off. "Have a good long lunch, ladies."

Indya was swept out of the office by two opposite but equally intractable forces who, even if she wanted to, refused to let her back out. But today, she wanted to be carried away by these two, her very best friends since she could remember. Self-righteousness and disappointment were giving way to melancholy and regret. She needed to get away from the constant nagging of those feelings, and being with her friends was the best way to do that.

As they moved toward the lobby, Rayne stopped in her tracks, eyes glued to the pool area just past another set of sliding glass doors. Indya followed her gaze and felt her heart squeeze at the sight of Santiago, brow furrowed in concentration as he tapped away at his iPad.

"And who, pray tell, is that fine specimen of a man?" Rayne asked, not-so-secretly checking him out.

Irritation surged through Indya. Rayne was not allowed to ogle Santiago that way. "That is my new facilities manager and you are strictly forbidden to go anywhere near him, man-eater."

Rayne's face twisted into an expression of comical disappointment, complete with large doe eyes, pouty lips and a foot stamp for effect. "But why not? He's such a dish."

"Because he is my employee and he has to remain my employee," Indya snapped. At Nyla and Rayne's surprised expressions, she took it down an emotional notch. "All I need is for you to dazzle him with your ridiculous sex appeal, make him fall in love with you and then crush his heart for me to be out of an excellent facilities manager."

Rayne put a hand over her heart in mock offense. "I would never!"

"Yeah, you would, *mala*," Nyla snorted, rolling her eyes at her. "You're a menace."

Indya was relieved that she'd thrown them off her trail. Santiago looked up at that moment and made instant eye contact with Indya through the glass. His gaze seemed to speak volumes, and their message was reserved only for Indya. He followed up with a chin nod before returning to work.

"Is that the only reason he needs to remain your employee?" Nyla asked, crossing her arms, scanning Indya up and down. "Or maybe he's the reason you forgot we were having lunch."

Indya winced. Nyla's words hit too close to home. "If y'all don't want me to cancel this lunch date, you better get yourselves together. Yes, please and thank you," Indya retorted, turning away from Santiago and nearly running out of the front lobby doors to the half-circle drop-off. She made a beeline to her convertible, but Nyla's long legs caught up to her. A gentle hand on her arm guided her toward a Jeep Wrangler instead.

"Uh-uh, sis, you're not driving. I'm not in the mood to fold my body into your little Matchbox car."

"Plus, we prefer you completely dependent on us," Rayne huffed out breathlessly when she caught up to their long-legged strides. Rayne was a tiny little thing, but she made up for her stature with a personality the size of Soledad Bay. "We are having an executive lunch today, whether you like it or not."

"But—" Indya began but was cut off by Nyla using her

fob to unlock the doors—if you could call them doors—of her Jeep. She really was being kidnapped by these two capricious women.

Rayne giggled, letting Indya have the front seat to accommodate her long legs while she happily took the back. With the top down, the leather seats had grown warm and baby soft. Indya shifted to help dissipate the heat against her thighs. Nyla started the Jeep, its motor purring to life, and pulled out of the parking lot, taking them in the direction of a wonderful '50s vintage-style diner right on the plaza that served breakfast and brunch all day and well into the night. How many times had Indya, Nyla and Rayne found themselves in that diner after a night of partying, sharing monster-sized platters of pancakes, French toast, eggs, bacon, sausages and all the fixings, before heading home to sleep off the excessive indulgence? Indya's life was tied up in every brick and slab of concrete in this town, from her physical family to her hotel family, her friendship circle, the birth of Indya's baby girl and the total combustion of her life with her ex. None of these things could be decoupled from the other and they made Indya who she was.

Yet somehow, she'd left it all when her marriage to Trent had fallen part. She may have come back because of her unwavering sense of duty to her parents. But she would stay because this would forever be her home.

They pulled into the diner, which had open-air seating looking out on the white sand and blue waves of the bay.

Once settled in at their table, they studied the already-familiar menu and chose their usual—salmon-and-vegetable omelet for Nyla, fish and chips for Rayne and a grilled red snapper for Indya. She glowered at her friends when three mimosas appeared at the table.

"I'm on the clock," Indya complained.

"No, you're not. There is no clock. The clock is dead," Rayne said with dramatic flair.

"I can't believe you killed off the clock," Nyla deadpanned, a small smile playing at the edge of her lips. Nyla had been so vivacious when they were younger. Between the three of them, she had been able to produce enough talk and noise to drown out everyone around them. But after spending two years in Miami, where she went to get her master's degree, she'd come back more subdued, and only lately seemed to be recovering her old ways again.

Indya took a sip of the mimosa, the fizzy sweetness tickling her nose. "Hmm, I needed that."

"Nothing that booze and fruit juice can't overcome," Rayne said cheerfully as she downed her mimosa in one gulp.

Nyla looked at her in open shock. "Did you even taste it?"

Rayne feigned giving the answer some thought. "You're right. I didn't. Guess I'm going to need another one."

Nyla pushed her untouched glass toward her. "It's a good thing for you that I'm driving."

"Your service," Rayne said as she picked up the glass by its delicate stem, "is greatly appreciated. So." Rayne turned her attention to Indya, which meant she might as well be under one of Nyla's microscopes. "Tell us all about this Santiago. Who is he? Where is he from? Is he single? Married? Does he want to be?"

"Rayne!" Nyla said while Indya shook her head. "She's just curious, that's all."

"Yeah, curious. Let's go with that." Rayne smiled, dimples creasing her cheeks, announcing all the mischief she was conceiving of at that moment. Indya really wished the food would come so Rayne could put something in her mouth to shut her up. Santiago was the last person she wanted to talk about.

Her face must have said it all because Rayne narrowed her eyes at her. "You really don't like that, do you?"

"Like what?" Indya asked, rearranging her silverware.

"The idea of me flirting with that man. It bothers you." She glanced at Nyla as if asking for her backup, which made Indya internally groan. She did not need her besties trying to read her that deeply.

"No, it doesn't bother me. I just want him to stick around."

Nyla tilted her head, her fingertips tapping at her chin. "I'm with Rayne on this one. Why are you being so weirdly possessive?"

"I'm not being weirdly possessive." Indya chugged at her water until there were only ice cubes at the bottom of her glass. She set it down, desperate to find a way to distract these two. "Carlos quitting the way he did was really traumatizing. I don't want a repeat of that experience."

The wind whipped through Nyla and Rayne's hair as they stared at her. She imagined this was what it must be like to be a lobster in boiling water.

Nyla sat up, tilted her head in the opposite direction, letting her mouth slowly fall open.

"You didn't."

Indya looked from Nyla to Rayne, whose face split into a terrifying grin.

"You...didn't," Rayne repeated, drawing out the words slowly as her voice dropped at least two octaves.

Indya was going to commit a crime. How did her friends always do this? She held their stares of shock for several more beats before she threw up her hands in defeat. "Okay. I did."

Nyla's whoop overshadowed Rayne's gasp, which, fair enough, was exactly the reaction Indya expected, but anyone who knew Nyla and Rayne in a casual context would anticipate the opposite, given their personalities. But Rayne was the quiet one in shock, while Nyla was as loud as a frat boy at a football game. The waitress finally appeared with their food, but it was too little, too late. Her friends were on her like white on rice.

"Ooh," Rayne said, jabbing a knife in her direction. "No wonder she's so possessive!" Rayne popped a piece of broccoli into her mouth, laughing at the face Indya gave her. "I can't believe you hit it! Didn't even wait for the man to finish out his probationary period." Rayne leaned toward Indya. "Such a boss bitch move."

"He was way out of his probationary period," Indya protested.

"Talking about bosses," Nyla interjected, bypassing Indya's clarification completely. "What's your status? Are you guys dating now? Is it a situationship? Friends with benefits?"

"What was he like?" Rayne asked, waggling her eyebrows.

"No comment, Rayne," Indya retorted before describing all the events leading up to Santiago becoming her employee and how they became lovers for only a few hours before their argument. Nyla's eyes seemed to grow wider and wider with each word Indya spoke, while Rayne was beside herself with glee.

"Your mom is always doing the most," Nyla said.

"Right?" Indya answered, relieved that her friend understood her frustration with Mami. "She keeps getting involved and she won't listen when I tell her that I have everything under control. It's so damned frustrating. His mother's no better. She planned a whole dinner to thank my family, and let us know barely a few days before."

"Yes, but the Mamis didn't tell you to bed the man, though, did they? That was your innovation," Rayne interjected.

"He sounds nice, I mean, besides the whole blowup." Nyla added, pointedly ignoring Rayne's comment.

"It was surprising, coming from him," Indya said slowly. She flagged the waitress down. Another round of mimosas was definitely in order. "He was always so chill and accepting."

Rayne nodded at this. "Do you like him?"

"Obviously I do or I wouldn't be telling you guys about him," Indya said, knowing that she sounded out of temper but it was hard for her to be otherwise because she was, in fact, sorely out of temper.

"So, go talk to him, cranky-pants," Rayne concluded.

Nyla's eyes were on Indya the whole time, examining her the way she might one of the many turtle nests she'd taken under her protection. "I agree. Why don't you just talk it out with him? Let him know why you're upset at him, and what he can do to fix it."

Indya squeezed her eyes shut. "I am not prepared to compromise on who I am. I already tried to twist myself into shape for one man. I won't do that for another."

"I can see how something like that can trigger you and remind you of your ex. But before you count him out, make sure he did what you say he did. The way you describe him, it sounds out of character for him, unless he was very clever about hiding his chauvinistic ways," Rayne said, sounding uncharacteristically serious.

"Yeah, you haven't dated in a long time, Indya. Make sure you're not coming from a place of fear of getting hurt,"

Nyla added, finishing off the remainder of her plate while Indya was still sitting on two mimosas and half of a red snapper.

"You seemed happier lately, you know?" Rayne concluded.

She had been, and she hated how dependent that had been on Santiago. "What if he turns out to be Trent 2.0?" Indya asked at length.

Nyla tapped the corners of her lips with a napkin. "Then we'll help you hide the body."

Rayne grinned, lifting her empty mimosa glass.

"That's not helpful at all," Indya scowled.

Nyla put a hand over her friend's. "Neither is being miserable. Talk to him. Put it to rest either way, once and for all."

"Yeah, you've never been afraid of anything. Don't start now." Rayne was sipping a glass of water, no doubt trying to dilute all the mimosas she'd drunk.

They didn't speak about it again as the conversation moved on to their lives, but Indya kept hearing the echo of Santiago's words at the back of her mind, a slow drip of memory whittling away at her resolve. Her friends were wrong. Indya was afraid of a lot of things—of being a bad daughter, a careless mother, an incompetent business owner, of not being enough or maybe being too much for any man to want her.

Her cell phone vibrated in her purse, and without thinking, she picked it up. "Indya Linares."

"Indya," came Trent's voice.

Speak of the literal devil.

Nyla and Rayne paused in their conversation. Their Trent-radar had been triggered and they did a bad job of pretending not to listen to Indya's conversation.

"Hi," she said, forcing cheer into her voice. "How's it going?"

"Good, good," he said. "I was calling about Gia's presentation."

"Yes, she's very excited."

"Yeah, she even invited the grandparents." He said it as if Gia was asking for a silly indulgence, and that set Indya on edge. The only other person who could set her off this quickly into a conversation was her mother.

"It's important to her," Indya said, instantly defensive.

"Yeah, she seems to enjoy it. I was calling to let you know that I'm gone next week and won't be able to make it back in time for her presentation."

"Flying out for work?" Indya said conversationally. Nyla and Rayne were speaking in low voices, every now and again glancing at Indya.

"No," he answered. Indya could imagine him scratching unconsciously at his jawline as he thought about what to say next. "I'm out on the boat with some of the guys. We're heading down to South Florida and I won't be back in time."

Indya rubbed her temple, fearing the headache that wanted to take root. "She's been working on this all semester. Can't you postpone your trip, even for a few days?"

"It's just a science project, Indya! I'll make it up to her when I get back."

"It's not just a science project. This matters to her."

"It matters to her now, but it won't define the rest of her life. I'm there for all of her little meetings and projects. I think I can sit this one out."

Indya's voice dropped low. "'Little meetings and projects'?" Her friends, noting the change in her tone, turned to watch her. "Everything Gia's done helps to build her college résumé and it offends me on Gia's behalf that you belittle the things that mean so much to her."

"You would be offended. I don't think it's as important to Gia as it is to you."

"What the hell does that mean?" Indya wanted to shout, but even out on the terrace where the sea breeze carried away the bluntness of her words, she was mindful of who was listening to her.

"Because that's how you are, Indya. You make such a big deal out of things that don't matter that she ends up doing the same thing. If she keeps it up, she's going to end up alone, too."

"I'm not alone," Indya snapped. "And I'd rather let Gia decide if something is important or not. Have a good fishing trip."

She clicked off the phone, her fury so palpable, even her friends didn't dare to tease her. Sometimes Trent could be such a kind, loving father. But there was a selfish streak in him, one that didn't hesitate to toss the responsibility for his decisions onto someone else if it meant that, in the end, he got what he wanted out of the situation.

"Did he just say that Gia was going to end up alone like you? Because she's excited about something that he doesn't care about?" Nayla asked.

"He should ask himself why he's still single, then, seeing as he doesn't care and still isn't coupled up," Rayne ground out.

Indya wanted to slam her phone against the ground. Trent knew how to sniff out her greatest insecurities and press on them like a fresh bruise. "Imagine deciding that something that matters to his daughter isn't important because he says so." She thought about Santiago's words, when Indya had given him a tour of his work area, and how they came to her now. "Our job as parents is to accept them for who they are and support their choices."

"Facts," Nyla said, offering her glass for Indya to clink against, which she did.

"Some people will never understand that," Rayne added.

"Santiago does," Indya said quietly. "He is taking all the steps to get his daughter to be here with him. And everything so far has been about respecting her choices and allowing her to be her own person in every way. And he's the same way with his younger sister."

Nyla exchanged a look with Rayne before saying, "Forget Trent. You can't protect him from the consequences of his own bad decisions."

"But Santiago is right there," Rayne added.

"I don't want to be wrong," Indya said, pain lancing through her at the thought. "Not this time."

"I don't want you to be wrong, either. But even if you are, you will get back up, dust yourself off and keep on keeping on. You're good at that," Nyla said, a shadow crossing her face. She looked quickly away, but Indya had seen it.

Indya took her hand. "Some day, you're going to tell me why you get sad when I say certain things."

"Someday," Nyla retorted. "But not today. Right now, it's about you."

Indya let it go. They were right about everything, of course. But that didn't keep Indya away from her mountain of doubts. She had to speak to Santiago, but she had to get right with her insecurities before she risked her heart one last time.

Chapter Nineteen

Santiago

It had been a very long time since Santiago set a table in his parents' house. Anxiety burned a hole through his stomach at the prospect of seeing Indya again. In addition, dinner with his father and a family with whom he was not personally familiar, outside of Indya, had him grinding his teeth in an effort to keep his stress level under control.

Of course he was grateful to the Linares family for giving him a chance at the hotel. They'd taken a leap of faith and he'd like to think it had worked out. But he also believed that he was competent in his own right and had a lot to offer. Indya, of all people, reducing what he did to "skill sets" and " résumés" when he knew that what he put into his work was so much more than was required, annihilated him. It was the most hurtful thing she could have said, and what made it more terrible was that she'd done so unconsciously, revealing a fundamental aspect of her thinking without intending to do so.

That didn't stop him from missing her.

Mamá bustled around him, wearing an apron over one

of her favorite Sunday church outfits—a cream-colored sleeveless dress with large roses printed across the cool fabric. She reached out to one of the glasses he had just set down. "Not so close to the silverware. They might knock it over when they are serving themselves."

"I don't think they are so out of practice with eating with silverware, Mamá," Santiago complained.

She sighed. "I know. I just want everything to be perfect."

"Everything *is* perfect. You specialize in perfect and always do everything just right."

Mamá patted his cheek. "You are a good boy, you know that? A very good boy."

"It feels like you are praising a dog," Santiago teased. "Should I bark and roll over?"

She slapped him on the shoulder. "*Tonto.* Don't twist compliments around to put yourself down. Now go bring the bread basket from the kitchen like a good boy."

"Woof," he joked, escaping her flying hand to head toward the kitchen and fulfill her request. Miriam and his father were still upstairs, getting ready, an observation that made Santiago more anxious. Miriam got so much more leniency than he did, which was understandable, given that she was younger. But it sometimes stressed him out that his father only allowed himself to show affection for his daughter while he seemed to have nothing but criticism for his son. Even a kind word would be enough for Santiago, but that had never been his father's way, and it didn't look like he would be changing anytime soon.

Santiago's mother would not be satisfied with anything less than perfection from a dinner she was hosting. She was a proud woman who possessed values and customs she would never betray. One of those was the principal of hospitality, and as Santiago looked out across the dining room table, he saw how those values had manifested in the beautifully set table, the smell of *sancocho*, freshly made *arepas*, *chachapas* stuffed with creamed corn and pork, *patacones* paired with avocados, and *pabellon* with *asado negro*. It was a feast that she and Miriam had been preparing for two days. While the stated purpose was to show gratitude, it also served to impress.

Miriam was fluttery and excited when she came downstairs to help her mother set out the last items on the table.

"Gia will be here soon," Santiago said, noting how Miriam stopped in her tracks at the mention of her best friend.

"I know!" she squealed. "I promised her I'd let her try some of my special homemade *tequeños*, not the ones we sell at the shop. I just hope she likes them."

Santiago patted his sister on the shoulder. "Don't worry, *chiquita*, she will love it just because you made it."

"I hope so." She blushed.

"What is it with my favorite ladies being so insecure all of a sudden?" He counted Indya in this group, even though she hid her own demons well.

Miriam opened her mouth to speak, but the doorbell cut them off. Mamá, who seemed to be running a mile a minute, slowed down, inhaling deeply. "They're here."

Miriam let out a shout of joy and raced to the front door before anyone could react.

"You would think they haven't seen each other in years," Mamá said.

"A day is like a year in teenage time," Santiago said as Miriam pulled the door open.

"Gia!" she shouted. Gia, for her part, threw an arm around Miriam's shoulder and smothered a kiss into her hair.

"Guess what? I brought dessert!"

"Oooh, what did you make?"

"Carrot cake with two inches of cream cheese frosting," Gia said gleefully. "My bestie's favorite."

"I can't wait to try it." Miriam glowed and Santiago found it endearing that his sister was so enchanted by the thought of cake.

Santiago waved at the two girls who didn't care if anyone else was around them. "Hello, Gia."

Gia snapped her attention away from Miriam and grinned, giving him a far-too-knowing look. "Helllloooooo, Santiago."

Santiago wasn't sure what to make of her greeting, but Indya's voice rooted him right back on planet earth.

"Hello, Santiago," Indya said with a formality that sounded like nails scraping down a chalkboard.

Santiago looked past them to watch Indya taking in the foyer and the interior of the house before settling her gaze on him. She was irresistible in a pair of black jeans, heeled sandals and a white button-down tied off at the bottom instead of tucked in. She had left one button undone at the top and he could just catch the swell of her breasts. When he looked up at Indya again, her eyes flitted away, as if she hadn't been watching him watch her.

"*Hola*, Indya," he answered.

"We dragged her with us. She almost didn't come," Gia said, oblivious to the tension that crackled in the air. Indya stood stiffly behind the two girls, eyes firmly fixed on them.

"I wasn't feeling well," Indya offered by way of explanation.

Santiago tried for levity. "Clearly, us *viejos* do not matter as much as your dessert."

"Yes, you do! I don't discriminate against the elderly," Gia answered.

"Gia," Indya scolded. Gia's smug expression did not entirely disappear, but she was more composed when she greeted Santiago's mother. *"Hola, señora."*

"Tan educada," Mamá said, approvingly. Mamá loved good manners. To Mamá, they were the highest courtesy a person could aspire to, even if Gia used them inconsistently.

Gia and Miriam chattered, uninterested in anything beyond what basic courtesy demanded. Santiago's mother stepped aside, dodging the young ladies, who were caught up in their own world as they made their way to the kitchen.

"Magdalena, thank you for inviting us," Oriana said. She handed Mamá a large aluminum tray.

"What is it?" Mamá asked.

Oriana smiled blissfully. "My granddaughter isn't the only one who can bake. It's a tres leches cake. I made it with the coconut cream that you like so much."

Mamá beamed. Santiago was sure that if she could hug the cake without ruining it, she would. "I can't promise I won't eat it all myself."

"As you should," Fermín, her husband and Indya's father, said. He was tall, like Indya, with the same dark skin and dark hair, his curls crisp and tighter than Indya's and Gia's. He walked slowly with the help of a cane because of a stroke he'd had recently, according to what Indya had told him about her parents.

Mamá, Oriana and Indya moved toward the kitchen, Indya resolutely ignoring Santiago before leaving him with her father. She looked just as good from the back as from the front. He tore his gaze away before he embarrassed himself by getting caught staring.

Fermín held a basket full of wine, cheeses, cold cuts, marmalades and crackers. "You must be Santiago. Gia and Miriam talk about you all the time. Here." He handed the basket to Santiago. "These are treats for later, once you have gotten rid of your visitors. Now, where is your grouchy father?"

"I'm not grouchy," came Papá's voice from behind Santiago. "I'm a serious man, as you should be."

"Ronaldo! Serious is for these young people," Fermín said, giving Papá a half hug, half clap on the shoulder. "The older you get, the sillier you should be. *Tanto*, nobody takes us seriously as it is."

"Es verdad." Papá turned to Santiago. "This is our prodigal son, Santiago. Have you met him yet?"

"We have only now been introduced," Fermín said formally, nodding at Santiago again. "A fine-looking young man. Are you as grouchy as your father?"

Santiago wasn't sure how to answer that, since in either case, he would have to acknowledge that his father was, in fact, a grouch. But Papá saved him from walking into that minefield.

"No, he lives more in the moment," his father said, clapping the other gentleman on the back.

His father's criticism stung. Not even for the sake of present company, could he restrain himself.

"That's not true," Santiago could not help but retort.

"Of course," his father said, almost perfunctorily before turning to Fermín. "Come inside, or will we have dinner in the foyer?"

Fermín gave a deep belly laugh. "What did I tell you, Santiago? A grouchy old man."

Santiago let the comment slide with the pretense of helping his mother.

When they were seated, Mamá passed the empanadas around the table, making sure the guests had first pick of the homemade treats. Everyone was arranged according to his mother's plan. Papá sat across from Fermín, while Mamá sat across from Oriana. That left Santiago next to Indya because Gia and Miriam had insisted on sitting next to each other.

This night would continue to toy with him.

"You have sooooo much gossip to share because it's been two long hours since you last spoke to each other," Indya teased.

"A lot can happen in two hours, Mom," Gia retorted, giving her mother a winning smile.

Santiago shored up his public face and said, "That smile promises only mischief."

"Every time," Indya answered, her eyes lingering a moment longer than necessary on Santiago before she returned her attention to the black beans, white rice and shredded beef on her plate. Dinner was going to be torture, though there was nothing but compliments for the meal. She savored a piece of *maduro*, lingering as she chewed. Santiago tried not to be mesmerized by the way she enjoyed her food, tasting each bite.

She cleared her throat and said, "Your mother is an incredible cook."

Santiago started. She hadn't said anything directly to him since she arrived. "Thank you. I think she's a wonderful cook, too, but I am biased."

"You're allowed to be." Indya leaned in close to him, and the smell of her fragrance—citrusy and sweet, which he imagined would taste wonderful on his tongue—stimulated all his barely repressed fantasies.

"I'll let you in on a secret," she said, careful not to be heard by anyone around them. "My mother only knows how to make three things well: white rice, waffles and that tres leches cake right there. I grew up eating in the hotel restaurant."

Santiago was surprised, not by her confession, but that she would enter into such an unexpected intimacy with him at all, especially after days of silence. He spoke carefully. "She must have worked a lot when you were young."

"They both did," Indya said, her expression growing wistful as she watched her parents laughing with Santiago's. "I complain about them, and if I am honest, they give me a lot of reasons to do so. But they have always done the very best they can for me. They worked, but they always made sure I was safe and well taken care of." She glanced down at her lap. "I think you are that kind of parent for Lisbet."

His heart swelled to twice its size. His daughter was everything to him, the reason for every decision he made. "Thank you."

Indya seemed to want to say more, but Mamá interjected, having overheard parts of their conversation while still engaged in her own—her own special superpower. "I cannot wait to see her again. It was so long ago when we last saw her, when we went to Venezuela on vacation, right? How long ago was that, Ronaldo?"

"Three years," Papá said. "Three long years since we have seen our only granddaughter." He glanced over at Fermín. "You don't know what it means to have your grandchild so far away from you. It is a torture."

Santiago's stomach sank. He knew that tone of voice. It was like he held his separation from his granddaughter against Santiago.

He couldn't keep from responding, though he knew better than to engage his father. "It's torture for me, too, Papá."

"Is it? Because you were never very good at doing what

you were told. You always chose your own path and look how it turned out."

"Ronaldo," Mamá said gently, but Santiago's father clearly had so much to say and relished having an audience to say it to.

"I told him to close up that business, take the money and open something similar in the US. At least here, if you work hard, you can go far. But he didn't listen to his family, who cares for him and wants his best. He followed his friend instead, and then his friend turned around and stole everything. Forced him to come here with nothing and to leave his girlfriend and daughter behind."

"Ex-girlfriend," Santiago corrected. The silence in the dining room was deafening. Even Miriam and Gia, who largely didn't care about anything that didn't directly impact them, were quiet and listening. Miriam with shame and Gia with shock.

"Maybe she would still be with you if you hadn't been so stubborn and left when you were supposed to, instead of staying behind just to lose everything."

Indya's expression darkened, but she continued to watch and absorb. It was the same look she adopted when she was handling a difficult customer.

"Papá," Santiago said firmly, keeping a tight rein on his anger out of respect for the Linares, for Indya, who he couldn't read at the moment. "I know that I messed up. Maybe the Linares are not interested in hearing that story."

"Yes, Ronaldo. I don't think this is something for us to hear, is it?" Fermín said, trying to calm his friend down.

"He ended up in the US anyway," his father continued, ignoring them, his cheeks growing red with anger. "With a daughter he doesn't live with and none of the money he could have made if he had sold the business when we told him to."

Santiago felt something fundamental snap inside of him. "You can accuse me of failing as a business owner, even as a son," Santiago said, pushing his plate away. "But you are not allowed to include Lisbet in my list of failures. She is the best thing that I ever created and I will not let you use her in any way against me."

His father slammed his hand down on the table. "Yes, but where is she? I have a granddaughter I haven't seen in years! If you had done things properly, she would be living a good life here with her family, and not lost in a country that is falling apart." Now he was pointing his finger at Santiago, cheeks flushed an ugly red through his beard. "I would be able to know the only grandchild I will ever have."

"Hello?" Miriam waved from her seat. "What about m—" But she was cut off by Gia, who shoved her elbow into her side.

"Mr. Pereira." Indya's voice cut across the dining room with a quiet force that silenced even his father. She spoke each word in eloquent, perfect Spanish. "I think what you are saying is unfair."

Indya hadn't raised her voice, and yet her words forced a silence to crash down over the room. She set her napkin next to her dish with deliberate measure. "People disappoint each other all the time. If my parents wanted to, they could air out a long list of all the ways I made both my life and theirs difficult."

"We would never," Fermín said firmly, and for the first time, Santiago saw real anger on the good-natured man's face.

"Nor can I speak to Santiago's past, which is not our business to know unless he shares it with us." The look she gave his father was pointed, the implication of her judgment incontrovertible. "But I do know Santiago in two important capacities, as a coworker and as a friend."

Santiago filled in *employee* in his mind, but the word felt wrong, because she had never treated him as just an employee. Suddenly, his words of that morning burned shamefully in his memory.

"And I can assure you," she continued, "in the short time I've known him, I consider him to be perhaps one of the best managers, maintenance or otherwise, who has ever worked in our hotel. He is honest, decent and kind with those around him. His coworkers respect him, and he impresses everyone he meets. He constantly talks about his daughter because everything he does is for her." She looked at him, offering him a small smile. "He's more than just an employee to me. He is sincerely one of the best people I've ever known."

Santiago was slayed by her words. They were as unexpected as they were touching, and he felt so unworthy of them, because he had spoken so unkindly to her the last time they were together.

"So are you," he said quietly.

She nodded and he knew they would have another conversation, away from present company. She turned back to Papá, who was shocked into incoherence.

"I hope you will learn to see your son for the wonderful person that he is."

Papá was not the only one caught by surprise. Mamá gazed at Indya with open admiration, her large, dark eyes glassy with tears. Oriana nodded quietly, as if this had always been her expectation and her daughter had silently fulfilled it. Fermín sat up straighter, satisfaction radiating from him at her words. Gia had a very proud expression—

teenagers of this generation really did enjoy a good callout, and Indya had done just that on his behalf.

His father downed a sip of wine before clearing his throat. "Well, that's—"

"You are right, Indya. He is a good man and we are very proud of him," his mother interjected, putting a firm hand over her husband's, squeezing hard to silence him. It threw Santiago even more off balance than Indya's defense of him. Not once, in all the years he'd been alive, had his mother contradicted his father in public. No matter what the conversation was behind closed doors, his parents believed in presenting a unified front to the world. If his mother had something contrary to say about a matter his father had decided on, she always did it in private. This was a gentle, but firm, rebuke and his father, no doubt overcome by the shock of it as well, slumped back in his chair, gazing at his wife with an expression at once surprised and chastened.

"More wine?" his mother asked, effectively ending the discussion. When all the glasses were filled, Indya glanced over at Santiago and raised her glass to him in silent toast. Santiago was more aware than ever of Indya and her proximity to him. Miriam and Gia twittered excitedly from their seats, no doubt dissecting the events of the last hour. Santiago, for once, pretended not to see the phone clearly hidden on Miriam's lap and left the girls to their own devices. What was the point of preaching about good manners when his father still found it so easy to throw them aside and mortify everyone with his words?

He leaned to the side, gently catching Indya's attention. *"Gracias,"* he said and meant it with his entire being. No one, outside of his mother, had ever stood up for him in front of his father. Miriam was too young and her voice was often drowned out or dismissed, despite how much his father doted on her.

"You didn't have to do that," he continued, keeping his words low to not draw the attention of his mother, who had the super hearing of a hunting dog.

"Yeah, I actually did. You deserve so much better than to get dragged by your own father." Indya's smile became brittle, the first time she'd shown any vulnerability this evening. "I happen to think you're rather wonderful and I hate that we argued the way we did."

Santiago swallowed hard. "If you keep this up, I might kiss you in front of everyone."

Indya's smile became mischievous. "Save it for when we are alone, *sí*? We've had more than enough excitement for one night."

He wanted to tell her that he had many, many kisses saved up for when they were alone, but Oriana asked Indya a question that drew her into a conversation with his Mamá. Papá still possessed a chastened air, but Fermín was discussing something soccer related, which slowly absorbed his attention. It would be a long time before Santiago would be able to tolerate a conversation with him.

The remainder of the night passed in a fog. They cut into Oriana's tres leches—Miriam was not interested in sharing Gia's cake—the coconut cream icing melting in Santiago's mouth. Oriana's cake had a sureness that came from long years of practice, even if it was one of the few things she knew how to make.

"It's delicious, *señora*," Santiago said.

Oriana smiled. "Thank you. It's just something I like to throw together every now and again."

Indya rolled her eyes and leaned toward him. "She made three different ones before deciding that this was the perfect version. We are going to have to donate the other cakes to the restaurant kitchen."

"What are you whispering about?" Oriana asked, side-eyeing her daughter with clear suspicion.

Indya gave Santiago a shrewd smile before schooling her face. "I was just telling Santiago how good it tastes when you add the pineapple filling."

"Oh yes," Oriana said, beaming proudly. "It's my own personal variation. It's featured on the restaurant menu, you know. I taught the chef to make it."

"Yes you did, Mami," Indya agreed. She and Gia shared their own look, both biting back laughter. Santiago suspected Oriana sometimes revised the truth when she needed to.

After another hour of conversation, Indya and her family took their leave. Mamá followed them to the door, thanking them for coming. Gia and Miriam clung to each other as if one of them were going to board a transatlantic ship across and never come back. Santiago offered Indya his cheek for the requisite formality, but instead of releasing the kiss into the air, as was customary, her soft, warm lips pressed into his skin. When she pulled back, her eyes glittered and her cheeks shone a rosy pink.

"Thank you for having us," she said softly.

His eyes slid down to her mouth, barely registering the ritual formality of her words. They were having another conversation underneath, made of long glances and simmering heat. "Thank you for coming," he murmured in return, unable to tear his eyes away from her.

She turned away, and suddenly, he found himself with a face full of Gia's hair.

"Bye, Santi!" she said, pulling away, tossing Miriam's nickname for him over her shoulder. He couldn't help but laugh at the way she flounced off, like a petal on the breeze. Santiago, Miriam and his parents watched them from the open door as they got into the sedan he recognized as Oriana's car. Indya, in the driver's seat, waited for everyone to get settled before she put the car in gear. She flashed her high beams, a last gesture of farewell, before she pulled out of the driveway, Gia waving wildly at Miriam as the car drove away.

"That was so much fun!" Miriam clapped her hands, her enthusiasm momentarily dampened when Papá quietly turned around and walked back inside. Miriam followed him, but Santiago held back. Mamá lingered as well, rubbing her arms even though it was far from cold outside.

"Need help cleaning up?" Santiago asked.

Mamá shook her head. "Your father will help me. It's the least he can do."

"Mamá," Santiago began but his mother put a finger over his lips.

"If you're going to apologize, I will chase you with my *chancleta*." They both chuckled at her threat. Santiago was sure that if he really did something ridiculous, it would earn him a flip-flop to the side of the head.

"The Linares were gracious and dignified in the face of something so embarrassing. I am tired of hearing what your father says about you. He forgets you are my son, too." Her eyes glittered with tears.

"Don't cry, Mamá," Santiago begged, his own throat closing up with the salt of his own. He never could handle it when his mother cried.

"It's okay." She wiped her eyes. "Your father needs to apologize to you," Mamá said. "And I will not speak to him until he does." She looked toward the house, as if she could see through the walls to wherever his father was inside the house. "I don't know why, but when it comes to you, he gets so intense." She looked back at him and shook her head. "I know he loves you dearly—"

"It's okay, Mamá. I know he loves me, too," Santiago said without real conviction. There was no way for him to know exactly what his father was feeling at any given moment, but he would go with her assessment, since she knew him better than anyone else. "I just wish he could see me as his son, not someone who went out of his way to defy his impossible expectations. I'm really nothing special in the end. Just…me. No more and no less."

"You are my son," she repeated with uncharacteristic ferocity. "You are very special to me. And if he refuses to see what a wonderful man you have turned out to be, despite all the obstacles you have had to overcome, so many of them on your own with no one to help you, then that's his loss." She swiped again at her eyes as if her tears had betrayed her by escaping. "Clearly, other people see it, so that makes him the blind one."

"Mamá—" he began, but she cut him off again.

"Indya cares about you. I can see it in her eyes." When he tried to cover his face with his hands, she pulled them down. "I am a woman, too, and I know when a woman is in love."

"I don't know if she's ready to call it *love*."

"The name doesn't make the feeling, Santiago. The action does. That was the action of a woman who has strong feelings for you."

Santiago needed time to absorb this, because his feelings for Indya ran deep as well.

"And another thing," she continued, oblivious to the crisis she'd triggered in him. "You be sure to remember this night so that, if someday, you feel like my granddaughter disappoints you, she will have an easier time of it than you did."

"Yes, Mamá," Santiago said, humbled by her words, by her faith in him and by the way she was already advocating for Lisbet. Loving his daughter well was the greatest gift anyone could give him. "I can't wait for you to see her again," he said, his heart squeezing at the thought of Lisbet in Soledad Bay and in his life for good.

"I'm going to spoil her!"

"As you should." Santiago gave his mother a kiss on the cheek. "Say goodbye to Papá for me."

"I'll give him a *chancletazo*," she retorted, and this time, Santiago was not so sure that her chasing him with a slipper was such an empty threat after all.

He gave his mother one last wave before pulling out. He had his father in his thoughts, but mostly, he couldn't stop thinking of Indya. She was like no other woman he'd ever met. So strong and so sure, yet so tender and gentle. He had adored women in his life, still adored his ex, Natasha, no matter what they were to each other now. But Indya was one of a kind.

He needed to see her, to thank her again, though he wasn't quite sure what more he could say. She'd shown up at seven in the morning to apologize for their date being ruined by this dinner, she could surely appreciate his impulse to see her. On the way to her house, he pulled into the lot of a twenty-four-hour pharmacy, parked his car and pulled out his phone. She would just be getting home. It was bold of him, but he couldn't leave it for the morning. He composed his text and hit Send before he could change his mind.

Chapter Twenty

Indya

Indya dropped her parents off at their house before driving home with Gia. The home they shared had once been a small duplex not far from the hotel that had been converted into a single residence when she bought it. Her parents still lived in their family home on the canal just two blocks inland, but Indya needed her independence to be able to take care of her daughter properly and build the life they both needed.

"That was a pretty impassioned defense of Santiago you gave back there," Gia said in a voice that sounded deceptively flat in its delivery.

Indya peeked at her out of the corner of her eye, but kept her focus on the road. "What his dad said didn't sit right with me. I had to say something."

"Hmm," Gia hummed, sounding thoughtful. "Wouldn't parents know their kids better than anybody?"

"In theory." Indya gripped the steering wheel, thinking of her own mother and her inability at times to acknowledge Indya's competence. "In some ways, our parents know us better than anyone else. But in other ways, being a parent can blind you to the way children grow and change over time. It's like being too close to the people you love makes it harder to see them the way that they are, sometimes. How would you feel if I treated you now the way I treated you when you were six or eight or even ten years old?"

Gia nodded. "I see that. Like how you give me a strict curfew even though I'm fourteen and ready to take on more responsibility. It's like you're not seeing me for the mature teenager I am."

Indya shook her head at the way her daughter loved to push her boundaries. "Not the same, little devil. Not the same."

"Hmm," Gia hummed again.

"What's all this humming for?" Indya retorted.

"Nothing, nothing," Gia said quickly. "So I guess that means you like Santiago?"

Prickles of heat flushed over Indya's skin at the thought of saying those words out loud. "I wasn't lying. He's a great manager. His suggestions to improve the hotel are realistic, and he supported everything with an action plan and a reasonable budget. His coworkers get along with him because he's reliable and fair."

"Yeah, okay, Mom, but do you like him?"

"Of course I do," Indya stammered. "What part of what I said implied that I didn't?"

"I don't mean like him. I mean, like *like* him? You know, the way people like each other when they have a crush on each other."

"Gia—" Indya warned.

"You know, it's okay to like someone. Santiago is good-looking for an old guy."

Indya snorted at this—he was only four years younger

than she was, but of course, Gia would see anyone over eighteen as ancient.

"He's got that Daddy energy going, you know?"

Indya choked on her own tongue. "Don't…don't ever say that again. Please."

Gia cackled, literally *cackled*, at Indya's reaction. "Okay, okay, Mom. But he's also nice and he works hard, you know? He's really nice to me. And Miriam told me he knows how to cook."

Indya side-eyed her daughter. "So you've been talking about this with Miriam, have you? Interesting."

"No, I haven't been talking about this with Miriam," Gia mimicked as if her mother were the slowest person on the uptake. "It just came up. God, Mom, you're so missing the point." Gia crossed her arms, huffing as she did so. "I'm just saying that if you had to get with anyone, Santiago would be all systems go. And he's totally into you. Anybody with two eyes in their head can see it."

Indya's hands shook as she pulled into the driveway of her house, and even jumped when the security lights automatically switched on. Her daughter was too observant for her own good. Did Indya wear her attraction on her face the way Santiago did? "You're exaggerating."

"Okay, Mom. Self-deception is not a good look, that's all I'm going to say."

Shutting the car off, Indya turned in her seat to face her daughter. "Let's not talk about this anymore. My brain is too tired for it."

Gia threw her hands up as if in defeat. "Whatever you say, Mom."

They gathered their things and stepped out into a temperate evening that sang with the sound of the soft surf rolling onto the beach. The moon, full and pregnant with light, shone like an eye winking on the ocean. Indya followed Gia up the walk, canopied with climbing ivy that wound in thick vines around the trellis framing their front door.

"I've never seen you with anyone except for Dad and I barely remember that," Gia said when they stepped inside the house.

Indya was taken aback by this. It had always been just her and Gia. Even her grandparents, whom she loved so much, were like satellites that orbited the center that contained mother and daughter, an unshakeable unit against the world. Indya should have anticipated that her too-observant daughter would notice the absence of even a boyfriend.

They took off their shoes, setting them in the shoe rack Indya had found in an artisan shop, an elaborately carved creation that was remarkably sturdy despite its intricate appearance.

Indya made her way to the kitchen, where she took two glasses from the cupboard. She filled them each with water and slid one over to Gia, who now seemed to hang on her every word. "I've never felt the need to be in a relationship. My life is full enough with my girlfriends, your grandparents, this hotel, and even—" Indya bopped her nose at this "—a little bit, with you."

"You're so corny," Gia said, but the smile of pleasure took the sting out of her words. "No, I just… Mom, are you like bi or something? Maybe lesbian, like Nyla and Jade?"

Indya set her glass down on the counter next to her. "Just because I'm not interested in a relationship doesn't mean I'm a lesbian or bi."

"Ace? Demisexual? Aromatic?"

Indya laughed. "No, none of the above. Not because there's anything wrong with any of those," Indya was quick to add. "That's just not where my orientation lies."

"It's okay, Mom. I know you're not a bigot. We have a lot of queer friends and you're super cool with all of them."

"Why wouldn't I be? I grew up with Nyla and Wil, and Jade is the best front-end manager of all time. Who they love has nothing to do with the way I feel about them."

Indya picked up a towel to wipe the counter when Gia stepped in front of her, arresting her movements. "What is it, baby?"

Gia studied her mother, a half smile on her face. "I just want to make it clear that if you want to date Santiago, you should."

Indya couldn't help but give her big-brained child a hug for her audacity. "Thank you for your permission."

"No problem!" Gia said, either ignoring or not caring about Indya's sarcasm. "Even old people need love."

"Wow, okay. How about a good-night, Gia?"

Gia grinned, leaving a loud kiss on Indya's cheek before heading up to her room, where she would turn on a fan for the white noise, lock her door and go right to bed.

Indya pulled a bottle of wine from the wine rack together with a wineglass. She uncorked the bottle, pouring out a generous amount. She had drunk a half glass of wine at the Pereiras', mostly passing on the alcohol as she always did when she was driving Gia anywhere. She padded over to the enclosed porch that cantilevered over the sand below and looked out over the sea. She made sure to turn the blinds down so that no light escaped into the night. It was turtle season and artificial lights from housing and street lamps along the beach only disoriented the creatures as they made their way from the sea to their nests in the sand. The city was strict about enforcing the Lights Out Ordinance to make sure there was minimal disruption to turtle mating habits. The only light tonight was that of a full moon, and it illuminated everything in its uncanny glow.

She took a seat on one of the cushioned chaise lounges, kicked off her house slippers, and stretched her legs out, her daughter's conversation commingling with thoughts of Santiago at dinner, the way he looked so handsome in his casual dress shirt, sleeves rolled up to his elbows, the tops of his large pecs flexing through the V of his shirt. Everything about him spoke of strength of body as well as of character and just the thought of all that strength brought to heel for her desires sent waves of heat to the deepest part of her. He deserved so much more than his father's disdain.

Maybe she was just as bad as his father, allowing one stupid argument to nearly end their entire relationship, just because she'd had the misfortune of having an ex-husband who couldn't accept all of her.

Her phone buzzed in her pocket. She glanced down to see a text message notification pop up. Santiago.

Drove by your house. Noticed the porch light was still on. Can I stop by?

The tips of Indya's fingers tingled where they hovered over the message. She glanced at the time. She was still dressed and it wasn't late. Gia was upstairs, likely already in bed. The idea of seeing Santiago made her shiver from a place deep inside her. She tried not to think too hard about whether her house was out of the way for him or not, ignoring the clear certainty that it probably was and how little that mattered to her.

Stop by.

She tossed her phone on the cushion next to her and was making her way through the house, pausing only to set out another wineglass, when she heard the soft rapping on her front door. Glancing at the security camera she'd installed on her doorbell, she confirmed that Santiago stood on the other side.

"Joyriding around Soledad Bay, I see," Indya said when she opened the door, stepping aside to let him in. He held a gold box in hand, Godiva chocolates, from the look of it. "Sounds like something our girls would do."

"I am afraid that is exactly what those two will be doing when it's time for them to drive on their own."

Indya closed the door behind him. "I planned on delaying the inevitable for as long as possible."

Santiago chuckled at this. "I brought something small." He handed the box to her. "It's nothing, really."

Indya was touched by the gesture, though not surprised. She, too, had been raised to not appear at people's houses as a guest without bringing something for the host.

"I didn't think they sold Godiva at the 7-Eleven," she teased, avoiding his gaze, which bore into her with an attentiveness that could burn a hole through concrete.

"Not the 7-Eleven. Walgreens." Santiago looked sheepish. "Thank god for twenty-four-hour stores."

"Oh," Indya said before breaking into a laugh. "And here I thought you'd planned this chocolate for me all along."

"If I had planned any of this," his voice dropped low, "I would have brought more than a box of chocolate."

She gripped the box in her hand. *"Ven."* She abruptly turned around, using his favorite word before switching into Spanish. *"¿Vino rojo?"*

"Red wine would be nice," he answered from behind, following her inside.

She held herself with impressive calm even as she felt every minute shift of his presence behind her. Each step, each sway of his strong arms and narrow hips was a finger stroke of awareness across her back and shoulder blades. She scooped up the glass she'd prepared for him as she passed. The porch where she'd been lounging earlier was a few short steps across her living room. Cutting off all the indoor lights as she walked, she was relieved when she stepped past the threshold into the moonlit darkness. She could finally face him, instead of feeling him, persistent and overwhelming, behind her. The warm air from the sea wound around her like a caress, smoothing down her anxieties until she no longer drowned in them. She felt different out here, as if she were overflowing the boundaries of herself, the world becoming as fluid and easy as the surf rolling across the sands. She poured red wine into the glass she held and handed it to him before taking a seat on the chaise lounge. She smiled up at him, and he instantly understood, taking the seat next to her.

"You're okay out here? We could go inside."

Santiago shook his head. "I think I could use some fresh air after tonight."

"Right." Indya turned to shut the thick curtains, blotting out even the vampire lights that forever blinked inside her home, and leaving them completely at the mercy of the light of the full moon. After clinking their glasses together, she took a sip, watching him over the glass.

After a silence full of expectation, she broke the ice and said, "So, interesting dinner, huh?" She suspected that this had been the reason he'd ventured to stop by her house this evening and preferred to spare him the discomfort of bringing it up.

Santiago swirled the wine in the glass, held snugly cradled in his large palm. "That is one way to describe it."

Indya nodded. "I'm still full from dinner. Your mother outdid herself tonight."

"Thank you," Santiago said. She was unable to take her eyes off him. He was radiant, even in the soft glow of the moonlight, with his bronze-tinted hair gleaming gold, and the outline of chest muscles that strained the fit of his shirt. He was wonderful in every way and if Indya was lucky, she'd get to spend more time getting to know this man.

Santiago sipped his wine, then set down the glass on a small table nearby, the deep, red liquid swaying gently. "I wanted to apologize for my father. He can be a little—"

"Unforgiving?" Indya interjected with a laugh. "If you're worried about any impressions your father might have made, you forget, I know your family and I happen to have a matching set of parents of my own. I am no stranger to unmet expectations."

Santiago nodded. "Yes, but I also wanted to thank you."

"No." Indya set her glass on the side table next to her. "I was only speaking the truth. I know we argued, but my experience of you has been far different from the one he described." She picked up the box of chocolate, looking for Santiago's complicity in opening it and finding it when he took the box from her and tore open the seal that held the packaging together.

"I meant every word and more," Indya continued. "You are everything good a person could want in a man."

"And you?" Santiago asked. "Am I everything good *you* could want in a man?"

Indya smiled, a bit breathless. She took the box from Santiago and dug out a piece of chocolate, only a part of her mind engaged in the task, the majority of it riveted on Santiago. "You are," she whispered before dropping her eyes to the candy she held before placing it in the box again. "In fact, I should be the one buying you chocolate."

Santiago shook his head. "No, you shouldn't. You showed me what you thought of me tonight, and that is more than enough for me. It was a stupid argument between us, nothing else."

"It wasn't stupid, Santi," she said, lifting a hand to his face, his skin both soft and rough under her palm. "It matters to me to be accepted by you, but I should not have been so quick to anger and assume that you didn't when you said what you did."

"Of course I accept you," he said, real pain marring his features. "I was just frustrated that you saw me as nothing more than someone who works for you when you are so much more to me than my boss. It felt a bit like what my father does to me every time he has a chance."

Indya had anticipated the possibility and it saddened her to remind him of someone who could so publicly hurt him. "I'm sorry I made you feel that way. I understand now how much that must have hurt."

"But I told you that a part of you was not welcome between us. This is unfair to you, and it is also dishonest." Santiago pulled her close to him. "I want all of you, Indya, not just the light and easy versions of you. I want the complicated and difficult parts, too. Life is hard and I want the scary and strong versions of you that you need to face down the world. All of it."

Indya's eyes glittered with tears. "That's all I've ever wanted."

"And you deserve everything you've ever wanted." Santiago's hand was now on her face, caressing her, making her feel loved and accepted in a way she never had before. "You are strong, intelligent and beautiful. I love you, *reina*."

Indya melted into his touch. "I love you, too, Santi."

She ran a finger over his lips, the tip catching on the bottom one. His tongue flicked out to taste her, then covered it with his mouth, gently suckling on it. Slowly, she leaned forward and replaced her finger with her lips. The gentle press of a chaste kiss changed into something fierce, the taste of him rich and sublime. She wanted to kiss and lick him until she'd consumed the very flavor of him.

Their kiss became increasingly frantic until Santiago pulled back, naked hunger flashing in his eyes.

"Reina," he murmured between kisses. "Tell me what you want and I will give it to you."

Indya shivered at the question. What did she want besides the obvious? She tilted her head to the side, a silent request for him to kiss her neck, which he did with lips as soft as fine cotton, and warm like the afternoon sun. She wanted this airy feeling of desire, but also the heaviness that came with dependability, of knowing that no matter what happened, she would have someone to count on. She wanted passion and fire, but she also wanted someone whose feet were firmly rooted to the ground.

She wanted to shine and have no one complain about how brightly she burned.

Santiago licked the tender skin behind her ear and nipped at the edge of her jaw, a tiny bite that sent pain and pleasure jolting through her body.

"What do you want?" Santiago asked again.

"I want you," she answered.

Santiago pulled back and gave her a smile that sparkled with pure, simple pleasure. "Then, have me."

Chapter Twenty-One

Santiago

Santiago followed Indya inside on silent feet. He had never been in her house before, but he assumed, like every other house in Soledad Bay, that all the bedrooms would be upstairs. He was willing to be as quiet as a church mouse if it meant not leaving her side. This whole night was already a study in euphoria—he didn't want to be anywhere else. Not ever again.

However, instead of heading toward the stairs, she led him to a room that looked out on the same patio they'd been on.

"Guest room," she said by way of explanation, closing the door and locking it behind her.

She didn't switch on the light, instead throwing open the curtains and the glass doors to the patio, letting moonlight and sea air stream in. Then she turned around and began to strip out of her clothes, inch by inch revealing that skin he couldn't get enough of the morning she came to him on the boat. Santiago stood mesmerized by her. She wasn't intentionally sexy or campy—she didn't pretend to sway to music or undulate her body in an attempt at seduction. But she held his eyes in a gaze forged of heat and expectation and didn't break eye contact until her clothes were a puddle at her feet.

She was a walking wet dream.

Her skin was a dark olive, its texture smooth, save for stretch marks which webbed out in delicate strands, caressing the slope of her hips. Her breasts were heavy, tipped in dark brown nipples that were tight with desire. Her stomach was soft and curved, her thighs rounded and her legs shapely and strong.

She let him stare at her until at length, she whispered, "Your turn."

Santiago spread his arms wide. "Help me."

Indya narrowed her eyes at him, studying him for several seconds until she stepped close to him and undid the remainder of the buttons on his shirt, pushing it slowly off his shoulders so the palms of her hands caressed the skin underneath the material. She couldn't know that one of his fantasies was to be stripped down by her, as if she couldn't get enough of him. She shivered as she undid his pants with one hand, sliding the zipper open and pushing both the trousers and his underwear down until they were nothing but a shadow of fabric at his feet.

"Now what?" he teased.

Indya laughed. "Do I need to be the one to tell you what to do?"

He pulled her suddenly forward, winding an arm around her waist. "No. In fact, you don't."

He dipped his head to give her a fierce kiss, plunging his tongue into her mouth. He could already feel the embers of his desire for her slowly igniting. He walked her toward the bed until the back of her legs hit the mattress.

She scrambled onto the bed, crawling backward to make room for him to follow.

She lay in the center, arms thrown over her head, gorgeous breasts crowned with the most perfectly shaped nipples he'd ever seen. He took them both in his hand, kneading their soft flesh and watched her eyes flutter closed with desire.

She was glorious in her abandon. He tweaked her nipples, pinching them gently, watching as her body jerked from the sensation. He chased the feeling with his lips, swallowing as much of her soft mounds as he could before toying with their hard peaks, sucking and biting them until her fingers were buried in his hair and she was pulling hard, whimpering for more.

He dragged his fingertips down the valley between her breasts, tracing a path from her rib cage to her belly button, over which he dragged the pads of his fingers. She flinched from the touch.

"Ticklish?" he whispered.

She nodded, unable to speak. He lowered his head and licked at the whorl of skin, dipping inside before dragging the tip of his tongue down over her belly, down and down farther.

"Santiago," she murmured, her breath coming fast and hard with anticipation.

"Yes," he said, letting his fingers slide lower, watching her face as he touched her again, this time without her instruction. "Am I doing it right?"

Indya nodded. "You're a quick study."

He moved faster, watching her climb. "Does that surprise you?"

She shook her head as he moved more quickly. "No. You've always been a fast learner."

She raised one long leg to run her foot up and down his side. She was magnificent, unfurled like a goddess beneath him.

He was determined to worship her.

Lowering his head, he licked at her, forcing her back to arch upward. He held her hips still with one arm while the other worked her the way she'd shown him. With his mouth and hands, he drew out those sounds she'd made him promise not to make, until she grabbed a pillow and covered her face, muffling her gasps of pleasure so only they could hear them. It was the best sound Santiago had ever heard.

Her orgasm, when it hit her, shook a cry that the pillow barely smothered. She clenched around his fingers, flooded him with the taste of her and drove him into the sky. He shook out a condom that he kept in his wallet and rolled it on as the waves of pleasure ebbed and flowed through her.

He lay over her body, removing the pillow from her face. She was flushed and breathless and so beautiful it made his heart ache fiercely in his chest.

"*Reina*, are you ready for me?"

Her eyes fluttered open. "I just came."

"And you will again, if you let me." He positioned himself at her entrance. "I want to give you all the pleasure you deserve."

Indya stared at him with the softest expression he had ever seen. "You're going to spoil me so well, I won't ever let you go."

"Then, don't," he whispered, pushing his way slowly inside her. He was falling into ecstasy and was ready to drown in it. "Tell me and I will never leave you again."

"Santi," she panted as he stretched her. His heart swelled and swelled with how perfect this was, how perfect she was. He didn't care if his father thought he was unworthy. She thought he was worthy, and that was more than enough for him.

He drew her leg over his hip, fixing the heel on his lower back. "I love you, Indya Linares." He pushed again, and this time her body pulled him in until his was flush against hers. Her eyes grew wide before fluttering closed. "From the very first moment I saw you. I loved you."

Indya's face withered into pleasure and passion, sweet and soft and so very agonized. "I love you, too." She gasped, her body writhing as if struggling to hold in so much pleasure and emotion at the same time. "I'm sorry it took me a little time."

"The timing was perfect," he said before plunging into her, rocking into her with a force that shocked his name from her lips. She made to speak again, but he covered her mouth with a kiss. It was enough for now.

All his pent-up need for her took, fueling him. He had wanted her for so damned long, now that he had her, he was going to make her his so that she never looked anywhere else for satisfaction again. The hard rocking of their bodies filled the air that already hung heavy with their moans until Indya bit her knuckle, burying her orgasm in the fierce clench of her fists. Santiago still moved, rocking her through the waves of her climax, drawing each one out. Unable to stop himself, he came as well, dissolving in his own ecstasy as she held him through it until they were both boneless and sated.

Santiago dropped his forehead into the valley between Indya's breasts, her lungs still working to drag air in and out. When he had sufficient control over his body, he pulled slowly away, making quick work of the condom, which helped him get a sense of his bearings again.

He adjusted his position so that Indya rested against his

chest. He ran a hand over her arm, smoothing heat into her skin. Another bit of shuffling and they were underneath a throw blanket that had been located at the foot of the bed.

This night had been a riot of emotions, some of which he could have done without. But not this. Not the part where Indya finally let him have her, not the part where he could lay with her like this, not the part where he could hold her in his arms until almost-morning.

"Hey," he spoke at length into the quiet of the night.

Indya shifted so she could gaze up at him, her hair a halo around her head. "Hey."

He chuckled. "So tell me, are you okay?"

Indya shifted, sliding a leg up over his. "I'm good over here. And you?"

He was happy, if thoughtful. "I still love you. That wasn't just me being excited."

Indya chuckled. "I still love you, too."

"Good." He shifted to look at her, carding a hand through her wonderful dark hair, pushing it away from either side of her face, because he wanted to look at it up close and study it. "Anything that I do involves my daughter. But you know that."

Indya nodded. "I do. And it's the same with me. Anything that I do must include my daughter."

"And my ex? She's the mother of my daughter and she will need my help as well."

"Santiago," Indya said quietly. "Baby."

Oh, he really liked that.

"I know your life already. When I said I loved you, I didn't mean I loved only the sexy parts of you. I meant all of you, everything messy and neat." She traced a finger down his chin. "Bring on your daughter and Natasha. Hell, I'll even take your Papá." At that, Santiago laughed again. " Give it all to me. Haven't I proven that I can handle them all?"

"You have, *reina*. I know you can handle that and more. And I love you, too. The messy and the neat parts. I'll take it all."

Indya slipped off his hips, snuggling up into his side. "Good. Now, get some rest. I want to go one more round before morning."

Santiago barked out another laugh. "And here I thought you were bossy only at work," Santiago said, dropping a soft kiss on the crown of her head.

"No, baby," she said, tucking them both in and he knew he would never get used to her calling him that. "This is just me all the time."

Epilogue

Indya

There was nothing like Florida in the early summer, before hurricane season got too serious, and the day of the competition was proof of that. The clear dawn promised an endless blue sky, and the weather report predicted that it would remain that way all day. It would be hot—there was no way it wouldn't be hot—but good sunblock, a hat and the inevitable sea breeze to cool the skin would do wonders. Gia and Miriam had appointed themselves official skin protectors of team Sea Warriors, their competition team name, after Glam Girls had been overruled.

"Hey, I expect commission on the use of my trademark," Nyla said when she and Rayne came to see them off at the marina before the first launch of the competition. Indya and Santiago's parents, as well as Natasha, Lisbet's mother, would be waiting for them at the end.

Indya had signed up for the competition with her tiny crew—Santiago, of course, Gia, and Miriam, who refused to be left on the sidelines. And, after reassuring her mother that she would be safe and well-cared for, Santiago's daughter,

Lisbet, a long limbed, pretty, now-eleven-year-old girl with bronze hair that sparkled like her father's and large, brown eyes that seemed to see everything, just like her mother's. After their immigration interview, the miraculous had happened and they were cleared to enter the US earlier than they had anticipated, sending Santiago into a whirlwind of last-minute preparations. Indya brought her organizational prowess to bear and was there when Natasha and Lisbet arrived, to welcome them into this new phase of their lives.

Indya greeted her two friends with a hug, while Santiago shook their hands. Indya couldn't help but catch the look of utter glee on their faces.

"Good luck getting a dime out of those two," Indya said to Nyla.

"Technically, I was inspired by the name of The Turtle Warriors. I did not actually use the club name," Gia answered. "According to fair-use laws, I can use it as long as it is not for profit or used to make money on the merchandising of that name."

"I can verify that. I looked up the law, too." Miriam high-fived Gia before they dissolved into laughter.

"The pair of you is a little too smart for your own good," Nyla said.

"Yes." Rayne looked them both up and down in assessment. "These two will either open a company or launch a criminal syndicate."

Gia shrugged. "Why not both?"

Miriam nodded quickly. "We already decided we're not getting married. We're going to live together, start a company and own at least ten cats."

"Ten cats?" Santiago looked at Indya in alarm.

Gia's grew wide. "How about a cat rescue? We could open a cat café where people can adopt cats!"

"Cat café? Say less!" Miriam and Gia got lost, creating plans for their newest scheme.

"Here we are," Natasha's voice came up the deck, a slim, petite woman wearing a white dress, her bright smile peeking out from under a large, straw hat. Lisbet followed close behind with her brand-new tackle box in one hand and a collection of rods in the other.

Santiago kissed his little girl on her sunblock-covered cheek before taking her things. Shifting the conversation to Spanish, he said, "I'm going to put this on the boat."

Lisbet nodded, a grin of excitement on her face.

Indya gave Natasha a hug before kneeling to speak to Lisbet at eye level. "We are going to get out there and drag in the biggest fish this boat can hold," Indya exclaimed. "You will never forget your first Salty Fish."

Lisbet, with her big brown eyes and sweet, round face, beamed at Indya in excitement. "And then we'll eat it!"

"I like the way you think," Gia said, taking Lisbet by one hand, while Miriam took the other. "So, what do you think about a cat café?" Gia's voice faded as the three girls boarded the ship.

Indya turned to Natasha, taking the backpack she offered her. "It's a change of clothes, a snack and extra water."

"Perfect," Indya said, slinging it over her shoulder. She paused, then said with more seriousness, "We'll take good care of her. I promise."

"I know you will," Natasha said, glancing at her daughter's retreating back. "She hasn't talked about anything else for days."

Indya's heart soared at this, remembering her own excitement when she was a young girl. "We'll see you in a few hours, hopefully with a giant fish," Indya said.

"I hope so. *¡Buena Suerte!*" Natasha waved them off before returning to the main dock.

Everyone boarded the *Gia Marie*, which now flew a banner with The Sea Warriors in rainbow designs and flowers painted across it.

Santiago helped the girls set up their rods. Indya tried her best to bring down her nervousness by concentrating on preparations for setting out to sea. Once they arrived in their first fishing spot, and the actual fishing got underway, everyone was focused in a way they usually weren't during their regular fishing trips. As usual, Santiago was indispensable, and his company became quiet and competent as they steered out beyond the bay. He helped Gia, Miriam and Lisbet with their snafus, making sure everything was in order, while Indya navigated, finding the best fishing spots. Gia and Miriam crackled with energy, happy as ever to just be in each other's company, and made space for Lisbet, who followed the girls everywhere they went. Indya's heart grew two sizes larger when both Gia and Miriam each wrapped an arm around Lisbet as they waited for something to tug their lines.

She felt the warm weight of Santiago's own arm around her shoulders. "They are really beautiful together, aren't they?"

Indya shifted her gaze to look at him. "They are. I grew up with Nyla and Rayne. I know how important it is to be surrounded by people who have loved you all your life."

Santiago shrugged, the locks that curled out from under his cap whipping in the wind. "Lisbet seems very comfortable with them."

"They are all lovely girls and they are lucky to have each other."

Leaving a kiss on Indya's cheek, he whispered, "You know who else is very lucky?"

Indya giggled. "Do tell."

Santiago ran his nose along Indya's neck. "You are, for having me."

Indya elbowed him in the side.

They caught quite a bit of fish, though none they could submit to be judged in the competition. Indya was fine with that. She was having the best day with her favorite people. Winning would only add a cherry to an otherwise enormous treat.

Just as Indya was calculating their remaining time before their return to the marina, her line gave a tug. Hard. She approached her rod, taking it in hand to steady it when it gave another violent yank. Sliding it out of the holder, she nearly lost it when the line jerked again, this time with real force that bowed the rod into a parabolic shape. Indya gripped the handle and braced it against her hip.

"Mom!" Gia said, watching her strain against the line.

"I think this one's a kicker!" Indya shouted. Some hapless fish had probably been drawn to her bait and a larger one had taken the opportunity to score a free snack.

The line bowed with tension as Indya struggled to reel in her catch. It lurched, sending vibrations up her arms and shoulders. She propped her foot against the ledge of her deck and pulled.

"Papá!" Lisbet called out after a particularly fierce wrench. "Indya needs help!"

With a speed she couldn't anticipate, his strong arms were around her, holding the fishing pole. Anchoring it. Anchoring her. His broad body was a slab of muscle and heat at her back, and it cocooned her even as it gave her the strength she lacked to struggle against the line.

"Ya, ya, te tengo," he murmured.

There, there, I have you.

His words momentarily fractured her concentration and she was grateful for the physical strength he gave her. The effort was evident in his quick breathing even as his voice remained calm and steady.

"¡Dios mio, es enorme!" Indya gritted out as they pulled and pulled at the line. Whatever they'd caught was fighting them with everything it had, trying its best to break away. But Indya and Santiago heaved together, Santiago steadying the line while she struggled with the reel, hoping and praying that the reviews she'd read about this particular fishing rod were true and that it would hold.

"Do you usually catch fish this big?" Santiago asked, his warm breath fanning in puffs along the skin of her temple as they fought against the fish.

"Never," Indya answered, breathless. "Not like this."

"Mom! Santiago! You can do it!" Gia shouted. "Let's go, *viejos*!"

"Gia! Just come help!" Miriam got behind Santiago, wrapping her arms around his waist, and pulled. Gia followed suit, fitting herself behind Miriam like a fish-themed conga line, with the small Lisbet wedging herself between the girls.

"Pull!" Lisbet shouted between giggles.

Indya strained, suffocating now in Santiago's muscles as they bunched around her. Sweat beaded Indya's skin, causing her T-shirt to stick in places. Santiago's chest was rock-hard with tension and strain. The adrenaline of fighting the fish exacerbated the more immediate distraction caused by Santiago's proximity. Even overheated and sweaty, he smelled like an edible dream and only the voices of the girls grounded her and kept her from turning around and licking the salt directly off his skin.

With a grunt, they finally yanked the rod upward. At the end was the most beautiful big eye tuna Indya had ever seen.

"Get it inside the boat before something even bigger tries to get him," Gia shouted as they dragged the still flopping fish onto the deck.

"It has to be at least two hundred pounds," Lisbet shouted as she jumped up and down. Indya dodged the fish's fins as she tried to get the line under control.

"I think it's closer to one hundred and twenty pounds," Santiago said.

"Pictures," Miriam said, laughing. "You have to show it off to Nyla, or she'll never believe you."

"Ugh, yes, her with her scientific skepticism," Indya said. Santiago pulled his phone out of his back pocket and swiped the screen.

"I don't think it's that, Mom," Gia said as she helped Indya hold the fish up. "I think she's just built that way."

Lisbet slid in between them, already posing for the camera. "Don't forget me!"

"How can we forget you, *chula*?" Indya practically sang.

"Does Nyla fish, too?" Santiago asked Indya as he raised the camera, taking a few random shots of them struggling with the fish.

"As a marine biologist, she has a conflicted relationship with fishing, but we've gone out together before," Indya said, the fish finally cradled successfully in their arms, like a bikini model lying on her side on the sand.

"Torn between her passion and conservation," Santiago murmured, distracted by the effort to get them all in the shot. Eyes fixed from behind the camera, he said "Smile, *mi reina y mis princesas.*"

"You need to be in the shot, too!" Miriam said. She grabbed Santiago's camera and hauled him to her side, wedging him between her and Indya.

"Hurry up! I'm getting cramps," Indya said through gritted teeth while she and Gia struggled to keep the tuna from tumbling out of their arms.

Affecting the most ridiculous pose imaginable, Miriam managed to get a selfie, the giant tuna's face squished against Indya's, ensuring that her hair would smell like fish until she took a proper bath.

"Do you think we can win with this one?" Gia asked.

Santiago took the giant fish out of Indya's arms, gazing at her with so much love, she glowed with it. "Just being out here together, we are already winners."

Once the boat had been cleared and the fish weighed— it would not win, but it was a respectable effort—Santiago pulled Indya down into the cabin of the *Gia Marie* after their crew were safely off board. He shut the door when he came inside and leaned against the wood dining table, cradling Indya's body between his open thighs.

He captured her lips in a kiss that ensured she would have to reapply her Guerlain lip gloss. Again. Why did she bother?

Oh, right, because Santiago's kisses were worth the risk of swallowing a pound of designer lip balm.

She gripped his shoulders as they kissed, opening her mouth to accept his silent invitation to join him in taking each other apart. Indya dived in, savoring him. He ran his hand over her bottom and squeezed hard, forcing her hips to surge forward. That was her critical error, because all she felt was the hardness of his desire straining against his pants, and it made her wet and achy, with little recourse for relief except to grind helplessly against him.

The kiss went on for an age as they both swayed with the boat's rhythm—Santiago really was too good at kissing to ever sleep alone—until Indya pulled away.

"Behave," she scolded, even as she clung to him even harder. Santiago stared at her lips, plump and wet from his kisses. Running his thumb across them, he licked his own, making Indya primed and ready for him. She wanted him everywhere, all the time, and wondered how she had lived so long without feeling this way. He locked eyes with her in a gaze so heated, it made her throat go dry. "What's your dream, Indya? What keeps you up at night?"

She was taken aback by his question. "I don't understand."

His voice dropped low, and he spoke into the shell of her ear. "What's your dream? What do you most want that you don't already have?"

What did Indya dream of? Most of the time, she thought she had everything she needed. She had a wonderful daughter, her family hotel, her overbearing parents and her wildly inappropriate friends. She had a man she loved and had acquired his tiny little family as well. What else did she honestly need out of life?

She gazed at Santiago, her tongue peeking out playfully between her lips. "Grilled grouper and braised potatoes. Sorry, but the thought of having that has been keeping me up all week."

Santiago barked out a laugh that was almost too loud to be contained in the boat's space. "I was thinking of something a little more special than that."

"Pompano?"

Shaking his head, Santiago dug a small box out of his pocket and held it palm up in his hand. Indya's chest grew tight with anticipation.

"Santi?" she half asked, half marveled.

"I know it's a bit soon, but I also know I've found something special with you, and I don't want to let it go." He opened the velvet box and took out a delicate ring with a single diamond. "Consider it a promise for now. We can take our time fulfilling it."

He took the ring and placed it on her finger. It sat, snug and pretty, twinkling in the bright afternoon sun that streamed inside the cabin.

"This is where we first met," Indya said quietly, taking in her boat with new eyes. "I love that this will be where we start our forever."

Santiago nodded, his eyes glassy with unshed tears. "Is that a yes?"

Indya flung her arms around Santiago's shoulders. They were covered in sea salt, sunblock and fish, but she couldn't imagine anything more perfect.

"I love you, Santi. Of course it's a yes."

Santiago nodded, not bothering to wipe away the tears that tracked down his face. And when she kissed him, she tasted her own as well, sharp and salty, like the endless promise of the sea.

* * * * *

Harlequin® Reader Service

Enjoyed your book?

Try the perfect subscription for Romance readers and get more great books like this delivered right to your door.

See why over 10+ million readers have tried Harlequin Reader Service.

Start with a Free Welcome Collection with free books and a gift—valued over $20.

Choose any series in print or ebook. See website for details and order today:

TryReaderService.com/subscriptions